Dornford Yates is the pseudony[...]
into a middle-class Victorian [...]
together enough money to sen[...] [...]ow. The son of a
solicitor, he qualified for the Bar but gave up legal work in favour
of his great passion for writing. As a consequence of education
and experience, Yates' books feature the genteel life, a nostalgic
glimpse at Edwardian decadence and a number of swindling
solicitors. In his heyday and as a testament to the fine writing
in his novels, Dornford Yates' work was placed in the bestseller
list. Indeed, 'Berry' is one of the great comic creations of
twentieth-century fiction, and 'Chandos' titles were successfully
adapted for television.

Finding the English climate utterly unbearable, Yates chose
to live in the French Pyrénées for eighteen years before moving
on to Rhodesia where he died in 1960.

DORNFORD YATES

B-BERRY AND I
LOOK BACK

HOUSE OF
STRATUS

This edition published in 2001 by House of Stratus, an imprint of Stratus Holdings plc, 24c Old Burlington Street, London, W1X 1RL, UK.

www.houseofstratus.com

Typeset, printed and bound by House of Stratus.

A catalogue record for this book is available from the British Library.

ISBN 1-84232-964-2

To the memory
of that brilliant novelist

'SAKI'
(H H Munro)

*whose first cousin I had the honour to be. It was a true honour.
Gently bred, aged forty-four, Hector enlisted on the outbreak of
the first great war. A very fine linguist, more than once he was
offered a Commission and an appointment to GHQ, but he
preferred to fight and die a corporal, in the front line.*

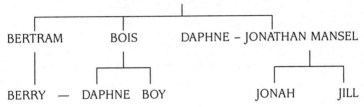

BERTRAM PLEYDELL
(of White Ladies, in the County of Hampshire)

BERTRAM   BOIS   DAPHNE – JONATHAN MANSEL

BERRY — DAPHNE BOY   JONAH   JILL

NOTE

Hardly had As Berry and I Were Saying *gone to press, when I began to remember occasions and incidents – all true – which might well have been related in that book. For what they are worth, here they are. As before, I have given them a fictional setting; for the many letters I received, thanking me for* As Berry *and* I Were Saying, *suggest that a memoir is more palatable when presented as a 'conversation piece'. As before, Berry contributes some monographs as well as a downright commentary upon the memories themselves: and the memoir is introduced by an account of a bereavement which he suffered less in sorrow than in indignation. Perhaps I may be forgiven for repeating that the memories themselves are strictly true and that I have exaggerated nothing.*

DORNFORD YATES

"I won't," said Berry.

"My darling," said Daphne, "you can't go on like this."

"Yes, I can," said Berry. "I can continue indefinitely."

"But supposing the pain comes back?"

"Don't dress it up," said her husband. "It wasn't pain at all. It was concentrated agony."

"Well, supposing that comes back?"

"The attack," said Berry, "which was as prolonged as it was venomous, coincided with a spell of the most vile and abnormal weather ever known in this temperate zone. Provided that Nature is no longer subjected to the impudent horseplay of the Bigger and Better Block-Busting and Blast Brigade, I have every reason to believe that atmospheric conditions will not reflect an ill-temper which was fully justified. In such circumstances, my teeth will not ache."

"But it's very bad for you. You can't bite up your food."

"I gnash it," said Berry. "I've got very good at gnashing. And so long as I'm not repugnant…"

"The X-Rays," said Jonah, "disclose – "

"I know, I know," said Berry. "According to them, I'm only fit to haunt a sewage-farm. But I've not yet been asked to leave any place of entertainment and, so far, no one has swooned when I have engaged them in talk."

"But it's bad for you, darling," said Daphne. "Terribly bad. You're being poisoned, day and night."

"Well, I feel very well on it," said Berry. "When I was Mithridates – "

"The agony," said I, "has passed. But we're talking of sailing the sea in two months' time. Supposing the pain returns when we're two days out."

Berry regarded me with great malevolence.

Then –

"I suppose," he said, "I suppose it's your legal mind. Be that as it may, your capacity for perceiving and indicating a bestial possibility is hideously disconcerting."

"I'm sorry," I said. "But, for all our sakes, I want you to weigh it up."

"D'you think I haven't?" said Berry. "I tell you, the scales of my brain have very near broken down. Three-score years and ten, and not a false tooth in my head. And now I'm to cast this record into the draught. And all the care I've lavished upon my jaws! Some teeth have been drawn, I know – and that, with a reluctance which I most heartily shared. But they clamoured to be removed – at least, I suppose they did; for, when they'd gone, the immediate agony ceased. But if but one more is removed, I shall be forced to employ auxiliaries. Otherwise, I shall repel all who see me; and my enunciation will be defective – the singular will become plural, against my will; and gnashing will present difficulty. All of which points to the poisonous conclusion that, since those that are left are failing, it would be common sense to make a clean sweep.

"And that is what fazes me.

"Hitherto, I have always reserved the finger-bowl for – "

A shriek from Daphne and Jill cut short the sentence.

"There you are," said Berry. "And a moment ago you were insisting that vivisection alone would save my life."

"We trust," said I, "that you will not construe any, er, acquisition which you may make as conferring a licence to abandon the decencies."

"Of course not," said Berry. "Of course not. But I may have difficulty at first. I may underestimate the pull of a *marron glacé* or the thrust of lobster *cardinal*." He frowned. "It would, you will agree, be imperative that in such a case the strain upon the mandible should be immediately relieved."

"But not in public," cried Daphne.

"Certainly not," said Berry. "In the bosom."

There was a pregnant silence.

Then –

"Is that a biblical allusion?" said Jonah.

"No," said Berry. "Familiar."

Jill began to shake with laughter.

"Of course," said Daphne, "if you're sure that you're now in no pain…"

"None," said Berry. "As I have said, it was the inspired malignancy of the weather that provoked my teeth. They're not as young as they were, and they saw no reason why they should be butchered to make an atom holiday. First, then, I have no pain. Secondly, though I lack several of my incisors, provided I avoid the less attractive habits of the bulls of Bashan, I give my neighbours no offence. Thirdly, in spite of the radiologist's report, my health leaves nothing to be desired. Fourthly, in case of accidents, Rodrigues has a mould of my mouth. In these circumstances, deliberately to purchase incredible inconvenience at a very high price seems to me irrational. I may be wrong."

"My darling," said Daphne, "all we want is to keep you well and happy and comfortable."

"The Women's Institute," said Berry, "assures The Old Folk's Home."

"You know what I mean. Now, if to bring this off, you've got to have them all out, then you must do it. I mean, if that's the price of your health. But if that's not necessary yet, I'm the last person to – "

"Let sleeping dogs lie," said Berry.

"I'm inclined to agree," said Jonah. "But the very next time they stir…"

Three days later, at half past four in the morning, the sleeping dogs woke. And more than woke. They stretched themselves and sat up. I'm not sure they didn't bark.

Grey in the face with pain, Berry stood the assault extremely well. But action had to be taken. At half past five that evening he entered a nursing-home.

Two days later we were seated about his bed.

"Mhat mife hmeebig mogs mow?" he demanded.

"Darling," said Daphne, "for heaven's sake don't try to talk."

Her husband seized his pad and wrote some words violently down.

Looking over his shoulder, Jill read the sentence aloud.

"I abhor my vacuum. How soon can it be filled?"

"Darling," said Daphne, "your poor gums have got to heal."

Berry made a noise like a cat. Then he snatched his pad and scrawled his riposte.

"Will you answer my question?" read Jill.

"Very soon, darling," purred Daphne. "Rodrigues is coming on Thursday to take the stitches out."

Berry looked dazedly round.

"Miggies? Mop miggies?" he demanded.

Daphne swallowed.

Then –

"Darling, he's done your teeth in the very latest way. This will ensure that your new ones fit like a glove."

Berry seized his pad.

"Gloves be damned. Exactly what has this butcher done to my mouth?"

"As I understand it," I said, "Rodrigues laid open your gums upon either side. This exposed the roots of your teeth. The latter were then picked out, instead of lugged. It was then very simple to swill the groove right out. When this had been done, the flaps were put back into place and stitched together. When they're healed, you'll have clean, smooth bars running right round your mouth."

Berry's face was a study.

After a moment or two, he picked up his pad.

"A major operation, without my consent. Supposing my heart had given out."

"Why should it?" said Jonah. "This is a vast improvement on lugging out tooth after tooth. Far less shock to the system."

"I should have been consulted," wrote Berry.

"My darling," said Daphne, "you weren't in a state to consult. I had to decide for you."

"I was mad with pain," wrote Berry. "America must have just found the carbolic bomb. Can I go home now?"

"As soon, my sweet, as you have the stitches out. Have you any pain now?"

"Well, I suppose you might call it pain. My mouth feels as if it had been recently flayed, after having been jacked up first."

"I'm sure," said I, "that Rodrigues knows his job."

"I'm glad of that," wrote Berry. "I mean after all this, it would be nice to find he didn't, wouldn't it? I suppose they counted the swabs. Of course it feels as if he'd left a couple of forceps behind."

"Oh, he'd've seen them," said Jonah. "It's only in abdominal operations that they leave their tools behind. Of course if he let a pair slip…"

"Emoove pvat mam," raged Berry. "Amome be mawpet. Mll mem my membiber ub."

We calmed him down and produced the backgammon board.

*

A fortnight later Jonah's Rolls stole up to the foot of the steps.

Carson alighted and opened the near-side door. And Berry got out.

"Thank you, Carson," he said. "Do they look all right?"

"They look a treat, sir," said Carson.

"Good," said Berry – and turned to us on the steps.

At the foot, he paused: then he uncovered and gave us a film-star smile.

"Marvellous," said Daphne.

And so they were.

"Are they comfortable?" said I.

"I keep on forgetting," said Berry, "I've got them in."

"Isn't that fun?" said Jill.

"Try and yawn," said Jonah.

The suggestion was enough.

My brother-in-law yawned. But his teeth never moved.

"That's a great triumph," said I.

Berry mounted the steps and embraced his wife.

"How does it feel to be kissed by a man with false fangs?"

"Very nice," said Daphne. "Do it again. And now come in and sit down. Tea's just about due."

"I see," said Berry, thoughtfully. "Tea. Yes. I could do with a cuppa."

"Bridget," said Jill, "has made a 'washerwoman's cake'."

"Oh, dear," said Berry. "I know. I'll have it upstairs."

"Don't be absurd," said Daphne. "They'll never move."

"I'm sure they won't. They might belong to my jaws. But I don't want to defile them – they look so nice and clean."

"They'll recover," said Jonah. "A little paraffin in the water, and no one will know they've been used. Carson'll do them for you: he's got to wash the Rolls."

As soon as he could speak –

"No," said Berry. "Supposing they dented the bucket… You blasphemous dog," he added, "wait till you see the gew-gaws. Their proper place is in the *Rue de la Paix*. And there's Bridget. Bridget, come and look at my teeth."

The housekeeper complied.

Then she turned to Daphne.

"Aren't they lovely, madam? And they make you look younger, sir. No one would take you for more than fifty now."

"Bridget's quite right," said Jill.

"Poor Faust," said Berry. "If only he'd known Rodrigues…"

Tea was proceeding quietly, when Berry let out a yell and clapped a hand to his mouth.

"My God," said Daphne, "don't say – "

"They're getting jealous," howled Berry. "They've bitten my tongue."

Before this contretemps, I confess that we all broke down.

"My darling," wailed Daphne, "it's only because you've been without them so long."

"Venomous swine," raved Berry. "That's what they are. Turning on the old hands like that. Have to have a false tongue presently."

To do the occasion honour, we drank champagne that night. Perhaps because of this, dinner went with a bang.

We retired just before midnight.

At a quarter past twelve my sister came to our room.

"Oh, Boy, it's dreadful," she whispered. "He can't get them out."

Scantily clothed, Jill and I repaired to the neighbouring chamber. Jonah saw us, as he came to the head of the stairs.

Kneeling beside his bed, leaning over a face-towel, Berry was manhandling his jaws.

"But why the posture?" said Jonah.

"In case I drop them," snarled Berry. "Then they'll fall on the bed and come to no harm."

"I should leave them," said I. "Swill out your mouth like hell, and leave them alone. I mean it's all to the good."

"Nonsense," said Berry. "Nonsense. Their bed of antiseptic is waiting. Besides, they haven't been out yet. Or am I thinking of dogs?"

Her face pressed into my shoulder, Jill fought not to laugh.

"I'll get a torch," said Jonah. "I expect there's a spring you press."

"What d'you mean – a torch?" said Berry.

"Well, I don't want to fumble," said Jonah.

Berry looked round.

"He doesn't want to fumble," he said brokenly. He laughed a hideous laugh. "I don't think he'd fumble long."

"Darling," said Daphne, "for God's sake leave them in. And ring up Rodrigues tomorrow and he'll tell you what to do."

"But my mouth must be cleansed," cried Berry. "Think of all the mess I've eaten tonight. And cheese straws and all."

Jonah laid a hand on his shoulder.

"If I wash my hands in Dettol, will you let me get them out?"

"Not on your life," said Berry. "You'll break the blasted things."

"Well, get hold of them and pull."

"You can't be rough with them," said Berry: "they're a very delicate job. A chaplet of pearls, they are. Two chaplets. Jewellers' work."

"Stronger than you think," said I. "Go on. Put it across them."

Berry bent to the bed and covered his face with the towel.

After some frightful contortions, he laid the towel carefully down and looked about him.

"Mell, matph map," he mouthed. "Mope a man ptmep mem mack."

*

I suppose it was very foolish, but all of us, Berry included, believed he was out of the wood.

It was nearly a month later, when April was ushering May, that, while we were having dinner, Berry clapped a hand to his mouth.

"What ever's the matter?" said Daphne.

Berry regarded his wife.

"D'you really want to know?"

"Oh, dear. P'raps we'd better not," she said.

"After all, why shouldn't you thuffer? There you are. I'm lithping now."

"But you never did that before."

"I know. It's delayed action. And there's a dirty one. I've just paid Rodrigues' account."

"I know what it is," said Jonah. "Your gums have shrunk."

Berry regarded him defiantly.

"What d'you mean – thrunk…srunk…SHRUNK? There you are. Perfect enunciation all my life. Clear as a blasted bell. And now I'm starting to lithp."

He covered his eyes.

"But what happened, darling?" said Jill.

"I was engaged in math – mastication – a very healthy pursuit. And the lower rank – the stalls – rose up, possibly out of zeal. Let us say they pursued their prey. But that's very dithcontherting."

"I expect it's the spinach," purred Daphne. "I mean, that is rather clinging."

"That's right," said Jonah. "The suction of the spinach was stronger than the suction of your teeth. When the gums have finished shrinking, you'll have to have a new set."

"And till then?" screamed Berry.

Jonah glanced at the ceiling, before proceeding with his meal…

Rodrigues, when appealed to, explained that that was sometimes the way. He would make a new set with pleasure, but not for three months.

On receiving the unpalatable news, Berry looked dazedly round.

"Three months?" he cried. "D'you mean to tell me I've got to have thethe – these interlopers frolicking about my mouth for the next three monthth?"

Worse was to come.

Before the week was out, if Berry bit anything hard, beneath the pressure his teeth began to tilt.

When this had happened twice during luncheon, Berry laid down his napkin, rose to his feet, bowed to Daphne in silence and left the room.

We followed him, naturally.

"Darling, I'm terribly sorry: but it can't be as bad as that."

As he lighted a cigarette –

"It's quite all right," said Berry. "You go and finish your repast. I'm going to fast for a bit. You know, like Mothadecq. Probably do me good. If I get too weak, I can be artificially fed."

"But, Berry darling," cried Jill, "if you don't eat you'll get ill."

"My sweet," said Berry, "at present I can still drink and smoke. At times I can speak with coherence. For the present, those mercies must suffice. The consumption of food, once an agreeable pastime, has become a hideouth penance, to which I am no longer prepared to submit. My mouth becomes the scene of a painful and vulgar brawl, which my tongue is unable or reluctant to control. I'm inclined to think it's reluctance. Its attitude is that of a servant who, having spent many years with the nobility, finds himself compelled to take service with *nouveaux riches*. His insolent contempt for their *gaucheries* has to be experienced to be believed. All that is going on in my mouth at every meal. In these circumstances, can anyone be surprised that I am, tho to thpeak, off my feed?"

Protracted consultations with Bridget produced a special diet – for Berry alone. Nourishing, no doubt, the dishes were distinguished by a dreadful similarity – so far as appearance went.

When we were served with roast duck, Berry was offered a casserole, containing a generous portion of beige-coloured slush.

Berry regarded it with starting eyes. Then he looked round.

"I thought you said the dog was well," he said.

This was too much.

"You filthy brute," shrieked Daphne. "Just because you can't eat – "

"My mistake," said Berry, helping himself. "But I've never eaten swamp before. I didn't recognize it at first. Am I to have a milk-pudding afterwards? Just as *la bonne bouche*?"

We began to count the days...

On the whole, he was very long-suffering. To celebrate Jill's birthday, he insisted on our visiting Lisbon and consuming at his expense as excellent a dinner as any connoisseur could devise. On mulligatawny soup, scrambled eggs and ice-pudding, he was the life of the party from first to last.

He went to see Rodrigues the following day.

A fortnight later, he saw Rodrigues again.

On his return to the quinta, he displayed a basket of fruit.

"I couldn't resist it," he explained. "You know that elegant shop in the Rua —. They do display their wares in a most attractive way."

"It's simply lovely," said Daphne. "How very sweet of you, darling. Mafalda, ask Bridget to come."

The bright-eyed maid went flying.

When the housekeeper appeared –

"Look at that, Bridget," said Daphne.

"Oh, isn't it lovely, madam. So perfectly arranged. I can make a fruit-salad for the Major."

"Shame," said Berry. "Such magnificent specimens must be done the honour of being eaten raw."

"Oh, you must have some of it, sir."

"I think you're right," said Berry.

With that, he picked up an apple and bit a piece out.

We stared upon him open-mouthed.

When he had bitten it up –

"As good as they look," he said. "Have we got any almond-rock?"

*

Once more himself, Berry revived a subject which he had allowed to lie dormant for nearly six months.

After dinner one August evening, he approached it boldly enough.

"No one, I think, will deny that my memoir was well received."

All four of us looked at him.

Then –

"What memoir?" said his wife.

Berry frowned.

"*As Berry and I Were Saying*," he said.

In his practice of the art of provocation, my brother-in-law could give a communist points.

Whilst Jonah and I were laughing, Daphne and Jill denounced him with a fury which knew no law.

Finally –

"It's simply monstrous," said Daphne. "It was a most generous title. All you did was to shove in some stuff about brandy which nobody read."

"And trustees," cried Jill. "Silly rubbish that lawyers are paid to do."

Berry looked uneasily round.

"The Sapphira Sisters calling. You really must be careful. How should we frame the announcement in *The Times*? 'Suddenly, as the result of subjecting the godly to an obscene libel...' I mean, it would look so unusual."

Before Daphne could get her breath –

"All this," I said, "is a screen of highly offensive smoke. By the time we emerge, the demand which he means to make will seem, by comparison, so modest that you will support him against me, when I refuse to play."

"What's his demand?" said Daphne.

"That a second memoir," said Berry, "should be begun at once."

There was a pregnant silence.

Then –

"It – it would be nice," said Jill.

"There you are," said I.

"Of course we must do it," said Berry. "Hardly had the book gone to press, when all manner of gems I'd forgotten came flooding into my mind."

"Matter of adjustment," said Jonah. "The ball-cock wouldn't close."

With an indignant stare –

"I cannot felicitate you," said Berry, "upon your choice of metaphor." He shrugged his shoulders. "It's not altogether your fault. If I had a mind like a greasetrap, who knows what indiscretions I might not commit."

Another of the arts which Berry has mastered is that of confusing his foes. He will offer them so many openings that they do not know which to take. Into one short sentence he will compress more inaccuracy, insult, self-praise and *suggestio falsi* than I would have believed possible.

Availing myself of his tactics –

"I don't suppose," I said, "that a memoir has ever appeared to which the author would not have added, had it not been too late. I, too, have remembered things which might very well have gone in. But, for one very simple reason, a second memoir, or sequel, will never appear. The reason is this. If you added our afterthoughts together, they'd run to some fifty pages, if as much. Well, you can't bind up fifty pages and offer them to the public for twelve and six."

There was another silence.

Then –

"How many pages," said Daphne, "was *As Berry and I Were Saying*?"

"Two hundred and eighty-three."

Even Berry was silenced by this disparity.

I continued to improve the occasion.

"If you want another reason, I'm busy. I've yet to finish the book I'm writing now."

"I should let that go," said Berry. "If it's no better than *Ne'er Do Well...*"

When Daphne and Jill had finished –

"As a matter of fact," said Jonah, "*Ne'er Do Well* was uncommonly good. Compared with most of Boy's stuff, it was not sensational. But it was a most accurate picture of Scotland Yard at work."

"I fear it was dull," I said.

"I didn't find it so."

"You're very good."

"The book took charge?"

"I'll say it did. I've never been driven so hard. After Falcon's appearance, it ran right away."

"Night after night," said Jill, "he was working till half past one."

"What *does* that mean?" said Daphne. " 'The book takes charge.' "

"It's terribly hard to explain. Something takes charge and tells me what to write. I can only suppose it's a sort of sub-conscious brain. And the conscious brain, which I'm using to talk to you now, accepts what it says and frames the sentences."

"And you don't know what's coming?"

"Never. In *Ne'er Do Well*, for instance, I'd not the faintest idea who'd committed the crime." Jill picked up the novel and put it into my hand. "That is revealed to the reader on page – wait a minute – on page one hundred and fifty-six. I think I realized who'd done it when I was writing page one hundred and fifty-one. It may have been later than that, but it certainly wasn't before."

"And one reviewer," said Jill, "said it was obvious from the first."

I shrugged my shoulders.

"His sight was keener than mine."

"Which is absurd," said Jonah. "I tried hard enough, but I hadn't the faintest idea."

"You say," said Berry, "you say it's the sub-conscious brain."

"In desperation," I said. "I'm quite prepared for a doctor to say that's rubbish. But I can't explain it in any other way."

"You must be mental," said Berry. "I've always thought there was something. When I tell you to rise above pain, you never do. You don't seem to get it, somehow."

There was an electric silence.

Then –

"I seem to remember," said Daphne, "that some ten days ago you didn't 'seem to get it', when I made a similar request. I never was so ashamed in all my life."

(When Berry is attacked by lumbago, nobody within earshot is unaware of the fact. On the last, unforgettable occasion, his roars and yells were actually reported to the police – who presently arrived in a car, in the belief that violence was being done.)

"That," said Berry, "was my sub-conscious brain. I never had the faintest idea that I was about to exclaim. When I heard my exclamations, the conscious brain was inexpressibly shocked." Before we could dispute this reading, he had thrown us another fly. "When will you finish the classic upon which you are now engaged?"

"Not for some time," I said.

"Is it any good?"

"I don't know. When it's done I shall make up my mind whether or no I should like to see it in print."

"Give it to me," said Berry. "I'll tell you in half an hour. And then, if I say it's tripe, you needn't go on."

"I'm much obliged; but I'd rather judge it myself."

"What about this?" said Jonah. "When you feel inclined, in the evenings, let's have the memoir piecemeal. Memory breeds, you know: and while you're relating one, another reminiscence will, as like as not, come to mind. By the time you've both done, you may have enough for a book. And then, perhaps, when it's finished, you'll read us your tale."

"Lovely," said Daphne.

Jill said nothing, but looked at me and smiled.

"I'm on," said Berry.

The others regarded me.

"On one condition," I said.

"Yes?"

"That no one shall interrupt me, whilst I am reading the tale. When I come to the end of a chapter, then you shall say what you please."

"Understood," said everyone but Berry.

I looked at him.

"But – "

"Nothing doing," I said.

"May I put up a hand?" he said. "That will mean that I have a question to ask – not that I'm seeking your permission to repair to – "

Submerged by a surge of protest from my sister and wife, the rest of the sentence was lost.

"You are disgusting," said Jill. "Just because – "

"As you were," said Berry, "as you were. The subconscious brain again. You know, I was quite surprised when I heard what I said."

"You wicked liar," said Daphne.

"Well, let's try again," said Berry. "Should I make an arresting gesture, that will mean that I have a question to ask or a precious statement to make."

"That's all right," I said, "provided you make no sound."

"I see," said Berry. "I see. Supposing you, er, don't see the gesture?"

"That will be just too bad."

"There you are," howled Berry. "He's going to ignore my gestures – cheerfully keep me waiting for hours on end."

At last, under duress, he gave his word.

In fact, this was just what I wanted – to 'try my tale on the dog'. I was not so sure of my judgment, as I had been in the past. I had hesitated a lot, before I let *Ne'er Do Well* go. I knew the new tale was 'all right': but I wanted to be sure that it was up to my standard, such as that is. If it was, the book would be published: if it wasn't, it would stay in my safe.

*

Berry was regarding the ceiling.

"If I remember," he said, "I allowed you to introduce into my memoir certain sordid recollections of the criminal courts. It was very weak of me."

"They sold the book," said Daphne.

"My love," said Berry, "how often have I told you that to be offensive, it is unnecessary to be mendacious? Never mind. I, too, have memories of the law: but, with one exception, I should not presume to recite them, arresting as they are. The exception concerns a matter of law in France. It was not a criminal case. We all know the singular rapidity and brilliance with which the French execute and administer the criminal law. The triple murder of the Drummonds leaps to the mind."

"Oh, don't," said Daphne.

"And then, if I remember, there was an English schoolmistress who was – unfortunate... But, as I have said, this was not a criminal case.

"We were in France for the winter, and, it being the fashion just then, we engaged a cook. If I remember, she knew her mystery. In other words, the meals which she presented were very good. Unhappily, her self-control left much to be desired. Indeed, so vile was her temper that, before she had been with us a month, she had to be dismissed. So Daphne fired her and asked me to pay her off. I paid her one month's wages and another month's wages in lieu of notice. That, of course, I need not have done: but we didn't want any trouble, and so I did.

"When I laid the money down –

" 'What's this?' said the lady.

" 'Two months' wages,' I said. 'Much more than you deserve.'

" 'I demand a year's wages,' she said. 'I was engaged by the year.'

" 'Rubbish,' I said. 'Take up your money and go.'

"After a painful scene, she took the money and went: but not before she had warned me.

" 'Monsieur will hear from my lawyer,' was what she said.

"We gave the matter no thought, for threats, however idle, are easy to make. But her threat was not idle at all, for a day or two later a *notaire*'s letter arrived. This declared – with many expressions of devotion – that, unless I paid the lady twelve months' wages, I should receive a writ.

"Well, I went to see Laborde, who had seen to our lease and one or two things like that.

" 'Have you ever heard,' I said, 'of any domestic servant's being engaged by the year?'

" 'Never, Monsieur,' he said. 'Neither has anyone else. The woman must be deranged.'

" 'She didn't give me that impression,' I said. 'Never mind. Please accept service and keep me informed.'

" 'Monsieur will have to go to Court.'

" 'That's all right by me,' I said. 'I never submit to blackmail.'

"Well, the proceedings took shape. He engaged a nice young counsel – he said it was better so. And the case was presently 'fixed' for an April afternoon. It was to be heard in a little village court-room some five miles off; and when the day arrived, I called for my young counsel and took him with me in the car.

"Our case was first in the list on that sunshiny afternoon, and I took good care to be there in plenty of time. I was given a nice front seat by my counsel's side. I didn't see the cook, but he said that she was there. When the three Judges, robed, came in, I naturally rose and bowed. I fear such reverence was not usually accorded, for all three returned my bow with their eyes on my face.

" 'Admirable', whispered my counsel, as we resumed our seats. 'Monsieur has nothing to learn.'

"I don't suppose the cook thought of bowing, and I am inclined to think that her case was dead as mutton from that time on. However, *pro forma* it was heard.

"Her solicitor said a few words and then put her into the box.

"When she said that she claimed a year's wages, the Judges stared upon her as though she were out of her mind. And then they fell upon her – all three, and all at once. They cross-examined her, they cautioned her, they rebuked her, they contradicted her, they interrupted her, they looked at one another and laughed very nasty laughs: and then they returned to the worry and tore and ate her again. But one thing they didn't do. They didn't daunt her. And I must confess to admiration for the way in which she rode out the storm, like a well-found ship at sea. After a quarter of an hour she was ordered to stand down, and the Judges sat back in their seats.

"My counsel rose to his feet, but the senior Judge waved him away. 'You've no case to answer,' he said. 'Judgment for Monsieur with costs.'

" 'I shall appeal,' cried the cook, from the back of the court.

"The three Judges laughed like hell. Then, 'All right,' said the senior Judge. 'You lodge your appeal.'

"Then the three of them rose, and everyone else got up. They all bowed directly to me, and of course I bowed back. And then they left the Bench and we left the court.

"I'd berthed the car under some limes, and as we were walking towards her, I turned to my counsel and spoke.

" 'Will she really appeal?' I said.

" 'I hardly think so, Monsieur. She may of course.'

" 'Where would her appeal be heard?'

" 'But here, Monsieur. Here, in this court.'

" 'And who will hear it?' I said.

"My question seemed to surprise him.

" 'But the same three Judges, Monsieur. They are, as you have seen, very able men.'

"I felt rather dazed.

" 'But not the same three?' I said. 'I mean, she's appealing from them.'

" 'The same three, Monsieur.' I put a hand to my head. 'Monsieur need have no fear. Their judgment will be the same.'

"I didn't pursue the matter. And while we were driving back I spoke of other things. But my brain was unruly. For some reason I kept on wondering what, if she did appeal, would be the cook's emotions when she first perceived the composition of the court.

"Now that is the plain truth. And Daphne will bear me out."

"It's perfectly true," said Daphne. "When he came back he was like a man in a dream."

"I believe you," said Jonah. "But I don't think everyone will."

"I'm afraid they won't," said Berry. "I should add that she didn't appeal. Possibly she inquired, as I did, by whom the appeal would be heard – and on being informed, as I was, decided that her chance of success was rather too thin." He looked at me. "Such procedure belongs to the Magistrate's Court at Fiddle in *The Stolen March*."

"That," said I, "is undeniable. In fact, if I'd known it in time, I'd have put it into the book."

"Well, that was France – some time in the nineteen-twenties. We can all remember many maddening examples of their unbelievable inefficiency: but until that afternoon it had never entered my head that their judicial system was distinguished by an absurdity so grotesque that even Gilbert would have hesitated to introduce it into one of his incomparable extravaganzas.

"And now it's Boy's turn."

"I can't approach that," I said.

"Something intimate," said Jonah, "that you won't get anywhere else. For instance, can you remember your first appearance in Court? As counsel, I mean."

I nodded.

"With considerable shame. I assume that you mean the first time I rose to my feet and lifted my voice."

"I do."

"It was at the Sessions at Maidstone. I appeared for the Crown in a very simple case. More. It was a plea of guilty, so I simply couldn't go wrong. More. The presiding Justice or Chairman was Coles Child, a member of my own Club. For all that and wide as my experience already was, I was quite painfully nervous. I didn't stammer, but I did everything else. I was quite unable to remember the conventional phrases and words – and Coles Child smiled very gently and put them into my mouth. I never felt so grateful – and so much ashamed."

"Darling," said Jill, "it was understandable."

"It wasn't, my sweet, for I'd seen so much of the Courts. For a year I'd been in one or the other every day – High Court, Police Court, Old Bailey. I knew the procedure backwards, as few young counsel did. And then, when my turn came, I went to bits."

"Did it happen again?" said Jonah.

"Never, thank God. That dreadful occasion cured me for good and all. I bearded Eve J once, when not even the head of my chambers would touch the brief. I was, of course, terribly lucky to be before Coles Child in the second Court. For he was a most charming man. Cranbrook, presiding in the first, would have been less tolerant. He got very cross with me when I was conducting the first real case I had. To be honest, I don't know that I blame him."

"Why d'you say that?"

"It was a miscarriage of justice. I was for the defence and I got my man off."

Jill put in her oar.

"Was he really guilty, Boy?"

"I'm afraid he was."

"And you sit there," said Berry, "you have the effrontery to – "

"Let's have it," said Jonah. "Boy's doing as I desired. Heaps of big shots at the Bar have written memoirs: but they never report the painful figure they cut when first they rose to their feet or how they fooled a jury into setting a felon free."

"Possibly," said Berry, "they had a sense of decency."

"Rubbish," said Daphne. "They didn't want people to know. Boy mayn't have been a big shot, but at least he's honest about it."

I began to laugh.

"There you are," said Berry. "He finds this outrageous memory matter for mirth. Never mind. Don't keep us waiting."

"As a matter of fact," said I, "I was thinking of something else. Jonah's words remembered the incident. I was present when a very famous big shot made his first appearance in court. I knew him quite well. He was called to the Bar before me – I was still a solicitor's pupil which was how I came to be at Bow Street when first he got to his feet. You see, I was with Muskett, who was appearing, as usual, for the prosecution; and Wilson, as I will call him, had been briefed for the defence. Quite frankly, he shouldn't have been briefed, for he was right out of his depth. But he'd been chucked into the water and told to swim. I think Sir Albert de Rutzen was on the Bench. He was, of course, lucky there. But I really believe he cut as bad a figure as I did – if that is possible. I was terribly sorry for him, but, of course, I couldn't help. And Muskett was so gentle – so very sympathetic. He never showed him up, as some would have done. As best he could, he covered him. But his flounderings made me writhe. I really never was so sorry for anyone. Happily the case was soon over. How the client felt about it, I have no idea. But it was terribly good for Wilson, for that is the way to get on – to be just chucked into the water and told to swim. And his rise was very rapid. He went to the war all right and put up a first rate show, and then he came back to the Bar and became a famous man, as he richly deserved."

"And you actually witnessed the very first struggles he made?"

I nodded.

"I did, indeed."

"Did they all begin like that? I mean, is that your belief?"

"I've no idea. I imagine some of them did. But I can't see the late Lord Birkenhead getting stage fright."

"And now let's have your confession."

"I'm not at all proud of it," I said, "and I think I'd better have some more port."

"Jumping powder," said Berry, filling my glass.

"Darling," said Daphne, "no end of people have done it."

"I know," said I. "But they have the sense to keep it under their hats. Never mind. Here we go."

"There was some sort of Show or Exhibition somewhere in Kent. It went on for a fortnight, I think, and a lot of tradesmen had stalls. The Show was closed every evening, as a matter of course: but the tradesmen could hardly be expected to remove their wares every evening and bring them all back the next day. Yet, their stalls couldn't be locked. And so they engaged a night-watchman, to discourage thieves. For all that, night after night, goods disappeared.

"No one could understand this – the night-watchman least of all. The latter inclined to the view that the thief attended the show and then remained behind when the public left. 'An' then he can watch me, you see, and seize his chance.'

"One stall-holder felt very sore, for his stall had been visited twice by the thief or thieves. And he said, 'I'll catch the —. I'll lie in wait myself.' And so he did. Two nights running the night-watchman let him in about half past nine, and he watched right through the night. But the thief never came. 'Oh, I give up,' he said. 'If you ask me,' said the night-watchman, 'you've frightened the — off.' 'Let's hope so,' said the tradesman. 'I can't go on like this.' But he could and did. On the third night he never came in, because he had never gone out. The night-watchman didn't know this…

"And so it came to pass that he caught the night-watchman red-handed with three of his precious exhibits under his arm.

"When he seized his man, the latter begged for mercy and put the goods back on the shelf. 'Let me go,' he begged, 'for the sake of my wife and children.' 'You dirty dog,' said the other, 'you're coming straight to the station here and now.'

"The night-watchman was accordingly charged and cast into jail. At the police-court he pleaded not guilty and reserved his defence: and so he was committed for trial, and I was presently briefed on his behalf.

"As you will have gathered, I hadn't a rag of a case. The stall-holder's evidence apart, once the fellow was out of the way no more thefts occurred. And he was most unattractive: he had a most shocking squint, his proportions suggested that he did himself very well, and he had an oily demeanour that made you feel slightly sick. He looked the rogue he was. He had no defence at all, except that the charge made against him was quite untrue. I dared not put him in the box.

"Well, counsel for the Crown did his stuff. He opened the case very shortly – and duly pointed out that, since the prisoner was paid to guard the stalls, it ill became him to play the thief himself. Then he called the stallholder…

"When the latter entered the box, I saw at once that he was a hot-tempered man, and so when my turn came, I decided to pull his leg.

"Well, he told his tale just as I've told it to you – how he'd waited two nights in vain and how on the third he'd caught the night-watchman out. Then I rose to cross-examine…

" 'Are you sure you didn't dream this?' I said. 'You were very short of sleep.'

"His reply was so violent that the jury began to laugh…

"All's fair in love and war, so I led him on – asking him questions designed to provoke his wrath. He rose to every fly, and the jury laughed like hell. But Cranbrook saw my game and began to get cross.

" 'What's the point of these questions?' he said.

"Well, I couldn't very well tell him. Besides, he knew. So I bowed and sat down at once – much to the jury's annoyance, for they were enjoying themselves. From their point of view, Cranbrook had spoiled sport.

"The stall-holder left the box, and counsel for the Crown summed up. Then I rose to address the Court.

"I can't remember most of what I said, but I do remember suggesting that, after the sleepless and fruitless nights, each followed by a tiring day, the stall-holder was ready to see anything and seize anyone who so much as approached his stall. I think I put it better than that, for the jury laughed quite a lot. Then I sat down, feeling quite hopeful; and when Cranbrook, who was fuming, summed up dead against me, I felt that the jury might take the bit in their teeth.

"And so they did. To Cranbrook's justified fury, they found the night-watchman not guilty – and that was that.

"Of course it was an outrage: but it wasn't a major crime, and I had only done what I was engaged to do."

"I can only hope," said Berry, "that you are ashamed of yourself."

"When I think of the stall-holder, I am. It was most unfair. But Cranbrook did his bit. I should never have got away with it before Coles Child."

"Why?" said Daphne.

"Well, he would have smiled with the jury and left me alone. And then, in his summing up, he'd have said, 'Well, we've all had a good laugh, gentlemen, but now I'm afraid we've got to get back to the facts.' Or something like that. And the jury would have done as he said."

"Nor," said Jonah, "would you have got away with it at the Old Bailey."

"Not on your life," said I. "A City of London jury would have put me where I belonged."

"Well, I'm glad he got off," said Jill.

"I don't expect," said I, "he was free very long."

Berry cleared his throat.

"After this shocking revelation – "

"Rubbish," said Daphne. "You know it's done all the time. Boy's job was to get the man off, and I consider he did it extremely well."

"He knew he was guilty," said Berry.

"I had no doubt," I said. "But he didn't admit it to me. If he had, I should have made him plead guilty, or else have returned the brief."

"Is that the law?" said Jill.

"The unwritten law, my sweet. A barrister's first duty is to the Court."

"Duty?" cried Berry. "You don't know the meaning of the word. You twisted an honest man's tail and then befooled twelve others. I don't wonder Cranbrook was cross. I wish you'd been before me. I'd have made you think. And now go back for a minute. Just now you mentioned Eve, the Chancery Judge. And you said you'd bearded him when no one else in your chambers would touch the case. May we have that reminiscence? Or is it as obscene as it sounds?"

I began to laugh.

"There's nothing obscene about it. It's really more of a side-light on the spirit and manners of the Bar – in 1913, any way."

"Proceed," said Berry.

"Well, a brief came into Chambers one Wednesday afternoon – pretty late, it was, I think, about five o'clock. The senior clerk was out, but the junior took it in. When the senior clerk returned, he saw at once that it was a Chancery brief.

"Now as, no doubt, you know, the procedure in the Chancery Courts is entirely different to that in the Common Law Courts and Chancery matters are handled by Chancery men. And Chancery's a very close borough – at least, it used to be. But we were Common Lawyers in Number One, Brick Court.

"The name of the head of my Chambers was on the brief, but he was down in the country doing some motoring case; so the senior clerk rang up the firm of solicitors who'd sent the brief, thanked them politely and said there was some mistake.

" 'No, there isn't,' said the managing clerk. 'We'd like Mr Harker to do it, although he's not a Chancery man.'

" 'Well, I don't think he will,' said our clerk. 'It's not his line. Any way, he's down in the country and won't be back till late. And I see it's fixed for tomorrow afternoon.'

" 'Well, try him,' said the other. 'It's only an application – won't take him a quarter of an hour.'

" 'What if he won't?' said our clerk.

" 'You've other gentlemen in Chambers. Give it to one of them. It's a loser, any way. Eve will never grant it. But it's got to be made.'

"So our clerk said, 'All right' and put it on Harker's table against his return."

"Nice sort of solicitors," said Berry.

"They were only acting as agents for a North Country firm. As like as not, they didn't do Chancery work. But they knew and liked Harker and thought it best to go to someone they knew. Besides, they were up against time.

"Well, Harker never got back till seven o'clock – to London, I mean. So he never came to Chambers, but went straight home. When he arrived the next morning, there was the brief on the table, waiting for him. He took it up and looked at the back-sheet.

" 'What's this?' he said. 'This ought to have gone to the other side of the road.'

27

"I'd better explain that saying. The Inner and Middle Temple are Common Law Inns of Court: and The Temple lies south of Fleet Street. Lincoln's Inn is the home of the Chancery Bar: and that lies north of Fleet Street and so, as we always said, 'on the other side of the road.' "

"What about Gray's Inn?" said Jonah.

"I can't be sure," I said, "but I think some Chancery men were members of that. Common Lawyers certainly were. Birkenhead's Inn was Gray's Inn.

"And now to go back.

"The clerk explained the position and Harker heard him out.

"Then –

" 'I'm not going to do it,' he said. 'I'd like to oblige them, but I've been at the Bar too long to go out of my ground and make a fool of myself in a Chancery Court. Before Eve, too. No thank you.'

"When the clerk brought it to me, I had a look at the back-sheet and shook my head. 'Nothing doing,' I said. 'Try somebody else.'

"Well, no one would take it on. So the clerk came back to me. 'They're all afraid, sir,' he said. 'Well, so am I,' I said. 'He can't eat you, sir. Have a look at the case.' Just then his telephone went, so he laid the brief on my table and left the room. I eyed it uncertainly. I wasn't sure Eve couldn't eat me, but I was rather ashamed of being afraid. Harker couldn't afford to make a fool of himself; but I had no standing at all.

"So I rang up a fellow I knew at the Chancery Bar. When I told him what had happened, he laughed like hell. (I think it was his derision that forced me up to the gate. When I heard his mocking laughter, I knew I should take the case.) 'Go and be murdered,' he said. 'Old Eve will chew you up. Besides, you're poaching. That's a Chancery brief.' 'That's not my fault,' I said. 'The solicitors like us best. Now be a sport and tell me what to do.' 'I'd love to be there,' he said, 'but I'm on in another Court.' 'Thank God for that,' said I. 'But how do I go to work?'

"Well, so far as I could make out, applications were made, as usual, after the luncheon adjournment at two o'clock. My job was to sit quite still and hold my tongue until the usher cried out *Any more motions behind the bar*? And if nobody else got up, then I must get to my feet and state my case."

"What does that mean?" said Daphne. "What is a motion and what is 'behind the bar'?"

"I didn't know then, my sweet, and I don't know now. And, frankly, I really don't care. The words are Chancery lingo and they can have them for me."

"Allow me to observe," said Berry, "that you ought to be in jail. Talk about obtaining money by false pretences..."

"Be quiet," said everyone.

"Well, then I read the brief."

"Only then," said Berry. "God give me strength."

"First things first," I said. "Besides, they'd said it was a loser...

"Well, when I read it, it gave me rather a shock. The motion or application – "

"There you are," said Berry. "You said a moment ago you didn't know what a motion meant."

"At that moment, I didn't," I said. "But now I do remember that, when someone makes an application to a Judge, he is said to be 'moving the Court' to do as he asks.

"Well, the motion or application which I was to make was on behalf of two sons to commit to prison their father for Contempt of Court."

"You do seem to have had some nice cases," said Berry. "Parricide now."

"I admit it sounds rather bad; but it wasn't as bad as it sounds. As far as I can remember, the position was roughly this.

"The father and his sons had a business in a North Country town. All three were partners. The sons, I may say, were hard-working, married men. A few months before, the three had agreed together to sell the business, as it stood. They had received an offer of twelve thousand pounds. This they had accepted. The father, as senior partner, was to take six, and each of the junior partners three thousand pounds.

"Well, the business was taken over, but the purchaser didn't pay. When the sons protested, their father said, 'That's all right. He only wants time.' Several weeks went by. At last the sons got impatient, and one of them went to see the purchaser. The latter said nothing, but rose and went to his safe. Then he laid before the son his father's receipt for the sum of twelve thousand pounds. This bore the very date on which the purchase money should have been paid.

"As you may well believe, that was more than enough for the sons. They went to Court forthwith, and the father was ordered to pay the two their share, six thousand pounds, within seven days.

"That order was made on Monday, so he had till Monday next. But now the sons had discovered that their father had booked his passage for South America, and that the ship was due to sail on Saturday next. So that, if no action was taken, on Monday next he would be out of the jurisdiction... Hence this application.

"There could be no doubt that their money had already been transferred to some South American Bank: so that if their father sailed, they would never see it again. So I was to ask for an order to apprehend him at once and put him into prison, so that he could not sail. His behaviour, of course, was gross Contempt of Court.

"There's no pretending that it was a savoury case. Sons don't ask for their fathers to be cast into jail. But fathers, as a rule, don't double-cross their sons: and six thousand pounds was a very great deal of money in 1913. The trouble was that Eve was not a Queen's Bench Judge. He was very old-fashioned and had nothing to do with crime. I don't suppose he'd ever been inside the Old Bailey. And he would be shocked to the marrow by an application which was redolent of such impiety.

"Well, I reached his Court in good time and sat down to wait for my cue. As the benches filled up, my neighbours regarded me. And not with sympathy. For I was a stranger – and I had a brief in my hand. Then a 'silk' turned round and favoured me with a stare. At last we all stood up, and Eve took his seat on the Bench.

"Some applications were made. Eve seemed to regard every one as a personal affront. He wasn't rude, but he granted them grudgingly: and he jumped on anyone who put a foot wrong. And he seemed to know most of the counsel – called them by name.

"And then at last my turn came. The usher said his piece, but nobody else got up. And so I got to my feet.

"Before I could open my mouth –

" 'And what do you want?' said Eve.

"That was rude – and the rudeness loosened my tongue.

" 'I'll tell your lordship,' I said. 'I'm here on behalf of two sons to seek an immediate order committing their father to prison for Contempt of Court.'

"As soon as he could speak –

" 'Well you don't think you're going to get it, do you?' barked Eve.

"As the Registrar gave him the affidavits –

" 'My lord,' I said, 'I venture to hope that your lordship will hear what I have to say. On the face of it, my lord, this is an impious request. But...'

"You see, the idea was to take the wind out of his sails. So I got in the word 'impious' before he did. I apologized for the motion and said that I hoped he'd believe that it was just as distasteful to me to make it as it must be for him to consider it, but that I had no choice: and that if he refused my request, two honest, decent men would be robbed of six thousand pounds.

"Well, he barked a good deal and was pretty rough with me. But the affidavits didn't leave anything out. Then he played for time, but I was ready for that.

" 'Today is Thursday, my lord; and the time is half past two. And the ship sails on Saturday morning. If your lordship adjourns this motion, such adjournment will cost my clients six thousand pounds.'

"He spoke with the Registrar and he hummed and hawed. But in the end he granted the application.

" 'With the greatest reluctance,' he said, 'I do as you ask.'

" 'If your lordship pleases,' I said, and resumed my seat.

"I never left a Court so quickly in all my life."

"Allow me to say," said Jonah, "that you did deserve to get on."

"I quite agree," said Daphne.

"My sweet," said I, "I've mentioned two occasions on which I came off. But I had so many failures – lost cases I ought to have won. But those I try to forget. Any way, I'm talking off the record. This mustn't go into a book."

"I disagree," said Jonah. "I'll tell you why. You're giving the low-down on the Bar – a thing that no legal memoir has ever done. You take us behind the scenes, revealing a state of affairs of which no layman dreams. Look at what you've just told us. Six thousand pounds at stake, and the sands running out, and clerks and solicitors and counsel all trying to pass the buck. To my mind this was a case for a powerful Chancery 'silk': instead, the lot falls upon you – who don't even know the ropes. A Common Lawyer, you have to ask the procedure, before you go into Court – to confront a testy Judge and endeavour to make him grant an odious request. A daw among peacocks, you get a hostile reception; and you only get home, thanks to your mother wit and the grace of God. And this is not fiction, but fact."

"Oh, yes, it's perfectly true. But – "

"I agree with Jonah," said Berry. "It is a side-light, of course, but its glare is most arresting. Have you got any more like that?"

"Not at the moment," I said. "And for Heaven's sake don't think that that memory is a fair sample of what in the ordinary way goes on behind the scenes. It was nothing of the kind. So far as I know, no other Chancery brief was ever delivered to us. And we did try to return it. If Harker had been there when it came, it would have been returned. But on Thursday there was next to no time for the agents to find someone else. They wouldn't have sent it to us, if they'd had a Chancery man. Any way, they were sure it was 'a loser', so what the hell?"

"Oh, it wasn't your fault," said Jonah, "your Chambers' fault, I mean. It mayn't have been anyone's fault, for the thing was so rushed. But if the unfortunate clients could have heard your conversation with your friend at the Chancery Bar – well, let us say that it would have spoiled their lunch."

"They'd have gone stark, staring mad," said Berry. "Give me the Inns of Court. They're worse than Harley Street."

My sister regarded her wristwatch.

"Give us something short, darlings, just to take us to bed."

I looked at my brother-in-law.

"It's up to you," I said. "I've talked enough tonight."

"There's something in that," said Berry. "Never mind. Let us pass from the squalid to the sublime, and consider for two or three minutes what are called Persian rugs."

"Why 'what are called'?" said Daphne.

"Because it is frequently a misnomer. The famous Tekke Bokhara is styled 'a Persian rug'. In fact, it is nothing of the kind. It is a Turkoman or Turkestan rug, and it has no more to do with Persia than had that beautiful Kulah that used to hang on the powder-closet's wall."

Jill cried out at that.

"You're not going to say that's not a Persian rug?"

"I am, indeed, my sweet. The Kulah came out of Turkey and it is a Turkish rug." He looked at Daphne. "And the Shemakha in your bedroom was a Caucasian rug."

"Well, I never knew that," said Daphne. "One always says 'Persian rugs'."

"I know. But considerably less than half the so-called 'Persian rugs' in fact come out of Persia. So the right word is 'Oriental'."

"But 'Oriental' means anything."

"I know. It's very awkward. All the same, you wouldn't point to a nice piece of Spode and say 'That's Crown Derby', would you? But that is what you're doing when you call a Tekke Bokhara a Persian rug.

"The meanest, modern carpet is so expensive today that the market for genuine rugs must now be extremely small. And there can't be many to buy. A few odd ones now and then, which come to be sold when death duties have to be paid. I suppose they go to collectors. Of course, quite a lot are offered."

"Fakes," said Jonah.

Berry nodded.

"As it was and ever shall be. And people are very stupid about Oriental rugs. They mayn't be experts – very few people are. But they've ordinary common sense. If they were offered an old master for forty pounds, they'd laugh in the salesman's face. But just because it's a rug, instead of a picture, they have it put in the car and drive home and write the cheque. And, as like as not, it came from a Japanese factory that turns out two hundred a day.

"The real Oriental rug which our fathers knew is now a thing of the past – has been a thing of the past for many years. It was, of course, hand-made; and the wool which was used to make it was dyed with vegetable dyes. The first thing to pass was the dyes. It must be about ninety years since aniline dyes began to reach the East. There they were seized upon, because they saved so much trouble. And now the secrets of the vegetable dyes are lost. But the rugs were never the same, for the colours were not so soft, and wool grows brittle when dyed with an aniline dye. And then, of course, came the machines…

"So another craft sickened and died. Of course, it was easy money – right down machinery's street. But no machine could do what the craftsman did. For he knew how to knot the pile to the warp, and he had infinite patience. His rugs are works of art and will see out Time. Upon the best of these, use will leave no trace. Some Tekke Bokhara rugs have nearly four hundred knots to every square inch."

Jill put a hand to her head.

"But how ever long did it take to make such a rug?"

Berry shrugged his shoulders.

"Half a lifetime," he said, "and sometimes longer than that. That's why they are worth having. They're human documents."

*

"How's the book going?" said Jonah.

"I can't complain," said I.

Berry looked up.

"Sub-conscious brain pulling well?"

"Like a train," said I.

"I think you'll love it," said Jill. "He's read me some."

"Alleged humour?" said Berry.

"Quite a lot."

"The conscious brain," said Jonah, "is really an amanuensis?"

"More than that," said I. "A kind of interpreter. For instance, not long ago the sub-conscious brain led me to a Roman road."

"Our Roman road?" said Daphne.

"No, my darling," I said. "I'd never seen this one before. Like ours, it had shrunk to a lane, but it had a gate in one side that gave to a lovely view. Well, I had a good look round, and then, with my conscious brain, I tried to describe the lane and the lovely view."

"And when you'd done that?" said my sister.

"The sub-conscious brain took over and told me how to go on."

"And till that moment," said Jonah, "you'd no idea?"

35

"None whatever," I said. "And I wasn't expecting what happened. I don't think you'll see it coming, when I read you the tale. And yet it's completely natural."

"I remember once," said Berry, "being led – no doubt by the sub-conscious brain, for I'd lost my way – to a very beautiful dunghill. I wasn't expecting that, either. And I didn't have to look round to describe how it smelt."

Jonah and I were laughing, but Daphne and Jill were not at all amused.

When they paused for breath –

"All right, all right," said Berry. "I was only seeking to embroider the hem of the Maestro's garment."

"You wicked liar," said Daphne. "And it wasn't your brain that led you to the dunghill. It was the homing instinct."

"Oh, the vixen," said Berry. "Now I shan't buy you those digitated bed-socks you wanted. More. I shall keep to myself the first of some handsome trifles I had in mind."

"What's this?" said I.

"Oh, it's too good, really," said Berry, "to go in a book like this. It's one of my *belles-lettres*. It ought to be bound in vellum and kept in a case. One hundred numbered copies at twenty guineas a go."

"Let's have it," said Jonah.

"Oh, not just like that," said Berry. "We ought really to have a fanfare. I suppose you couldn't go on your knees."

"We'll leave that to posterity," said Jonah.

"That you may do," said Berry, "with every confidence."

With that, he emptied his glass and sat back in his seat.

"The average man," he observed, "has little inclination and less time to read what are commonly called 'the standard works'. I mean, they've got to be got down to." He looked at me. "Your comic strips make no such demand upon the intelligence. And so, since today the average man is always tired, they and their like offer him an easy escape from the trivial round. Which is, of course, why you sell your rotten books. Jane Austen is still read, and so is Trollope; but not by everyone. And there are many authors of even higher standing whose works the average man never considers."

"That," said I, "is undeniable. But that is because, as you have pointed out, leisure is a dead letter today."

"As is liberty. Never mind. L seems unpopular. Now the point I am seeking to make is this. Neither you nor I are qualified to appraise the masterpiece: but we do know something about them. And since the treatises which are written by the great about the great are invariably beyond us, I make bold to assume that they are, often enough, beyond the average man. Yet for the masterpiece, there is a great deal to be said."

"It's like pictures," said Jill. "No one's ever got time to go inside a picture-gallery. But, if they did, they'd have to be turned out."

"Exactly. And since the average man today has no time to study Velasquez or Spenser, I feel that an effort should be made to offer him, say, a slice of one of those glorious loaves. That can't be done by a high-brow: he is too big a man. But the low-brow's forte is the low-down..."

"I think you should take Chaucer," said Daphne.

In a silence big with suspicion, Berry regarded his wife.

Then –

"You will now," he said, "have the privilege of listening to the first of my collection of *belles-lettres*.

"It's funny to think of somebody having a keen sense of humour six hundred years ago. Especially Dan Chaucer. (Why Dan? His name was Geoffrey: but Spenser calls him Dan.) For his portraits insist upon a reverend, sad-faced, bearded bloke, soberly apparelled. Yet he was a humorist of the first water. That his humour is sometimes broad, I frankly admit: but it's damned good. Of course, till you get the hang of it, he isn't easy to read: for his perfect English is old – 'pore persoun' for 'poor parson', for instance – and he uses many beautiful words, now out of currency. But he was not only a very great poet. He found time in his life to be a courtier, a soldier, a diplomat and a member of parliament. Geoffrey Chaucer, MP."

Jill put in her oar.

"I never knew they had MPs when Chaucer – What's the word, Boy?"

"The high-brow term," said I, "is 'flourished'."

" 'Did his stuff'," said Berry. "This is a low-brow book. Well, they hadn't been going long. Anyway, as everyone knows, Chaucer's most famous work was *The Canterbury Tales*. He was a very quiet fellow and, I think on his own admission, he kept his eyes upon the ground. But he didn't miss much – *The Canterbury Tales* show that. They show beyond all argument that his knowledge and understanding of human nature were most exceptional. There are the pilgrims before you, in their habits, as they lived – the squire, the parson, the doctor, the lawyer, the undergraduate, the sailor, the carpenter, the ploughman, the cook and the gay widow of Bath. And others. Quite apart from the glorious entertainment of the tales they tell, their portraits are most beautifully presented – and all, in exquisite verse.

"The Wife of Bath was rather deaf, which, says Chaucer, was a pity. She was very jealous of her standing, and if any other lady of Bath presumed to precede her, such lady was never forgiven. She was bold-faced, handsome and raddled. Her stockings were scarlet and were always nice and tight. She had had five husbands and, in her youth, had never looked at another man. Her middle age, observes Chaucer, is no affair of ours. To tell the truth, he adds, her teeth were set wide apart. She was a traveller: she had visited Jerusalem, Rome and Cologne – which is more than most of us can say. She rode well and easily – astride, of course, but her spurs were sharp. For decency's sake, an ample apron was girt about her substantial hips. Finally, says Chaucer, among friends she was excellent company. 'In fellowship well could she laugh and talk.' But, as a mistress, you could teach her nothing. 'Of that art, she knew the old game.'

"Whether that can be beaten as a portrait, is not for me to say. The fact remains that it was written in 1389.

"Yet, so often as I think of Chaucer, the first thing that always comes to my mind is his haunting picture of the poor parish priest – 'a pore Persoun of a town'. And especially the last two lines, which I have by heart. 'But Cristes lore, and his apostles twelve, He taughte: but first he folwed it himselve.'"

"Quite perfect," said Daphne. "And only a very nice man could have written such lovely words."

"Of such," said Berry, "was 'the well of English undefyled'. At least, so Spenser called him; and he was a pretty good judge."

"Is that all?" said Jill.

Berry nodded.

"I don't want to bore: I just want to whet the taste. When the lords of the films read that, they'll send a man over at once, contract in hand. Not to see me. To find Chaucer and get the rights. And while he's on the way, they'll retain the rage of Broadway to play The Wife of Bath. I think I'll do Smollett next. And now let's hear some more about British Justice."

"One moment," I said. "I believe it to be a fact that, when Playfair revived *The Beggar's Opera*, Somerset House sent an income-tax form to John Gay."

"What does that mean?" said Jill.

"Well, he was the author, my sweet. And as the revival was an immense success, Somerset House thought they'd have a slice of his royalties. But he wasn't in the telephone-book, so they sent the demand to the theatre. But he never got it, for nobody knew where he was. You see, John Gay had been dead for two hundred years."

"Tell us," said Daphne, "about the case you did that Whitsun weekend."

I smiled.

"Fancy your remembering that."

"Well, it was a great triumph, Boy."

"It was for me. But then I was very small fry."

"You gave all you'd got," said Daphne, "because it was touch and go. When you got to White Ladies that night – well, I'd never seen you so done."

"It had been worrying. And, as the Duke would have said, 'it was a close-run thing'."

"Who was against you?" said Berry.

"No mortal man, but a very dangerous opponent who cares for no rules of law. We call him Prejudice."

"Let's have it," said Jonah.

"I warn you," I said, "it was not spectacular. I didn't save anyone's neck. And I don't suppose it was reported, except in the local Press."

"Proceed," said Berry.

"The Whitsun weekend," I said, "in 1914. Saturday morning – a very beautiful day. I was just going out of Town, when the telephone went. When I took the receiver off, I heard the voice of my clerk. He said that the matter was urgent – a motor car case. He couldn't get hold of Harker, who had already left Town: so the AA would be glad if I would help them out. An inquest at Laidlow that very afternoon. A cyclist was dead, and a chauffeur stood in grave danger of a verdict of manslaughter. Local solicitors had been instructed on his behalf, but this was a case for counsel. The solicitors would hand me a brief. Would I undertake the case? If so, a train for Laidlow was leaving in half an hour. An AA official would meet that particular train and put me wise."

"Laidlow," said Daphne. "Where's that?"

"I've changed the name, my darling. You know the town quite well."

"I understand."

"I said, Very well, I'd go – and put the receiver back... And I'd hoped to lunch at White Ladies...and then go on to play tennis at Merry Down...

"I sent a wire to Daphne and managed to catch the train. The AA man met me at Laidlow, as arranged, and we drove at once to see the solicitors."

"How did you get your robes?"

"Counsel don't wear robes in the Coroner's Court. Nor, of course, in the Police Court. At a Court Martial, they do."

"Usedn't you to carry your robes in a dark-blue bag?"

"Seldom, if ever, out of London. The bag was all right, so long as it only contained your robes and your brief. But when you had to take volumes of Law Reports, it became very unwieldy: and so, for the sake of convenience, you used a small, leather kit-bag – at least, I did."

"What was it made of – the blue one?"

"Well, it looked like damask," I said. "I should say it was figured mohair – I may be wrong. But it was very strong. You closed the neck by drawing two cords together – two stout blue cords. When your progress at the Bar had attracted the attention of a 'silk', he would tell the robe-makers to deliver to you a red bag, with his compliments. I need hardly say I never received that attention."

"I wonder Charles Gill didn't send you one. I mean, he did ask you to enter his Chambers."

"He probably didn't think of it. And I'm much more proud of that than of any red bag."

"You ought to have had one," said Jill.

"Quite honestly, my darling, I don't think that I deserved it."

Jill sighed.

"You always say that," she said, "about everything. What about – "

"My sweet," I said, "I beg that you'll leave it there. And now let's get back to Laidlow.

"The solicitors received me very kindly. The brief was non-existent – they'd had no time. So they gave me a back-sheet, and, what was more to the point, the use of a very nice room.

Would I like to see the chauffeur? 'Not yet,' I said. 'Please tell me about the case.'

"Well, we all know Laidlow – as it was, and the line of the London road... Out of the town and up a long, straight rise – with side-roads on the left, running very sharply up-hill.

"Two days before, the chauffeur had driven to Folkestone and seen his master and mistress on board a Channel steamer, *en route* for the South of France. His orders were to drive the car back to London and then take a fortnight's leave.

"The car was a landaulette and a powerful car.

"Once clear of the streets of Laidlow, the chauffeur is popping along, up the long, straight rise and well on his left-hand side. Then a cyclist, moving fast, swings suddenly out of a side-road, only a few feet ahead. The cyclist is bound for Laidlow and so he bears half-right. He has to do that, you see, to get to his proper side of the London road. In a frantic endeavour to avoid him, the chauffeur bears to his right... In fact he ends up on the pavement and knocks a lamp-post down. But he can't quite clear the cyclist, who hits the near-side panel right at the end of the car. And the poor fellow breaks his neck.

"There were one or two witnesses, but none were valuable. They swore, of course, that it was the chauffeur's fault. Cars were unpopular then, and that particular stretch was inviting speed. Just clear of the town, you know, a good straight road ahead and a steady rise. Many a time I've put my foot down there."

"So've I," said Jonah. "I'm afraid we were lucky – that's all."

"Well, what did the police find? A cyclist dead in the road of a broken neck: and the car that did it not only upon its wrong side, but with one of its wheels on the pavement and half a lamp-post upon its canopy.

"And now for the strong stuff.

"The cyclist was a Laidlow man and immensely popular: a modest, hard-working joiner and everyone's friend. He was very happily married – with seven children, the eldest of whom was fourteen. Side-road and main road – he knew them as the palm of his hand, for, while he worked in Laidlow, the side-road led to his home. In other words, for more than seven years he had rounded that fatal corner at least once every day.

" 'I take it,' I said, 'that feeling is running high.'

"The solicitor made a wry face.

" 'I'm afraid it is, Mr Pleydell. Very high. And most of the Coroner's Jury certainly knew the dead man.'

"I nodded.

" 'And the Coroner?' I said.

" 'We're all right there. He's very good at his job and he's nobody's fool.' He hesitated. 'I'm sorry to have to say that the chauffeur is badly rattled.'

" 'He's afraid of the verdict?'

" 'Yes.'

"This was natural enough. As I have said, cars were unpopular then, and verdicts of manslaughter were frequently returned. It didn't follow, of course, that whoever was driving went down: but he had to stand his trial at the next Assizes. And if the case went wrong, he was sent to jail. And not for six months, either.

"He gave me a few more facts and showed me the police report.

" 'Well now,' I said, 'will you have the chauffeur in?'

"He was a nice-looking fellow, aged, I think, thirty-five. His licence was clean, and we'll say that his name was Blake.

"The solicitor introduced us.

"Then –

" 'Blake,' I said, 'I'm here to look after you. And I'm going to do my best to get a verdict of accidental death. But I can't do it, Blake, unless I have your help. And the only way you can help is by telling the absolute truth. Never mind if the truth is against you. I've got to convince the jury that you are an honest man. If I can do that, we're home. But that is our only chance.'

" 'Very good, sir,' said Blake.

" 'And now please tell me what happened from first to last.'

"Well, he told me what I've told you. And he kept on saying, 'He never gave me a chance.'

" 'I know what you mean,' I said: 'but tell me what you mean in so many words.'

" 'Well, I did all I could, sir, but he did nothing at all. If he'd turned sharp to his right, he might have had a spill, but he wouldn't have hit the car.'

" 'I quite understand,' I said. 'Was the road behind you clear?'

" 'Nothing behind or in front, sir. No cars, I mean.'

" 'And now tell me this. What speed were you going, when the accident occurred?'

" 'Twenty miles an hour, sir,' said Blake.

"I knew he'd say that, of course. For twenty miles an hour was the speed limit then. (At least, I think it was. Any way, it was very low and was regularly ignored.) And everyone going over twenty was out of court. And I mean what I say. That was the end of his case.

" 'Blake,' I said, 'you're going to be asked that in court. And if you give that answer, you'll get a verdict of manslaughter, sure as a gun. Why? Because they won't believe you. I don't believe you, myself. You were going twice that speed, and you know it as well as I.'

"Blake put a hand to his head.

" 'But I can't say that, sir,' he said: 'because, if I do, I'll just be cutting my throat. Anything over twenty's against the law.'

" 'We're not in court now,' I said. 'Tell me here, in this room, what was your speed, when the cyclist hit the car.'

"Blake looked over his shoulder. Then he took a deep breath.

" 'About fifty, I'd say, sir. I never 'ad time to look. But – '

" 'Why were you going so fast?'

" 'Because I was tryin' to clear him. I shoved my foot right down. But for the lamp-post, I think I might of done it. Not that I cared about that, but it checked my speed. I couldn't avoid it, of course. They would put one just there.'

" 'That's a very good answer, Blake, and I want you to say it again. Why were you going so fast?'

The chauffeur repeated his words.

" 'Good. That is the answer you're going to give in court. And, if you give it, Blake, I believe I can get a verdict of accidental death.'

" 'But – '

" 'Listen, Blake. If you give any other answer, I think you'll go down. You see, *that answer rings true*...and it shows you were doing your utmost to save the cyclist's life. You saw the lamp-post ahead, but you didn't care about that.'

" 'I was over the speed-limit, sir.'

" 'I know you were. But why? Because you were doing your best to save a man's life. And now let's leave the matter. Tell me this. Was the cyclist moving fast?'

" 'Come out like a flash, sir. As if he had the road to himself.'

" 'I shouldn't say that in court. I'm not saying it isn't true. I think it probably is. But the jury won't like it at all – because it is a reflection upon the dead man. You see the point?'

" 'Yes, sir.'

" 'Very well. My answer to that question would be, 'I'm afraid he was. Very fast.'

" 'I'm afraid he was. Very fast.'

"After half an hour I'd got him pretty well schooled. Finally, I said, 'Don't be afraid of the truth. It's the strongest card you've got. If the jury thinks you're honest, I don't think they'll send you down.'

"When, about an hour later, I entered the Coroner's Court, I hoped I was right. The hostility made me feel cold. I don't think I've ever been so conscious of an atmosphere. And the court was crammed. Three of the orphans, stony-faced and wearing the deepest mourning, sat in the front row. Happily, I had told Blake to wait outside the court, until I sent for him.

"When the AA man appeared, a minute or so after me –

45

" 'Blake tells me,' he said, 'that you've told him to stay where he is. Don't you think he ought to hear the evidence of the police?'

" 'Yes,' I said, 'I do. But we'll have to let that go. If he is to sit in this court for half an hour, he will be all to bits when he enters the box. But once he's being examined, he won't notice the atmosphere.'

"When the Coroner took his seat, he looked very grave, but I saw at once that he was a proper man. When the jury took their seats, they looked very grim.

"Well, the case took the usual course – identification of the dead man, police statement, surgeon's evidence. Mercifully, nothing was said about the deceased's familiarity with the roads. I never opened my mouth – I mean, I asked no questions. I fear the AA man felt that I should have questioned the police; but the wicket was so sticky that I let the loose balls go."

"Were you wise?" said Berry.

"Yes, I think I was right. I might have got an answer that didn't suit me at all.

"Then the chauffeur was called...

"I rose at once and requested the Coroner's permission to examine him. This he gave. To my immense relief, although he was very nervous, he did very well. I led him as much as I dared. In the Coroner's Court, you can get away with such things."

"When you say 'led him'," said Jill, "what exactly d'you mean?"

"This, my sweet. I put to him 'leading' questions. A 'leading' question is a question which indicates unmistakably the answer you wish to receive. That you may not do in examination-in-chief. I mean the Judge will stop you – at least, he should. For instance, I said to the chauffeur, 'To see the cyclist emerge from the side road so fast must have been a very great shock?' And the chauffeur replied, 'A very great shock, sir.' '*You* saw the frightful danger?' 'I did, sir. But he didn't seem to see it. He held straight on.'

"But the Coroner was very decent. He was, of course, well aware of the prejudice which I was fighting, and he was a just man. He let me say a few words before he summed up: and the direction he gave was very fair. Then the jury retired. They were out for about twenty minutes, if I remember aright. And then they came back and said 'Accidental death.'

"So that was all right. And I do think justice was done. I quite believe that Blake was – well, popping along. But for a cyclist to whip out of one of those side roads on to and *across* the London road was – well, suicidal. Be that as it may, it was a very near thing. As I have said, the prejudice in that court made me feel quite cold. I knew it was coming, of course, and, again as I think I've said, I'd already made up my mind that the only thing that could break it was transparent honesty.

"I remember that I said to the jury, 'I'm not here to ask any favours. Subject to the Coroner's direction, you will bring in the verdict which you think you ought to bring in. I have come down to see that the chauffeur's case is fairly and squarely presented, to show that he did his utmost to save this valuable life. And don't forget, gentlemen, that he would be dead himself, if he hadn't had that canopy over his head.' "

"That was very skilful," said Berry. "And now tell me this – if you'd failed, and they'd returned a verdict of manslaughter, he'd have been committed for trial. Would he have got off at the Assizes?"

"I think he would. There wouldn't have been the same prejudice there, you see. And counsel would have lammed in the fact that the cyclist never gave him a chance – which was, of course, perfectly true. But that was a card which I was afraid to play, because of the prejudice."

"I give you best," said Jonah. "It was a very good win. Even better than it looks."

"Why d'you say that?" said Daphne.

My cousin looked at me and smiled, and I smiled back.

"He said it, my darling, because he is very shrewd. I concentrated the Court's attention upon the accident itself. I did my utmost to keep their eyes fixed upon that – because I was deadly afraid of one very awkward question."

My sister leaned forward.

"What was that question, Boy?"

"Well, supposing somebody'd asked the chauffeur this – 'You tried to save the man's life by putting your foot right down. Why didn't you try to save it by applying your brakes?' "

My sister clapped a hand to her mouth.

"Exactly," said I.

"D'you know," said Daphne, "it never occurred to me."

"For the same reason," said I, "that it didn't occur to the jury. I kept your eyes on the accident all the time."

"Talking of Coroners," said Jonah, "what is 'The Coroner of the Verge'?"

" 'The Coroner of the Verge' was the Coroner of the Royal Household. I use the past tense, because I believe the old title is now no longer used. 'Within the Verge', originally meant 'Within ten or twelve miles of the Sovereign's Court'; but by the time of HM King Edward the Seventh, 'The Verge' had come to mean 'The precincts of the Sovereign's residence'. If anyone died in those precincts and a doctor felt unable to give a death certificate, an inquest was held by 'The Coroner of the Verge'. The idea was, no doubt, to preserve the privacy of the Court. I think the office survives, but that its holder is now known as 'The Coroner of the Queen's Household'.

"I remember Montague Guest's sudden death in King Edward the Seventh's reign. He was a very nice man, a close friend of the King's, and was staying at Sandringham. One day he went out with the guns, though he wasn't shooting himself: and he had a heart attack and died on the spot. It was expected that an inquest would be held by The Coroner of the Verge: but Guest's doctor came down to Sandringham and signed the death certificate, because he had been attending him for heart trouble for a long time and was not at all surprised by his sudden death. Walking over the fields had been too much for him."

"Were you often in the Coroner's Court?"

"Only about half a dozen times, I'm thankful to say. It's atmosphere is unpleasant, as you may well believe."

"Sordid," said Berry.

"It's not exactly sordid. At least, it's no more sordid than that of some Metropolitan Police Courts I could name. But the *raison d'être* of the Coroner's Court is death – sometimes a dreadful death. And many tears are shed there, and painful evidence is heard. The only occasion on which I didn't notice the atmosphere was at the inquest on Belle Elmore."

"The Crippen Case?"

"Yes. It was all so dramatic and there was so much excitement that it didn't seem like a Coroner's Court. Then again there were no relatives. Even Crippen wasn't there."

"Why not?"

"I think he was on the high seas. There was no reason why he should be there. Human remains had been found. Very well. It was the Coroner's duty to inquire into the circumstances of that unfortunate person's death. Whether or no Crippen was involved remained to be seen."

"Did the jury return a verdict of wilful murder?"

"I think so. I can't be sure. It didn't make any difference, for he was already under arrest."

"What evidence was given?"

"Well, the police spoke to the discovery of the remains. And the police-surgeon gave evidence. Pepper, the Home Office expert, may have been there. I think Mrs Nash gave evidence – she was a friend of Belle Elmore's and was really responsible for setting the ball rolling. But for that courageous lady, nothing would have been done. Oh, and Le Neve's landlady went into the box."

"That's interesting. What did she say?"

I hesitated. Then –

"Well, it's all in the files of *The Times*, so I may as well say. She said that one night Le Neve 'had the horrors'. What precisely she meant, you can guess as well as can I. A severe emotional outburst – tears and wailing and lamentation. Any way the landlady ministered to her, and after a long time she managed to calm her down. But she never forgot that night – or that painful scene. If you'll forgive me, I'd like to leave it there."

There was a little silence.

Then –

"This," I said, "has remembered something else. It's only a side-light on a certain *cause célèbre*, but it may interest you.

"A man was arraigned for wilful murder at the Old Bailey. He was defended by Marshall Hall and he was acquitted. He did very well in the box. He was very cool and collected. The first question Marshall Hall asked him was, 'Did you murder Agatha Collins?' I think the question surprised him as much as it did the Court, for he hesitated a moment. Then he shrugged his shoulders and simply said, 'It's absurd.' Which was, of course, a very good answer – and a very much better one than Marshall Hall deserved. Most men would have just said, 'No', which would have cut no ice. I may say that 'Agatha Collins' was not the victim's real name."

"Why didn't Marshall Hall deserve it?"

"Because in asking that question he took a great risk. And counsel for the defence shouldn't take any risks. That was a question from which Marshall Hall could have hoped to gain nothing, which, coming from his own counsel, was quite liable to shake the defendant up. It might easily have provoked an outburst: and when a man loses control, he may say anything.

"You and I are so familiar with the procedure, that such a question wouldn't worry us: but the average man knows nothing of courts of law: everything's strange to him, and, if he is on trial for his life, formidable. In this case, he'd just been sworn – sworn on the Word of God to speak nothing but the truth. And then came this awful question…

"I remember that a member of the Bar who was in court said to me afterwards, 'Did you see him hesitate? He didn't know whether he ought to say yes or no.' "

Jonah began to shake with laughter.

"Yes, he was being funny. All the same, it was a very dangerous question. In this case it came right off. But Marshall Hall was lucky to get away with it.

"I'm well aware that I'm criticizing a man whose little finger was thicker than my loins, who was very kind to me. He was a splendid and famous advocate; and, as such, deserves to be remembered. But he was impetuous: and now and again, as I have said before, he would do a foolish thing. Still, he was in the front rank of his contemporaries, and not one of his successors has come anywhere near him."

"What of Patrick Hastings?"

"He was not in the same street. Such was his reputation between the wars that I made a point of going to hear him in a *cause célèbre*… I believe he was very successful; but, quite honestly, he simply didn't compare with Marshall Hall. With all his faults, Marshall Hall had a great and compelling personality, and I'm very proud to have known him."

"Did the prisoner in a murder case always go into the box?"

"As a rule, he did. I mean, it looked damned bad if he didn't. Even Crippen went into the box."

"When you say it looked bad," said Daphne…

"Well, it suggested very strongly that he wished to avoid being questioned by Counsel for the Crown. If you were accused of something you hadn't done, would you be afraid of cross-examination? Of course, you wouldn't. Your one idea would be to get into the witness-box. But if in fact you were guilty, the prospect of being cross-examined by a trained lawyer in open court would be, er, less attractive."

My sister covered her eyes.

"I should be frightened to death," she said.

"Exactly. So you would have to decide whether to face that ordeal or to leave upon the jury's minds the dangerous impression that you were afraid to face it. Your counsel would probably decide for you. Or, at least, advise you which to do, for the choice is really yours.

"Counsel for the Crown is not allowed to comment, in his final speech, on the fact that a prisoner has not gone into the box. But the Judge may – and in my time almost invariably did. After all, the Judge's function is to direct the jury and unless the prisoner is, for instance, labouring under great emotion or a singularly stupid man, it is his duty to remind the jury that he has not seen fit to enter the box and deny the charge upon oath. But times have changed. I remember a case of murder which was tried long after I had left the Bar. Counsel for the defence must have passed sleepless nights, trying to make up his mind whether to call the prisoner or no. If ever there was a case in which the accused should have been called, it was this one. I mean, that stood out. Yet the material for cross-examination was – well, deadly. In the end his counsel decided not to call him – and if I may humbly say so, I think he was right. To be perfectly honest, I think he put his money on the Judge. And did he romp home? For the Judge actually directed the jury to *pay no attention to the fact* that the prisoner had not gone into the box."

"Why on earth?" said Berry.

"You can search me," I said. "For the prisoner was very much all there. But, as I say, times have changed."

"What happens," said Jill, "what happens if the jury can't agree?"

"Well, in the old days they used to keep them shut up on a diet of bread and water till they did agree. But now the Judge has them in and asks if he can help them and then sends them back to have another shot. But if it's no good, then the jury is discharged and the prisoner is tried again at the next Assizes or the next session at the Old Bailey."

"The unsolved murder," said Berry, "seems not so uncommon today. Were there many in your time?"

"I don't think so. To be perfectly honest, I only remember two: but I expect there were more than that. The word 'unsolved', of course..."

"Let me confess," said Berry, "that the phrase 'the unsolved murder' is an unpardonable piece of jargon. What I should have said was, 'the capital crime, whose author was never discovered'."

"That's very much better," I said. "You see, if no one is convicted of or possibly even arrested for the crime, the public naturally assumes that the murderer is unknown. But that isn't always so.

"Now, before I go any further, please bear this in mind – that in all I am going to say I am referring to capital crimes which attracted attention, that is to say were accorded the dignity of headlines in the daily Press. I have little doubt that there were others; but to those I cannot speak."

"That," said Berry, "is understood."

"Well, in the years immediately preceding the outbreak of the first Great War I can only remember two murders, the authors of which were never found. Only two. One was the case I referred to in *As Berry and I Were Saying*, which attracted little attention because of the Crippen Case. Only the lady in the case knew who the murderer was: and she wouldn't talk. The other was the case of Kensit. Kensit was a very Low Churchman. As such he deeply resented the High Church practices of the Incumbent of St Cuthbert's, Earl's Court. His resentment blossomed into fanaticism and again and again he led a number of supporters, whom he had inflamed, to the precincts of St Cuthbert's – and sometimes into the church itself – where he and they protested violently against the ceremonial observed. As a natural result, supporters of the Incumbent of St Cuthbert's were mobilized, to deal with this unwarrantable behaviour, and since religious feelings can run very high, serious clashes took place. On the last occasion, although the police did their best, there was a battle royal and Kensit was killed. A file, driven into his eye, entered his brain. Such was the *mêlée* that the police never saw the blow struck. Possibly no one did. The fact remains that no one was ever arrested for that great wickedness. Still, the murder sobered both factions, as well it might: and that was the last of the clashes with which, in the name of Religion, the Sabbath Day was profaned.

"Well, there are my two. Some of my contemporaries would probably suggest that there were more but, unless my memory is letting me down, I am inclined to think that my figure is correct. You see, they would include some cases which I do not. Regarding some of those cases, I shall say nothing, and I must beg you to let me leave it at that. But in the period which I have mentioned there were, to my knowledge, two cases in which the murderer was known, but *in the public interest* was never brought to trial.

"And now just let me say this. First I am telling you something which I did *not*, repeat *not*, learn in the course of my duty – that is to say, while I was with the Solicitors to the Commissioner of Police or with Treasury Counsel. I was told it years afterwards by a man who is now dead, whom I came to know very well. And I have the best of reasons for believing that his report was true. Secondly, in neither of these cases was there any question of shielding anyone, or of sparing the feelings of the well-to-do. The persons involved were not rich and their names were virtually unknown. But the circumstances of both crimes were so demoralizing that no one who knew the truth could condemn the decisions taken by the authorities.

"Now of the first case I am only going to say that it was a most painful affair and that no injustice was done by not making an arrest. Of the second, I shall say more, but not very much. This appeared to be an ordinary, straightforward case:

the victim was dead: his assailant had made himself scarce. With little enough to go on, the CID got down to it, and after some excellent work by Detective-Inspector — the man was found. But before he was so much as arrested – let alone charged – the man made so startling a statement that Detective-Inspector — decided to hold his hand. Arranging for the man to be watched, he hastened back to the Yard and made his report. The man's statement was investigated and found to be, if anything, less than the truth. These facts were immediately communicated to the Authorities and it was decided that, in the public interest, the case must be dropped."

There was a little silence.

Then –

"When you say 'dropped'," said Berry…

"Well, so great was the man's provocation that, had the case come to be tried, there can be no doubt that the charge of murder would have been reduced to one of manslaughter. All the same, he stood in jeopardy, and I assume that he was told that, provided he left the country, the warrant for his arrest would stay on the file. Any way, I have reason to believe that he emigrated within the month.

"Now please don't think that I don't realize that I have in no way substantiated my statement that it was in the public interest that this case should be suppressed. For that, I can only ask you to take my word: for it would be most improper for me to defeat the object of the Authorities, to achieve which they went such lengths. I can only say that, in my humble opinion, they were more than justified. The victim did not deserve to be avenged and the consequent revelation of a very great and far-reaching scandal would have done irreparable harm."

There was another silence.

Then –

"Most interesting," said Jonah. "Detective-Inspector — was clearly an exceptional man."

"For that, I can vouch," I said.

"And what a relief," said Berry, "to know that, where the public interest was at stake, the Authorities were prepared to take the responsibility of driving a coach and six through the Criminal Law."

"I entirely agree."

*

I looked at my brother-in-law.

"What about a few words about Cheiro?"

"Ah," said Berry. "Cheiro. A very likable man. And very talented. I knew him fairly well. He wrote me a very nice letter shortly before he died." He stopped there and looked at Daphne. "Another small wet of port would spare the vocal cords."

"It's just as likely to give you gout," said his wife.

"I'll take the risk," said Berry. "Er, would you mind, er, passing the decanter?"

"If," said my sister, "I could reach it without rising, I shouldn't mind at all. As it is…"

Berry looked round.

"Will nobody succour the head of their house?" he said.

Jill, beside me, began to shake with laughter.

"That's right," said Berry. "Derision. When Boy wants another snort, you get it quick enough."

"He's got a game leg," said my wife. "With you, it's laziness."

"No port, no Cheiro," said Berry.

Jonah got to his feet.

"It happens," he said, "that I want some more port myself."

"You shall have my blessing," said Berry. "I'll make a note of your smell. That's what Isaac went by. He was stung, I know. But then he went by the clothes. Esau probably kept his in naphthaline. As they all had BO, the flesh itself was no help."

"That's right," said Daphne. "Be bestial. And now that you've got your port, what's Cheiro done?"

Her husband sat back in his chair.

"It is not my practice," he said, "to patronize soothsayers – much less to pay two guineas to have my fortune told. For that was Cheiro's fee. But more than once Cheiro told my fortune – and never would let me pay him a penny piece.

"In his day, of course, he was a very big man. He was consulted by many most eminent people – that I know. His Majesty King Edward the Seventh was one of these. And the King commanded Cheiro to tell him the date of his death."

"Never," said Daphne.

"He did, indeed, and Cheiro begged to be excused. But the King was insistent. In the end Cheiro begged him to be very careful indeed when he was sixty-eight. Now on the sixth of March, 1910, the King left London for Biarritz. It was a Sunday evening. Whether His Majesty travelled by special train or the Royal coach was attached to the ordinary boat-train, I do not know: but, as he was crossing the platform, his quick eye caught sight of Cheiro, who had come to the station, I think to see somebody off. So Cheiro was summoned. 'Well, Cheiro,' said the King, 'here I am, in spite of my sixty-eight years.' Cheiro smiled. 'I'm only too thankful, sir, to see your Majesty looking so very well.' 'I may prove you right yet,' said the King. 'That, sir, I decline to believe'. The King chatted with him for a minute of other things… Two months later, to the day, His Majesty died, aged sixty-eight years and six months.

"I don't think that sad story has ever been told before."

"It was so terrible," said Daphne. "We were at White Ladies at the time. We heard he was ill on the Thursday and left for Cholmondeley Street on the following day. You went straight to the Club, to get the latest news. After a while you rang up, to say you were dining there. And you came back soon after midnight, to say he was dead."

Berry nodded.

"It was a bad day for England. So long as he lived, Germany dared not make war. The Kaiser feared his great personality. If he'd lived six years longer, the Kaiser would have been out. His own people were sick of the tiresome mountebank. He had erected a lot of statues of his ancestors, real and imaginary, in the Tiergarten of Berlin. Three months before war broke out, every one was defaced. I saw the King's funeral *cortège* pass up St James's Street. It was a flawless, summer's day. Eight Kings rode behind the gun-carriage – it may have been nine. Not in ranks – they all went by in a bevy, a truly historical sight. And Caesar, his wire-haired terrier, was led by a Highlander directly in front of them. The *cortège* was headed, of course, by the Earl Marshal, the father of the present Duke. He had a truly mediaeval beard and he looked like something out of the picture-books. And now we must get back to Cheiro."

"One minute," said Jill. "You saw Queen Victoria's funeral?"

"Yes," said Berry, "I did. That was in January – a cold, grey, very gloomy day, with a promise of snow. I remember King Edward riding behind the gun-carriage, with the Kaiser on his right and the Prince of Wales on his left. It was not a brilliant sight, for all the troops were cloaked or were wearing their great coats; but it was most impressive."

"Was the King wearing his cloak?"

"I think so. I can't be sure. But, if he was, it was open. I remember his scarlet tunic very well – and how he diminished the Kaiser, riding beside. For all his airs, the latter looked as if he was playing a part, as, of course, he was. But the King was the real thing. It's the only time I ever saw him on horseback: but he looked magnificent."

"Wasn't there some trouble with the horses drawing the gun-carriage?"

"Yes. But that was at Windsor. The second gun-carriage had been waiting for the train to arrive, and the horses were cold. When all was ready the signal was given for the *cortège* to start. At once all sorts of orders rang out. Now the leaders of the gun-carriage waited for their particular order, 'Walk march': but the wheelers heard the other orders and, impatient because they were cold, acted on them. And the weight was too great for two horses, and so the traces snapped. There were no spare traces, and a very steep hill to come. Prince Louis of Battenburg at once suggested that the naval guard of honour should take the horses' place. But there were no ropes. However, they managed with what was left of the traces. But they had three sailors on each wheel, in case the traces snapped."

"What a most unfortunate show," said Jonah.

"Yes, it was. For the troops ahead went on, not knowing that anything was wrong. They were very soon stopped, of course. There was a delay of about ten minutes. Everyone was very sorry for the Gunners, who were mortified to death. And now we simply must get back to Cheiro.

"It was Madame de — who introduced me to Cheiro. She dabbled in palmistry and expressed some interest in my hand. So she wrote to Cheiro and asked him to see me when I was next in Town. She had known Cheiro for years, and he certainly had a great regard for her. I rather imagine she had helped him, when he was still unknown. And this was what she told me of how he came to start. I've only her word for it, but I believe it to be true.

"As a young Irishman, Cheiro had just enough to live on, but nothing to spare. Then he was left a respectable legacy. This he decided to blow on seeing the world. So he wandered across the Continent, where he met Madame de — , and presently fetched up at Cairo, to stay at Shepheards Hotel. One night he was invited to dine at the Mohammed Ali Club... After dinner he was so indiscreet as to play. Now the members of the Mohammed Ali Club were immensely rich and the play was immensely high. It follows that at two in the morning Cheiro returned to Shepheards, broke to the world. He hadn't even the money to pay the hotel what he owed.

"Later that morning he saw the Manager. As may be believed, the latter took his news very ill. After all, the young man had been living extremely well. But Cheiro asked him politely to hear him out. 'I've got an idea,' he said. 'Ideas,' said the Manager, bluntly, 'won't pay your bill.' 'I think this one will,' said Cheiro.

"Well, he'd always had a flair for palmistry: so he suggested to the Manager that he should be furnished with a table and a chair and a screen, that these should stand in the lounge and that he should practise his art for the patrons of the hotel – at, let us say, one hundred piastres a time.

"After a little persuasion, the Manager agreed to let him try…

"He had to have a name, so he called himself Cheiro. And very soon he was doing extremely well. And there he stayed until he'd paid what he owed and amassed enough money to get him to England and keep him for two or three months. And then, despite the Manager's entreaties, he took his leave. And on his return, he set up as a soothsayer in London.

"Before very long he had a big clientèle, and I don't have to tell you that he published several books.

"I found him very modest about his undoubted gift. He always insisted that he was no more than a student. 'I'm only groping,' he'd say. 'One day, more capable men than I will open astrology up. And then – well, the impression of every child's hand will be registered at his birth.' He laughed. 'For once, I'm playing the prophet – and that's all wrong. Never forget that I am not a prophet: I'm an interpreter. Your destiny is written in your horoscope and the palm of your hand: and I try to read what is written. Sometimes the writing is very sharp and clear: at other times it's blurred, and then I can only tell you what I believe it says.'

"That was fair enough," said Jonah.

"I think so," said Berry. "Cheiro was very honest. His gift was, of course, amazing. He told me about my past and he never put a foot wrong. And what he said of my future has always come to pass. I'll only mention two things. He told me that seven was my good number, and eight my bad. When he'd said that, he smiled at the look on my face. 'You can't swallow that,' he said.

'But you will in a little while. Your good days are the seventh, sixteenth and twenty-fifth of each month: your bad days are the eighth, the seventeenth and the twenty-sixth. Bear that strictly in mind, and you'll find I'm right.' "

"When you came back," said Daphne, "and told me that, I begged you to forget it, for I said such a thing was absurd." She sighed. "In less than six months, I'd come to dread those bad days, for if anything ever goes wrong, it's always on one of those dates."

"It's painfully true," said Berry. "And so I always take what petty precautions I can. I don't let these rule my life, but on those days, for instance, I'm more than usually careful, if I'm to cross a street. I won't write an important letter on one of those days. But I can't help receiving one. And, as sure as Fate, if bad news is on the wing, it fetches up on the eighth or on one of the other two.

"Well, that's the first of the things I was going to mention. This is the second...

"I think it was on the last occasion on which we met that, under pressure, Cheiro admitted that something which was anything but pleasant was going to happen to me when I was fifty-five. (I was then, I think, forty-six.) 'I'm bound to tell you,' he said, 'that I don't like it at all.' 'My death?' I said. 'It might be. I can't be sure. It's a very unfortunate conjunction' – I think that's the word he used. He wouldn't have told me, of course, if he hadn't known me well. But he knew that I wasn't the sort who'd brood on a matter like that. I never told Daphne, of course, or anyone else. But I was perfectly sure that some time during that year my life would come to an end.

"Well, we all know it wasn't my death that Cheiro saw. But when I was fifty-five, we had to leave Gracedieu, our justly beloved home... I may be forgiven for adding that the fall of France occurred on the seventeenth day of the month."

There was a little silence.

Then Jonah lifted his voice.

"Wasn't he known as Count Hamon in private life?"

"Yes. Of the Holy Roman Empire. But he was most unassuming. The last time I saw him was not long before he left for California. Before we parted, he wrote down his future address and gave it to me. 'You might feel you wanted to write.' "

"How very nice of him," said Jill.

"Yes, it was very nice. When we shook hands, he held my hand very tight. 'I think you know,' I said, 'that we shan't meet again.' 'I don't think we shall,' he said. 'But you will go over seas.' 'Ah, but you're going for good.' 'So will you,' said Cheiro, 'one of these days.' "

"Amazing," said Daphne.

"Yes, he had the gift. And it wasn't second sight – like that of Deborah Crane. He could read the report of the stars which control our destiny."

"What secrets he must have learned."

"Yes, indeed," said Berry. "When he was in his prime, before the first war, half Society must have repaired to his house. They talk about old Sir George Lewis, and all the secrets he knew. But Cheiro's knowledge was of another sort. Of those who consulted him, when he knew the date of their birth and had studied the palm of their hand, he knew their very nature and much of what they had done and of what they were going to do. He knew that this wife was unfaithful and that man a murderer born. He saw that X would succeed and that Y would fall by the way: that this lady of high degree would suffer a violent death: that this highly respectable peer would be sent to jail. I don't suggest that he was infallible; sometimes, as in my case, the writing he was reading was blurred and he could not be sure of its burden: and then he said as much. What do you say of him, Boy?"

"I agree with all you've said. To my mind, Cheiro was unique."

"Darling," said Jill, "you know what he said to you."

"He said a lot, my sweet, and it all came true."

Jill looked round.

"Boy only went to him once. It was when he was at the Bar. He'd written a short story or two in his spare time: but the Bar was his profession and all that he cared about. And Cheiro told him his name would be known all over the world."

"Astounding," said Daphne.

"It's a fact," said I. "When I protested, Cheiro only smiled. 'There's no doubt about it,' he said. 'I know I'm right.' "

"Did he know that you wrote?"

"No. I never told him. It never occurred to me to tell him. He knew I was at the Bar. I couldn't understand it at all, for I couldn't believe I should enter politics. That I should ever write for my living never even entered my head."

"And no one has taken Cheiro's place?"

"No one," said Berry. "But Cheiro was a product of the golden age. So were Winston Churchill and Frederic Henry Royce. And Forbes Robertson and Kipling and Cromer and Cecil Rhodes." He sighed. "I'm glad to have seen it, you know. Mark you, I'm not comparing Cheiro with giants like those. He didn't approach them. But, in his way, he was a distinguished man; and I'm not in the least surprised that neither the chromium-plated age nor the plastic age has produced his like."

"Oh, dear," said Daphne.

Berry leaned forward.

"You'll never look it, but be your age, my love. The state of things in half the world today is more absurd than anything Gilbert wrote." He shrugged his shoulders. "And please remember the adage – 'Whom God wishes to destroy, he first sends mad.' "

Jonah looked at me.*

"Capital punishment," he said.

---

* The passage which follows was written some months before the recent Homicide Bill became law.

I smiled.

"I don't think I'm qualified to express an opinion on that."

"Allow me to say," said Berry, "that capital punishment is one of the very few things upon which you are qualified to speak. I'll tell you why. First, for two full years you had a close acquaintance with crime. You were able to observe the demeanour of several murderers and of very many felons, charged with offences less grave. Yet the law has not been your profession for forty years. During those years you have almost certainly lost any bias you may have had: yet you have always retained the legal mind. Secondly, all your life you have studied human nature as have very few men."

"So be it," said I. "One moment… No, I'm sorry. I can't remember something. Never mind. I once had a very good text-book on Criminal Law; and I remember that it had a chapter on Punishment. I also remember that it set out the four objects of punishment. Unfortunately, I can only remember three of them. Here they are…

"First, to deter the potential criminal. Secondly, to inflict upon the offender a just penalty for his crime. Thirdly, to assuage the feelings of the person or persons injured by the crime."

"Very interesting," said Berry. "And if you ventured to declare that last object in public today, you would be branded as a barbarian."

"I know. Such hypocrisy is the vogue. To desire that the brute who saw fit to murder your wife or child should receive his deserts is a natural, healthy emotion, of which no man need be ashamed. It is, of course, a priest's duty to remind the bereaved that they must try to forgive him: but it ill becomes the odd layman to denounce as improper an outlook which many a priest would find it hard to condemn.

"But that is all by the way.

"Arguments for and against the rope bring us straight to the old, old question – *Which of the two do you propose to consider, the community or the convict?* Boil it down and skim off the emotional scum, and it's just as simple as that. If you are to consider the community, then, for every reason, the man should be hanged.

"Before I go any further, perhaps I should say just this. In such a matter, statistics prove nothing at all. They are completely valueless, and as such not evidence.

"Hanging is an immense deterrent: of that, to my mind, there is no question at all. And I think I know the outlook of the criminal class rather better than the most fervent abolitionists. Those who insist that hanging is barbarous, seem to ignore the barbarity committed by felons every day – murder, attempted murder, grievous bodily harm, aggravated assault and the rest. If these crimes are to be discouraged, then not only should hanging be retained, but flogging should be commonly awarded. 'Barbarous' again, of course. But I am thinking of the community. And I say here and now that if murderers were regularly hanged and flogging was awarded for all other brutal crimes, in six months' time the crimes of violence would have fallen by eighty per cent. Of that, I am as certain as that I'm sitting here.

"Finally, the question of mistake. It is, of course, perfectly clear that, once a man has been hanged, you cannot restore him to life: so that, if a mistake has been made, it is irreparable. On this point let me say, first, that I have yet to learn that in the last sixty years any innocent man has been hanged. And that, secondly, bearing in mind the value of hanging as a deterrent, it is better that one innocent man should suffer that shameful death than that scores of innocent people should lose their lives at the hands of brutes who have no gallows to fear.

"Now, if some people were to hear what I've said, they would load me with abuse, quote from Holy Writ and support with a cloud of clichés their horror and indignation. My withers would be unwrung. To such, I would suggest that they apply to Scotland Yard for permission to inspect the photographs, now usually taken, of the unhappy subject of murder before their poor clay is removed. That might divert a little of the sympathy which they lavish upon a convict, who is unfit to live, to his innocent victim and the family so brutally bereft. They might even compare in their minds the quick, clean end on the scaffold with the agony of the death struggles to which their hero has subjected his prey.

Certain politicians still flaunt that catch-penny jewel of jargon, 'To make the world safe for democracy' – incidentally, I do hope they're pleased with the results they have so far achieved: but if we were to flog and hang, we should at least make England safe for honest men."

"Insanity," said Jonah.

"Ah," said I. "More than two-thirds of the murderers found insane are no more insane than you or I. They plead insanity in the hope of avoiding the gallows."

"And the remedy for that?"

"Is very simple. First, can anyone suggest that a homicidal maniac is fit to live? Well, the obvious answer is 'No'. But if he is truly insane, then it is unfair to stigmatize him with the rope. So a modified sentence of death should be passed and he should be painlessly destroyed in some other way. Secondly, make the plea of insanity equivalent to a plea of guilty. You wouldn't get many pleas of insanity then: and quite a lot of felons would come to their proper end."

"Allow me," said Berry, "to felicitate you upon every word that you've said. Many people would call you outspoken and worse than that. The truth is that all you have said is hard, common sense. But few today have the courage to face the facts."

"I wholly agree," said Jonah. "It simply amounts to this. Crimes of violence are barbarous crimes. As such, they are committed by barbarous men. Barbarous men fear corporal punishment, as they fear nothing else. If, therefore, they know that crimes of violence will meet with the rope or the lash, they will not commit them. That's all."

"I entirely agree. And now let's forget the matter. I remember a case with which I had something to do. And it has a curious tail-piece, to which only I can speak. The trouble is that, while I can remember the details, I can't remember the form which the action took."

"That doesn't matter," said Berry.

"It does to me. If I get it wrong, in a lawyer's eyes it will vitiate the reminiscence."

"You're not drawing an indictment," said Jonah.

"I know; but – "

"Darling," said Jill, "your memory is terribly good but who could look back forty years and never make a mistake?"

"Some people can, my sweet. Or used to be able to. Modern conditions don't favour remembrance. But Asquith, for instance, had an astonishing memory."

"That I can believe," said Jonah. "Did he never refer to his brief?"

"I couldn't tell you," I said. "I never saw him in court. But somewhere or other I read that he once performed a truly astonishing feat – so astonishing that, if one may take it as a sample of what he could do, even for his great days he must have been outstanding."

"Let's have it," said Berry.

I hesitated.

"All right," I said, "but we'd better not put it in. I don't think I read it in a book: I think I read it in a letter which somebody wrote to some paper: but, although I'm sure it's quite true, we must not run the risk of its being already in print."

"If we haven't heard it, I think you might chance that," said Jonah.

"Well, we'll see. I think it occurred at a house-party at his home, two or three years after the end of the first great war. Several people were gathered about the fire and were discussing racing. Asquith, who had probably never been on a race-course, held his peace. Presently an argument arose as to what had won the Derby in, say, 1902. Nobody could be sure, but somebody suggested Rock Sand. Then a quiet voice said, 'Ard Patrick. Rock Sand won the Derby in 1903.' Yes, it was Asquith. As soon as he could speak, 'Are you quite sure?' said someone. 'Quite sure,' said Asquith, and, with that, he proceeded to name every single Derby winner from 1890 on. Naturally, everyone was staggered – and I don't blame them at all. I can only suppose that he'd always seen the name on the posters or in *The Times* and that every year it had passed automatically into a special compartment in his memory. The real marvel was that he could identify that compartment and could draw upon it when he pleased."

"A great achievement," said Jonah. "The astonishing thing being that racing meant nothing to him. How many million compartments did such a memory hold? I daresay Winston could do it: but then he likes racing – and has always been far more human than ever Asquith was. But with that great exception, I find it hard to believe that there is anyone, other than an expert, who could do such a thing today."

"Or I, either," said Berry. "Didn't Rock Sand win the Triple Crown?"

"Yes," said Jonah. "It was won three times in five years – by Flying Fox, Diamond Jubilee and Rock Sand – but thirty-two years went by before it was won again. Then Bahram brought it off. I don't count the war years, of course, for the courses were not the true ones."

"Has a filly ever won it?" said Daphne.

"I don't think so. Sceptre came very near."

"I'm sorry," said Jill, "but what is the Triple Crown?"

"There are five classic races," said Jonah. "The Two Thousand Guineas, The One Thousand Guineas, The Derby, The Oaks and The St Leger. To win the Triple Crown, a horse must win The Two Thousand Guineas, The Derby and The St Leger. Sceptre won every classic, except The Derby – a really wonderful show. And now let's get back to the Old Bailey."

"Not the Old Bailey," I said. "The High Court. I believe this was called an action for an account. That doesn't sound right somehow; but I will explain what I mean. Incidentally, if justice could have been done, this case would have been tried at the Old Bailey. But that's by the way.

"There was once a wealthy young waster, aged about twenty-five. He was not the type that takes the bit in his teeth, but he was just hopeless. His family could do nothing with him. He had, I need hardly say, an unswerving belief in the virtue of alcohol.

"Well, he had his own money, so the family couldn't cut him off. But if they could have taken such action, he'd simply have sunk into death. The poor fellow was docile enough, but he had no guts. So the family decided that he should make a world tour – in sober company. Money, I may say, was no object. Accordingly, they procured a tutor. His references satisfied them that he was a dependable man. The case was explained to him: he proved to be most understanding; and the youth was committed to his charge. The two were to do the thing properly. They were to proceed to the East, visiting Cairo and Colombo on the way to China and Japan. They were then to make for Honolulu and from there proceed to the Americas, South and North. The tutor was to render reports and to discharge such expenses as were incurred. In other words, he was to hold the purse, for to give the youth money was to cast it into the draught.

"Well, the two set out. No expense was to be spared, so they travelled in luxury. The tutor quite understood that the youth was to have the best that money could buy… The weeks went by, and at every port at which the liner touched the tutor posted a report upon their progress. The reports were comfortable. Three weeks at Cairo had proved extremely expensive, but the youth was enjoying himself and behaving well. The relations, sitting at home, cabled more money to Colombo with sighs of content.

"At last the two reached Honolulu. After a fortnight there, the tutor reported by cable that his charge found the spot so attractive that, if there was no objection, they proposed to extend their stay. 'But, of course, it is very expensive.' 'Never mind that,' said the relatives, and cabled another thousand there and then.

"Ten days later, the tutor reported by cable that his charge had unhappily died.

"More money was cabled for the funeral and 'to settle outstanding accounts' and the tutor was instructed to return to England at once.

"On his return, he, of course, reported in person. But the interview, though protracted, was unsatisfactory; and it was then, for the first time, that the relatives began to wonder whether, after all, their estimate of the tutor had been at fault. So they called their solicitors in…

"Of course, there are people like that. At least, there were. Rich, fond, trusting – fair game for any rogue.

"The first thing the solicitors did was to cable to Honolulu for a copy of the death certificate. This revealed that the youth had died of drink. When the tutor was confronted with the damning document, his explanation was so halting and so patently valueless that the solicitors were given a free hand. So they instructed a reliable private detective to make the very same tour. They were rather afraid that the scent, so to speak, might be cold; but as money was still no object and the furious suspicions of the relatives were mounting every day, they felt that they might as well try. They need have had no fear. Cairo, Colombo and the East had by no means forgotten the visits paid by the two gentlemen; they were, indeed, memorable. Seldom had such riotous living ever been witnessed before. It was the same thing at every port at which the liners had touched. Again and again, the two had had to be carried on to the ships. One might have been forgiven for thinking that to paint Honolulu red would present considerable difficulty. One would have been mistaken. The two had taken that formidable fence in their stride. Here a certain lady had taken them into her house. Let us say they became her guests – no doubt, though the tutor denied this, her handsomely paying guests. Be that as it may, the parties she threw for them went on for days at a time. I must be careful here, so I'll call her Margery Daw. And then the detective found himself out of his depth. Perhaps it would be better to say that he ran into fog. Fact dissolved into rumour and rumour was denied. The lady herself was not available. People found themselves unable to remember. Even the doctor was extremely vague. However, the evidence collected was very much more than enough to brand the tutor as a callous and unprincipled rogue, who had aided and abetted the youth to run his tragic course.

"Naturally enough, the relatives demanded vengeance. But vengeance cannot be bought. Of course there was no contract and the man could not be shown to have broken the criminal law. All the facts were laid before counsel, and after a lot of thought Harker advised, I think, an action for an account. This meant that, if the action succeeded, the tutor would have to account for the moneys which he had received. It goes without saying that he was a man of straw: so the only satisfaction the relatives could obtain was that the knave would be harassed and, for what it was worth, exposed and, presently, made bankrupt. But that, they felt, was better than nothing. A fifth of a loaf was better than no bread.

"So dim is my memory that I cannot remember what happened. I imagine that the action succeeded. I don't think it can have failed. But I saw the tutor in court, and if looks are anything to go by, he'd paid a part of his debt. I never saw anyone so hang-dog in all my life. Guilt, shame and fear looked out of his shifty eyes. After all, he had betrayed a solemn trust, robbed his employers right and left and helped to his death the young man committed to his charge.

"And now for the tail-piece, which I remember well.

"About three months later I dined in Cavendish Square. Among the guests was a man who resided abroad, whom the hostess had been asked to receive by a very old friend. 'You'll find him very amusing.'

"So we did. He made us all laugh very much. But I found him hard to place. As the women were leaving the table, I managed to ask my host who the stranger was. He whispered back, 'He's a fashionable GP – practises in Honolulu.' When we sat down again, I found myself next to the man."

"I'll bet you did," said Berry.

I laughed.

"I admit I probably worked it. I can't remember now. Be that as it may, after some general conversation, he and I were talking quietly by ourselves. Presently, 'Tell me,' I said, 'have you ever heard of a lady called Margery Daw?'

"My words might have been a spell. I can see the fellow now. He had been about to drink; and there he sat, still as death, with his glass halfway to his lips. With the tail of my eye, I watched the blood leave his face. Then he pulled himself together and set down his glass. 'Never,' he said, 'What makes you think…I should have?' 'Oh, I don't know,' I said. 'I know she lives in Honolulu, and I thought you might know her name.' 'No,' he said, 'I've never heard of her.' Then he drank up his port and wiped his face.

"I never saw a change so sudden and so pronounced in all my life. All his assurance had left him, as if it had never been. I had shocked him – raised some spectre he'd never expected to see. Fate, in my innocent person, had tapped him upon the shoulder. And he had been unready – had never dreamed that Fate could so dog his steps.

"As I entered the drawing-room, I saw him approach his hostess and bid her goodbye. She protested, of course, but he made some excuse or other and took his leave.

"So I cut short a very good evening, so far as he was concerned.

"Now what was the explanation, I have no idea. As like as not, it had nothing to do with our case. I can't remember his name, but it was not that of the doctor who gave the death certificate. And I never pursued the matter. To tell the truth, I felt very guilty about it."

"Darling, it wasn't your fault."

"In a way, it wasn't. But Margery Daw was clearly a lady of ill report. And since I knew nothing of the stranger, I ought not, perhaps, to have mentioned her name as I did. I mean, I might have led up to it."

"I don't blame you at all," said Berry. "He was clearly a man of the world and you gave him every chance. He could perfectly well have replied, 'No, I don't think I know anybody of that name.' You might not have believed him, but the matter would have been closed. As it was, he lost his nerve – and gave himself clean away. Did you mention the occurrence to Harker?"

"No, indeed. I thought I'd done enough harm. By asking an idle question I'd raised some dreadful ghost, which the poor fellow thought was laid."

"Very curious," said Jonah. "Whatever the trouble was, he must have been pretty deep in to take it so hard. Speculation, of course, is vain: but yours was the sort of question that someone from the Yard might have asked."

"That occurred to me at once. And I am inclined to believe that when I, er, spoke out of turn, he thought he was under surveillance and that he had been asked to dinner at my request. Which would account for his manifest consternation.

"Well, there we are. I'm sorry I can't remember more of the proceedings themselves; and I fear that, as a story, it's rather disappointing. But the tail-piece does go to show that truth can be just as strange as fiction; and, in fact, the stage was set for a thriller that might have been worth reading, if someone had been disposed to follow the matter up."

*

"I feel," said Berry, "that a very few words on the English spoken today would not be out of place. And when I say spoken, I mean spoken publicly, particularly on the broadcast and in the House.

"First, as regards the reading of 'the news'.

"I have always felt that, in view of the very high standing of 'The BBC News', and of the fact that it is relayed all over the world, not only should the composition of the bulletins be above reproach, but those appointed to read them should be masters of the English tongue. If this would necessitate the employment of a small, special staff, then this should be done. Such a measure would be well worth while, for in a very short time men, women and children all over the world would come to be taught to regard 'The BBC News', not only as reliable, but as a model of excellence – fine prose, accurate pronunciation, flawless enunciation and delivery.

"But, although the composition of the bulletins could be improved, it is the reading of them with which I wish to deal. This is by no means what it was. Stuart Hibberd was impeccable. On all the thousands of occasions on which I listened to his golden voice, I never once heard him fail in any particular. Pronunciation, enunciation, delivery – all were always perfect. The same can by no means be said of his many successors. None enunciate their words as he did. Some make mistakes in pronunciation. I have heard 'controversy' pronounced with the accent on the second syllable, and 'remonstrate' pronounced with the accent on the first. I have heard 'formidable' pronounced with the accent on the second syllable. Only the uneducated made those mistakes when I was young. And pray remember that such solecisms – intolerable in polite conversation – are being received all over the world. Millions of people, who know no better, are going to accept as orthodox those vulgar parodies. I have quoted but three examples, because, to be honest, I can't remember the others which I have heard: but, though I don't say that such mistakes are frequent, my point is that not one should ever have occurred. (Oh, I've just remembered another – 'alleging' with the accent on the first syllable. Can anyone beat that? And yet another – 'revolt', with the 'o' pronounced not as in 'jolt', but as in 'jolly'.) The enunciation, again, leaves much to be desired, while the impression that the announcer is speaking against time is painfully insistent – an impression which is not only very trying to the ear, but, quite honestly, indefensible. In a word, if an item of news is deemed worthy to be communicated to the world, then let it be presented with dignity.

"Secondly, as regards public speech.

"It is too much to expect that the admirable English once spoken in Parliament should distinguish the House of Commons today. And, of course, I can say nothing of the delivery of the speeches made – though I have an uneasy feeling that Winston stands alone. But one grammatical fault, I can expose. It is often to be heard on the floor of the House and in speeches made elsewhere by eminent men.

"This is, shortly, the use of 'will', where 'shall' should be used, and of 'would', where 'should' should be used. I am not going to set out the reasons why the one is right and the other wrong, because, in the first place, I couldn't do it, and, in the second, Fowler has done it for all time: but this I can say – that if I had made such a mistake at my private school, I should have been immediately corrected. To my mind, it is a matter of instinct." He looked at Daphne and Jill. "I'm quite sure that neither of you two sweethearts could begin to defend your particular use of these words; but never in all my life have I heard either of you go wrong. In the old days, it was a recognized peculiarity of a Scotsman that he would sometimes say 'will' or 'would' where we should say 'shall' or 'should': and this peculiarity was regarded with interest and amusement. But now the solecism – for that is what it is – is committed by Englishmen of standing every day.

"You may say that it doesn't matter. But English is admittedly the very finest language in all the world, and that is, to my mind, a heritage worth having. It would be too much to expect all those who use it to respect it as we do. After all, aliens scrawl their names on the stones of Westminster Abbey and The Tower. But it ill becomes our own stock to deface the English tongue."

Unbidden, I rose, fetched the decanter and replenished Berry's glass. Then I drank to him, and Jonah did too. And Berry drank to us. There was no need of words. Neither scholar nor pedant, my brother-in-law had hit the nail square on the head. *It ill becomes our own stock to deface the English tongue.*

"And now," said Berry, "the Queen's Bench of today and yesterday."

"Sorry," I said. "Of the Judges of today, I know almost next to nothing. They're probably very good. One or two, I know, are outstanding. But how they compare with those of The Golden Age, I cannot tell." I hesitated. "A photograph I once saw made me think. It was taken in the early thirties, and it was a close-up of the two Judges who were taking some Summer Assize. They were walking side by side in procession from their coach to the doors of the Court.

"I think we've all seen that procession – I've seen it many times. As the Judges leave the coach, a fanfare of trumpets is blown and they pass slowly up the steps, with the High Sheriff walking before them, wand in hand. The little ceremony is one of the shreds of pageantry which survive, and it can be very impressive.

"Well, now for the photograph – of Her Majesty's Justices in Eyre.

"The taller of the two cut a very dignified figure, wearing his robes with an air, looking straight before him – and wholly ignoring his 'brother', who was poking his head towards him, talking as if they were strolling in some back-garden, with his right hand thrust up and out, to emphasize some point. He made me think of a charwoman arguing with a statue; and, remembering other days, I was profoundly shocked. I mean, it showed that the dignity of his high office, the tradition with which it is endowed and the honour which was at that moment being done it meant no more to him than did the bananas which were probably being hawked half a dozen streets away."

"A very vulgar exhibition," said Berry.

" 'Vulgar,' I'm afraid," said I, "is the appropriate word. After all, the Red Judge is Her Majesty's representative, and the honour and dignity which he is accorded is rendered to him as such. To disregard it is, therefore, offensive. If the Lord Chief saw the photograph – and it was certainly in *The Telegraph*, if not in *The Times* – I hope and believe that he fairly put it across him."

"Who was the Lord Chief then?"

"Trevethin, I think. How he did, I don't know: but he wasn't up to Alverstone's weight. I remember him as Lawrence J. I may be prejudiced, for he once gave me a bad time."

"How was that?" said Daphne.

"Well, I was defending a fellow at, we'll say, the Lewes Assizes. His crime was pardonable, and I did my best to get him off. And Lawrence embarrassed me by interrupting – not once, but again and again."

"Please tell us the facts."

"The accused had been a grocer's assistant. Then he was left a legacy – five hundred pounds. So he determined to set up for himself.

"Now, before I go any further, I think I should make it clear that he was a full-marks fool. Not a knave. There was in the man no guile. He meant to be 'The Poor Man's Grocer' – and make his own fortune in his peculiar way.

"The first thing he did was to get a shop in a poor quarter of the town. Then he went to an established grocer. 'What is the price,' he said, 'of, say, 'Rainbow soap?' 'Threepence a cake,' said the grocer. 'What's the price to me, if I take a thousand cakes?' Well, after a little discussion, the grocer sold him a thousand at twopence a cake. So he carted them off to his shop and started to sell Rainbow soap at twopence halfpenny. You see the idea? Small profits, quick returns. He did that with all kinds of goods. But it didn't occur to him that no one, not even a grocer, likes being under-cut. Still less did it occur to him that the wholesale price of Rainbow soap was a penny a cake. But it certainly shook him up, when he found one afternoon that a cake of Rainbow soap was being sold for twopence at every shop except his. And it was the same thing with everything. The grocers showed him what undercutting meant. After all, it was only a temporary measure. As soon as he was broken, the price of soap would rise.

"Well, the poor fool tried to go on. With the inevitable result that he ordered more stuff than he could pay for. He had to sell much at a loss, to pay his bills. And in the end he was summoned for obtaining goods by false pretences. In fact, he'd been robbing Peter to pay Paul.

"I tried my best to make the poor man plead guilty, but that he would not do. So the case came to be tried. I had only one good card – and that was this. That before he started business, he'd been to see the Chief Constable of the Borough, laid his plan before him and had asked whether there was any objection in law to what he proposed to do. And the Chief Constable said there wasn't and wished him luck. And now that same Chief Constable headed the list of witnesses for the Crown.

"Well, you may imagine that when I rose to cross-examine, I didn't spare him. To my mind, he'd failed in his duty. When the accused had submitted his scheme, it was for him, as Chief

Constable, to tell him not to be a fool and that, if he really meant to set up his shop, he must buy his stock from the wholesalers. But he didn't even do that: he said that the absurd idea was unobjectionable and wished its creator luck. And so, as I say, I didn't spare him. You know. 'When you applied for a summons against the accused, did you tell the Bench that this scheme had been submitted to you and that you had approved it?' 'No.' 'Why didn't you?' 'I didn't think it was necessary.' 'Necessary or advisable?' Well, it was easy money – at least it should have been. But Lawrence kept pulling me up. 'What's the point of that question, Mr Pleydell?' Well, it's distracting you know, to have to stop and explain – and then pick up the thread. To a more experienced counsel, it wouldn't have mattered at all. But it greatly embarrassed me: and it helped and encouraged the witness, who naturally felt that the Judge was taking his part. When he'd interrupted me for about the fourth time, I looked at him in silence. Then, 'My lord,' I said, 'my task is difficult enough… If your lordship feels that it is not for me to question the propriety of this officer's behaviour, so be it.' He looked damned hard at me, and I looked back. Then, 'Go on,' he said. And he didn't interrupt me again. But I found the flurry upsetting – inexperience again, of course – and so I lost a case which I think I ought to have won."

"You have all my sympathy," said Berry. "If Lawrence had left you alone, your cross-examination would have won the case."

"I don't know that mine would. That of a better man would have got the prisoner off. Still, if he'd have pleaded guilty, I think I could have got him bound over. I mean, he'd lost all his money, and, generally, I had a very strong case for mitigation. But, there you are. That is the way things go."

"But what was biting Lawrence?" said Jonah. "I mean, the Chief Constable merited censure for what he'd done."

"I've no idea," I said. "Channel would have put it across him – I'm sure of that. Lawrence may have had some notion of maintaining the dignity of the police."

"And Lord Alverstone?"

I laughed.

"I'll tell you what he would have done. He'd have taken the cross-examination out of my hands, asked four or five deadly questions and then told me to go on. And I should have bowed and sat down."

"No reflection on you, I hope."

"Oh no. He'd have done it to anyone – any junior, any way. In one of my books, somebody says, 'Have you ever watched a fool untying a knot?' Well, Alverstone's brain was so great and his discernment so swift that in court he continually found himself in that most trying position. Hence his impatience, which I have mentioned before. But I never saw him lose his temper. And considering that, compared with him, nearly all men were fools, I think that does him infinite credit."

My sister lifted her voice.

"Wasn't it rather frightening to appear before him?"

I shook my head.

"I never found it so. I was always conscious of the benevolence of his tremendous personality. And so I was never afraid. There's room for a fable there – 'The Mouse and the Elephant'."

"What about Darling?"

"Darling was nobody's fool. If he'd been trying the case, he'd have asked the Chief Constable if he'd ever heard of Machiavelli. And when the Chief Constable said no, he'd have said, 'Oh, I only wondered. He was rather a believer in not letting his right hand know what his left hand had done. There's a lot in it, you know. According to the best traditions, you did your alms in secret. And then to go and tell the Bench would have spoiled everything.' "

"Lovely," said Berry. "Lost on the jury, of course."

"I'm afraid so. But the Chief Constable would have felt he was being got at and have got all hot and bothered, as a result."

"I think it was a shame," said Jill. "After all, he'd lost all his money. What did the Judge give him?"

"I can't remember," I said. "I think perhaps three months. Darling would have given him one, which would have meant that he was immediately released, and the Lord Chief, I think, would have done the same."

"Why," said Daphne, "would he have been immediately released?"

"Because, my sweet, he'd lain in jail for a month, waiting for the Assizes."

"Supposing he'd been found 'Not Guilty'. He'd have been in prison a month, although he was innocent."

"I know. But that can't be helped. A man must await his trial. And if he can't get bail – well, that's just too bad. It's just one of those things. It's obviously impossible to try every prisoner the instant he has been committed for trial. And those who are acquitted are so glad to get off that they never worry about their temporary detention.

"And now please let me qualify something which I have just said. I think that in my day the sentence of one month would have meant the prisoner's immediate release. But I may be wrong. In any event to ensure his immediate release today, the Judge would have to sentence him to two days' imprisonment only."

"Why two days?" said Berry.

"Because today – and possibly in my time – all sentences passed at the Assizes run from the Commission Day, which is the day before the Judge opens the Assize."

"I see. So that if a man is given fifteen years on the first day he will have the consolation of knowing that he's only got fourteen years three hundred and sixty-three days to serve. I wonder what his reactions are when he is told of that munificence."

"I don't suppose they tell him till the last week. By that time it's a pleasant surprise."

"I see," said Berry, thoughtfully. "Oh, and I do wish you'd remember better. These afterthoughts are most distracting."

"How dare you?" said Daphne. "He remembers wonderfully. And it's only because he's so anxious to be accurate – "

"All right, all right," said Berry. "But I had a most valuable question on the tip of my tongue, and now – "

"Exactly," said Daphne. "Two minutes later you've forgotten what it was. But Boy goes back fifty years."

"That," said her husband, "is a perversion of the – Oh, I know. I've recaptured it. What a *tour de force*! Never mind." He addressed himself to me. "Protests such as that you made to Lawrence were rarely made?"

"In my day they were. Counsel had to be pretty desperate before taking such a course. I remember that Lawson Walton, the very distinguished 'silk' who was defending Whitaker Wright, protested to Bigham J in much the same way. But his plight was worse than mine, for, as I have said elsewhere, all through that case Bigham showed a remarkable bias against the accused. I have never understood this, for Bigham was a very good Judge. There was then no Court of Criminal Appeal. If there had been, and Whitaker Wright had appealed, I really believe that the Court would have quashed the conviction upon that ground. Still, no injustice was done, for Wright deserved to go down.

"But that's by the way. To have to make such a protest upset me very much. And I was very uneasy, in case I had gone too far. After all, a Judge is a Judge, and I was very young. But Arthur Denman was there, as Clerk of Assize, and he never looked at me or summoned me afterwards: and I think that he would have done both, if he'd disapproved. And so I was comforted."

"Denman was a stickler?"

"An unofficial *elegantiae arbiter*. His own manner was above reproach. No man did more than Denman to uphold the dignity of the Court. He had a great admiration for Darling – an admiration which, as you know, I shared. And I often feel that, when people speak lightly of Darling as a Judge, they would do well to remember the high esteem in which Arthur Denman held him. And Denman was the son of a High Court Judge and the grandson of a Lord Chief Justice of England."

"Am I right in saying," said Jonah, "that the Lord Chancellor is a Judge?"

"You are, indeed. He seldom sits now, except to deal with appeals to the House of Lords. But he can sit anywhere. In *Bleak House* the Lord Chancellor is sitting as a Chancery Judge in Lincoln's Inn Hall. And in our own time, shortly after the first great war, Birkenhead sat in the Law Courts day after day. I always think it did him great credit."

"How so?" said Berry.

"Well, the Lord Chancellor's job is quite tiring enough. But during the war the Divorce Courts got terribly behind with their lists. All the time, more and more divorces were being sought. So morning after morning Birkenhead came down and helped to reduce the lists. He was very expeditious and stood no nonsense at all, with the happy result that very great progress was made and the lists which had been so swollen, began to assume their normal proportions."

"What about Jeffreys?"

"So far as I know, he never sat as a Judge after he became Lord Chancellor. When he behaved so ruthlessly in Somerset, he was Lord Chief Justice. I don't think it's realized that he was an extraordinarily brilliant man. He was called to the Bar when he was twenty, rose very fast, became Common Serjeant when he was twenty-three and Recorder of London seven years later. Five years later he was made Lord Chief Justice, and two years later Lord Chancellor. For a short life of only forty-one years, I don't think that's too bad."

"I should think it's a record," said Daphne.

"Isn't it a fact," said Jonah, "that he was not so bad as he's painted?"

"I believe that's accepted now. He was sent on the Bloody Assize with instructions to 'weigh it out', and he certainly did. I'm not defending him, but the times were hard times and the unhappy people he tried were charged with high treason. 'Judge Jeffreys' is, of course, a misnomer. He should be known as 'Jeffreys, LCJ' or 'Lord Jeffreys'."

"The Garrick Club," said Berry. "Weren't some members of the Bar members of that?"

I nodded.

"Only a few, I think. Treasury Counsel, mostly. Marshall Hall was a member, I know."

"Why Treasury Counsel?"

"I fancy it was because they belonged to the Criminal Bar, and their cases were, therefore, more dramatic than those of the Civil Courts. And, while Marshall Hall was a Common Lawyer, I don't have to tell you how often he was briefed for the defence of those committed for trial. I was a guest at the Garrick once or twice. It was a very nice Club. But it really belonged to the Stage and to those connected with the stage. If you couldn't keep the hours the Stage kept, to my mind it wasn't much fun. I mean, a feature of the Club was the great supper table, at which members would sit to all hours; and at eight or half past, when most people used to dine, most of the members of the Garrick were on the stage. Then, again, a member of the Bar could seldom sit over his lunch. But it was a great institution, and they've got some beautiful pictures."

"Who took you in?"

"I can't, for the life of me, remember, but it wasn't a member of the Bar. It may have been Arthur Bourchier, or, possibly, Harry Irving. Or both, on different occasions."

"Tree?"

"No. I never went there with Tree." I hesitated. Then, "But the mention of Tree has made me remember something. Dion Clayton Calthrop once told me that it was his father, John

Clayton, who taught Tree how to make up. I think that is of interest: for Beerbohm Tree was famous for his makeup."

"How did you come to know Calthrop?"

"He was the Master of the Robes of the Oxford Pageant. I don't suppose you could have had a better man. He was a delightful fellow, and very talented. His book on English Costume is still *the* standard work upon that subject."

"Shall you ever forget Tree's make-up as *Fagin*?"

"I shall not. Nor his interpretation, either."

"Don't," said Daphne.

"The death of *Nancy*?"

"Yes. It was the most dreadful thing that I've ever seen."

"It was very shocking," said Berry. "But you must give Tree full marks. It's not in the book, of course. It was his idea."

"I never saw it," said Jonah. "I was abroad when he put up *Oliver Twist*."

My sister rose.

"Well, they can tell you about it. Jill and I'll go on up. But do come up when it's done – it's long past twelve."

My wife laid her head against mine.

"Mustn't I hear it, darling?"

"I don't think I should, my sweet."

She got to her feet.

"All right. But don't sit up."

As the door closed behind them –

"Well, you know the story," said I. "*Nancy* is overheard putting a spoke in Fagin's wheel. Although pressed to do so, she refuses to give the gang away. But *Fagin* is so mad at having his plans spoiled that he tells *Sikes* that *Nancy* has betrayed them all. And *Sikes* murders her. The murder is done off stage, but the audience hear it take place. This was the scene. *Fagin* is standing in a passage, listening, beside a closed door. The stage is dark, except for the candle which *Fagin* is holding, close to his face. You hear *Nancy's* frantic protests of her innocence and then her pleading for mercy: then you hear her struggles, as she tries to avoid her doom, and, finally, her screams as the murderer has his way. But all you ever see is *Fagin's* face, and the hideous satisfaction which lights it, as the screams sink to whimpers and then die out. When the last whimper has died, with a smile of extraordinary evil, the Jew blows the candle out."

"Shocking," said Jonah.

"Yes, it was a terrible scene."

"Tree was a fine producer?"

"Very good indeed. Some of his Shakespearian productions were really lovely. He fell down sometimes, of course."

"Was he the best producer of his time?"

I shook my head.

"Of straight plays, I think Asche was the best producer before the first war. *Before*, mark you. His productions of *The Taming of the Shrew*, *As You Like It*, *Count Hannibal* and *Kismet* were as near perfect as anything I've seen. His production of *Kismet* made Knoblauch, who wrote the play. In *Kismet* the curtain rose upon a busy street scene in old Bagdad. And at every performance, before a word was spoken, the roars of applause kept rising and falling for as long as two minutes at a time. And then, when you thought they were over, they'd break out again. And the tribute was richly deserved. He had imagination, of course, but his attention to detail was infinite. But with the outbreak of war, he seemed to go to bits. *Chu Chin Chow* had a record run, but that was because there were a lot of scantily dressed ladies and the war was on. As a production, it was dreadful. The music was the best thing about it." I got to my feet. "And now let's redeem our promise and go to bed."

*

"To return to Tree," said Berry. "Was he a great actor?"

"Undoubtedly," said I. "The trouble was that, when he'd played a part for a week, he got bored with it. So, if you wanted to be sure of seeing Tree at his best, you had to go on one of the first few nights. Of course he played some parts which he should never have played. His *Hamlet* was fearful: it really gave you a pain. And his *Benedick* was frightening. Bourchier, who couldn't bear Tree, asked me if I'd seen it. I said I was going next week. 'Well, don't go,' said Bourchier, 'unless you want to see a coloured hermaphrodite.' And W S Gilbert said of his *Hamlet* that 'it was funny without being vulgar'."

"What a shame," said my sister, laughing.

"Yes, it was in a way. But he did stick out his neck. For all that, Tree was a great man, and he did a great deal of good. On the whole, his productions were lovely."

"He couldn't bear Bourchier, could he?"

"No, indeed. A rehearsal was in progress at His Majesty's when a tyre burst in Charles Street, outside. Everyone jumped at the noise. 'I knew it would happen,' said Tree. 'That's Bourchier's head.' "

" 'On the whole,' " said Berry.

"Well, some were better than others. But he did slip up once, I remember. I can't remember the play, which was not a success, but the scene was laid in some South Sea Island or other, no doubt a very beautiful spot. That great scene-painter Joseph Harker – the father of Gordon Harker – painted all the sets, as usual. I don't think Tree ever went to anyone else. The first act and the last act were played in the same setting. This was upon some sea-shore. The back-cloth, a mighty bay, was very handsomely done, but, to everyone's horror, there was a British man-of-war, painted into the back-cloth, apparently lying at anchor, quite close in."

"Good God," said Berry, and everyone else cried out.

"Yes, but there's worse to come. The last act was played after the sun had gone down, and when the curtain rose, there was the cruiser lighted up."

As soon as he could speak –

"I don't believe you," said Berry. "Not at *His Majesty's*?"

"It's true," I said laughing. "It wasn't Harker's fault, for he'd only done as he was told. Tree had demanded a cruiser, so Harker painted it in. I've no doubt he protested: but when Tree wanted something, he usually had his way. You may imagine the critics' reactions, for, if they could get at Tree, they always did. It wasn't very long before the first war, and Germany was growing insolent. One of the critics wrote, *I have seen that cruiser before: and then the funny man showed it a sausage and it sank.*"

As the laughter subsided –

"Well, anyone can tell you those things, but here is another tail-piece, which I don't think most people know. Tree was upset by these criticisms and pretended, of course, that Harker was to blame. After the play had come off, which it very soon did, he spent a few days in the country. One afternoon he drove out in an open car. Except for one companion, he was alone. He was still very much depressed and refused to talk. Then the car breasted some rise, and there was a magnificent sunset – a most arresting sight. Tree called upon the chauffeur to stop: and the three of them sat in silence, contemplating the glorious spectacle. Tree touched his companion's arm and pointed. 'Harker at his worst,' he said."

"Brilliant," said Jonah.

"Sorry," said Jill, "I'm not there."

"It's very subtle, my darling. What Tree meant was that, if Harker had rendered that sunset, all the critics would have said it was overdone."

"That," said Berry, "was very quick. But you've said before that most of his wit was studied."

"That's quite true. Very different to that of Paul Rubens. I'll tell you of him in a minute. I haven't quite done with Tree. I didn't know him very well, but he was always very nice to me. When he came up to Oxford to see the pageant, I asked him to lunch with me first. During luncheon he inquired how we were going to get to the pageant-ground. 'I've ordered a hansom,' I said. 'It's such a lovely day. Could we have a landau?' 'Of course,' I said. 'If you'll excuse me, I'll give the order at once.' So I went off to telephone. (In those great days, it was as easy as that. You could have a special train for less than fifty pounds.) When we took our seats in the carriage, Tree turned to me. 'I have visited Oxford many times, but never yet have I seen a good-looking girl.' 'I can believe you,' I said. 'But, then, Oxford's a monastery.' So it was in those days. 'There must be one,' said Tree, beginning to look about him. 'After all, Sodom and Gomorrah could produce just one good man.' I began to grow uneasy. Tree was in a mischievous mood. Sure enough, 'If I should see one,' he said, 'I shall rise and take off my hat.' 'I beg,' I said, 'that you'll do nothing of the kind.' 'Oh, but I shall,' said Tree. 'That's why I wanted a landau.' Well, we got down The High all right, though we had to go very slowly because of the crowds. I need hardly say he was recognized right and left. But he spotted a winner, as we were going over Magdalen Bridge. She was in some scene in the pageant and was wearing mediaeval dress. 'There you are,' cried Tree and, steadying himself on my shoulder, got to his feet. Then he swept off his hat with a most magnificent gesture, brought the hat back to his heart and bowed as low as he could. I had to laugh, but I never was so much embarrassed. As he sat down, 'Probably down for the day,' he said. 'Perhaps she'll be on the train. D'you think she'll know me again?' 'I imagine so,' I said. 'She'll talk about this for years.' 'D'you really think so?' said Tree, as pleased as Punch.

"One more memory of this really great man at play. He asked to luncheon a man whom he wanted to please. Luncheon in the Carlton Grill. He ordered very special food and a particularly rare wine. To his dismay, his guest's reception of the *hors d'oeuvres* showed that he was no *gourmet* and that a cut off the joint at Simpson's and a tankard of beer would have served him just as well. Tree was in agony. To see such superb dishes devoured as if they were provender drove him half out of his mind. Then the wine was served. God knows what wine it was or how much it was worth. But their glasses were filled with every reverence. Tree's guest, who was thirsty, seized his glass which he plainly proposed to drain. This was too much. With a stifled scream, Tree caught his arm. 'Don't drink it all at once,' he cried."

"But how do you know this?" said Jonah, wiping his eyes.

"I knew the guest," I said. "He was one of Tree's backers. And he was, very unkindly, pulling Tree's leg."

"Poor Tree," said Jill. "What a shame!"

"It was. A damned shame. But Tree did ask for it sometimes."

"How was it that some of the actor-managers sometimes produced such bad plays?"

"That's a question on which I never can make up my mind. They didn't often do it: but the fact that they did it at all surprised me very much. I'm not talking of failures, for many a good play has failed. I'm talking of rotten plays. (And, if you please, I am talking of things as they were before the first war. For a rotten play then was doomed: it didn't run for two years, as they do today.) I have seen some plays put up on the West End stage that almost any one of us here could have predicted would fail. But the management couldn't see it. Sometimes, I think, the big shot saw a part for himself which he liked so well that he could see no further. Sometimes I've wondered whether such a play was put up out of obstinacy – just because somebody else had ventured to say it was no good. It has occurred to me that such plays were put on, because they were the best they could find and, if nothing had been put on, the theatre would have been standing idle. But none of those reasons seem to me good enough. The fact remains that these highly intelligent men did on occasion go to very great expense to produce a play that you or I could have told them was no damned good. Fortunately for their pockets and for those of their backers, such an occurrence was rare; but that it did happen is beyond argument."

90

"Just now you mentioned Paul Rubens."

"Yes. He had a very quick wit. He was an Old Stager, and I met him at Canterbury. The men used to stay at *The Fountain*; and night after night we would sit up to all hours while Paul Rubens moved between the supper-table and the piano, playing and telling his tales."

"He was very talented," said Berry. "I would sooner listen to his light music than to that of many of his successors."

I nodded.

"His early death was a tragedy. Apart from his brilliant work, he was the life and soul of any company he kept. And he was very modest. He had an immense fund of side-splitting anecdotes in which, according to him, his brother played the lead. I was always quite sure that it wasn't his brother at all – that it was himself. But that was Paul Rubens' way.

"His sister was a close friend of Mrs Willie James, who was one year a member of a house-party at Sandringham. She suggested to the King and Queen that the Rubens should be asked down for two nights to help in some amateur theatricals. Their Majesties agreed and the visit was arranged. Paul Rubens' account of their adventure into such exalted society was one of the funniest tales I have ever heard. Their troubles began at Wolferton Station, for, by some mistake, no carriage had been sent to meet them and the station-master had not been warned to expect them. The latter flatly refused to believe that the three had been invited to stay at Sandringham House, and it took them twenty minutes to persuade him to allow Rubens' sister to use his telephone. I should have said that it was a bitterly cold night and that there was at the station no transport of any kind. At last the station-master gave way and the sister was connected to Mrs Willie James. 'Is that you, Eva?' she said. 'Oh my Gawd,' said the station-master. 'Bill, light the fire in the waiting-room.' Well, it was all like that...

"One very quick back-answer has always stuck in my mind. (He told it of his brother, of course, but I shall tell it of him.) One evening he dined at his father's table. It was a party, and, since one of the guests had dropped out, an odd man that the family knew had been asked to take his place. Paul and his brother couldn't bear the stand-in, who was a sycophant. When the women had left the table, the sycophant seated himself beside Paul and began to do his stuff. 'Devilish good port, this, my boy.' 'Yes,' said Paul Rubens, 'I think the governor's changed his grocer.' "

As the laughter subsided –

"Darling," said Jill, "What's a sycophant?"

"A toady or parasite, my sweet. And now I've remembered a quick one of Darling's. I wasn't in the case, but I happened to be in court. It was a motor-car case, and the plaintiff was a nice old fellow who lived in the country and believed that roads were made for equipages and regarded motor cars and all who used them with the most violent hatred and contempt. He was quite rabid on the subject; besides, his four-wheeled dog-cart had been hit by a motor car. Under cross-examination, he became so excited that his tongue ran away with him. 'I tell you,' he cried, 'that I have seen much murder done by drivers of motor cars.' Darling leaned down from the Bench. 'What, many murders?' he said. 'Many murders, my lord,' cried the witness. Darling sat back. 'Ah, well,' he said. 'Some people have all the luck.' "

"George Alexander?" said Jonah.

"I never met him." I said. "Frankly, I never understood why he had the success he had. To my mind, he was not a great actor. He was quite good in a society play, but his rendering of *Rudolf* in *The Prisoner of Zenda* was dreadful. And that is by no means a difficult part to play."

"Ellen Terry?"

"There was no one like her. There's been no one like her since. She was incomparable."

"Is it a fact that she never could remember her lines?"

"That's putting it rather high. But neither she nor anyone else ever knew when she was going to break down – or, as they call it on the stage, dry up. Her failing was most disconcerting and used to drive Irving mad. It was never in the same place. I heard her do it once. The first intimation I had was her agonized aside, 'Oh, what *do* I say? What *do* I say?' Then somebody gave her her words and she recovered at once.

"Which reminds me that the only time I ever saw Muskett gravelled was when he was cross-examining a daughter of hers. (You will remember that I was once his pupil and that he was the Solicitor to the Commissioner of Police.) The lady – would it have been Miss Ailsa Craig? – had been subpoenaed by the Militant Suffragists to give evidence on their behalf at Bow Street. I need hardly say that the evidence which she had been summoned to give was utterly irrelevant. However, she looked very charming, very faintly reminiscent of her mother and absurdly out of place. When she had given her evidence, Muskett rose to cross-examine. 'What time was this, Miss Craig?' With a charming smile, 'I'm so sorry,' she said, 'but, you know, I can't appreciate time.' I began to laugh, but Muskett seemed utterly dazed. He kept looking at her and then at the Magistrate. And then at last he sat down and turned to me. 'What the devil's the woman mean?' he said. Then he saw I was laughing and laughed himself."

"You know," said Daphne, laughing, "you did have a lot of fun."

"I did, indeed, my darling. Far more than I deserved."

"Pity you didn't keep a diary."

I wrinkled my brow.

"It would be useful now: but I'm far too lazy for such an exercise."

"Most people are," said Berry. "I did once – for a month; but I was truly thankful to lay the swine down. Self-discipline's all very well: but the effort of writing up one's diary is formidable indeed. Thank God Sam Pepys did it – though how such a lad contrived to keep it going for ten full years, I never shall understand. Evelyn, of course, was exactly the sort of bloke who would keep a diary. But not Sam Pepys.

"I remember once, many years ago, lunching with the old squire of a little village in Kent. When luncheon was over, we sat in the library. I'd just been staying at Ruth with Nicholas John and, when the old fellow heard that, he got all excited because he had known his mother, when she was a little girl. Then he rose and passed to a bookcase. He took down three or four volumes, all handsomely bound in calf, and after a little search, he found the entry he sought. 'Drove over to —, and lunched with the —s. An excellent luncheon; roast goose, stuffed with onion farce, and apple sauce: cold steak and kidney pie; plum pudding. Miss Fanny much perturbed by the loss of a favourite cat...' and a lot more of the same sort of stuff. Miss Fanny was the future Duchess. I think there were more than fifty volumes, all of which he had composed in the sweat of his face. Well, I don't know, but where are those volumes now? And I'm perfectly sure that he never read them himself."

"I think," said Jonah, "that the old fellow deserved full marks, for he made a considerable effort for many years. Supposing those volumes survived a world catastrophe – to be found five thousand years later... They'd be invaluable. I admit that, as like as not, they have already been pulped. But that is not his fault. He made his effort, poor man. And if Pepys and Farington and Greville hadn't made their efforts, how very much poorer the world would be today."

"I withdraw," said Berry. "You're perfectly right. The diarist does a duty which nine out of ten of us cannot be bothered to do. We can talk about being too tired or not having the time. But that won't wash. Pepys was pretty busy; but he always made the time – and ruined his sight by writing up 'his journal' night after night." He sighed. "That old squire was a better man than I am – and that's the truth."

"Eleanor Carson," said Jill.

"True again," said Berry. "Consider the very great pleasure her diary presently gave to Vivien and Pip. And they were contemporaries." He looked at me. "By the way, how's the new book?"

"I can't complain," I said.

"Darling," said Jill, "you know it's going strong. Do let them hear the first part."

"Why not?" said Berry. "Then if it's no good, we'll tell you and you needn't go on. How many parts will it consist of?"

"Only two," I said. "The first is told in the first person, and the second in the third."

"That's rather interesting. Has it ever been done before?"

"I really don't know. I expect so. The tale goes straight on. The first part ends on a Thursday afternoon, and the second begins the next morning at eight o'clock."

"Why did you change over?"

I shrugged my shoulders.

"The same old answer," I said. "I never saw the change coming. I did as I was told. But please don't dress this up. I'm sure that a lot of authors have written in just the same way. As I've said before, I know that Kipling did."

"I find it remarkable," said Jonah. "Did Dickens write like that?"

"How can I tell?" said I. "I have a feeling that Maurice Hewlett did. *The Forest Lovers* always suggests to me the same technique. I may be wrong, of course; but I always feel that, when *Prosper le Gai* rode forth to seek his fortune, Hewlett had no idea what fortune he was going to find. The dovetailing is so perfect that I simply cannot believe that that magnificent story was ever thought out."

"A book so written is better than other books?"

"You can't expect me to say that. But that technique does work."

Jonah leaned forward.

"Your sub-conscious brain must see the book as a whole."

95

"I'm forced to that conclusion. Again and again I have recorded an incident to which at the time I attached no importance at all, which, many pages later, has played a big part in the tale. To be honest, in the old days when some reviewer was kind enough to say that the story had been 'well worked out', I used to feel ashamed – for I hadn't worked it out."

"Your sub-conscious brain had."

"I suppose it must have: but it took care to keep me in the dark."

*

"I once had," said Berry, "a most painful experience. It was in no way my fault, although I occasioned it. I don't think I've ever mentioned it to anyone. But to this day its memory makes me feel cold. It won't upset you, for you didn't suffer it. But I think it will interest you. So here we go.

"You may remember that early in the first war two volumes of our set of *Punch* were damaged by water from a burst pipe."

"Both 1847," said Daphne. "You got replacements in the end."

Berry nodded.

"But not for some years. Nothing, of course, could be done till after the war. And then I began to try. Advertisement proved hopeless, but since, if we couldn't get them, the whole of our set was spoiled, I felt that something must be done."

"Very difficult," said I. "Original publisher's cloth."

"You're telling me," said Berry. "And a lot of good you were. Said your job was to write books, not to seek them. And Jonah was after some thug in the worst of France. Any way, I started in.

"Somebody advised me to try a bookshop south of the river. This was, I think, about 1923. Well, I had the address and one afternoon I set forth. I found the shop, a sprawling, rambling place, with a very jovial fellow of about my age in charge. Not at all like the traditional bookseller. Big, broad, well-covered and full of fun: jesting with his assistants and using their Christian names. And they were all laughing. I'll say it did me good to enter that shop. He'd fought, of course – a sergeant in the —s. And I'll lay he was a good sergeant and pulled far more than his weight. We were very soon changing hats. But he knew his job all right. Sergeant or no, he was a bookseller now.

"Well, he had a lot of 'Punches' which he had bought as job lots, with the idea of meeting such demands as mine. He and I went through them together, talking all the time and remembering other days. But the ones we needed weren't there. There were scores of volumes and many duplicates; but Numbers Twelve and Thirteen were not among them. At last he pushed back his hat. 'Everything else,' he said, 'and that's so often the way. But I've got some more in a garage – say, five minutes' walk. Shall we have a look there?' 'I'd be more than content,' I said, so off we went. When I saw the stacks of 'Punches', I thought we were home. So we were – halfway. The last volume which I picked up was Number Twelve. But Number Thirteen wasn't there. I paid what he asked for Twelve, but that was little enough. And I was rather upset, for he'd taken no end of trouble. But when I said as much, he clapped me upon the back. 'That's all right, sir,' he laughed. 'I'll have it next time you come. You must give me a chance, you know. Come back in six months.' 'If the pubs were open,' I said, 'I'd ask you to have a drink.' 'We'll wait till we find it,' he said, 'and then we'll have one or two.' Then we shook hands and parted.

"It must have been eighteen months before I went back again. You know how it is – you remember and then you forget; and then you remember again when you're out of Town. However, at last I got there, on a dull November evening…

"I'd been looking forward to seeing my jovial friend again, and paid my visit late, for I meant him to have his drink. But the moment I entered the shop, I saw that it had changed hands. It was ill-lit, dingy and cheerless. From being gay, the atmosphere was depressing. More. The definite air of dejection hit me between the eyes. I very nearly withdrew – I wish I had.

"I was the only customer. As the door closed behind me, a hang-dog assistant came forward. 'Yes?' he said listlessly. I glanced to where an older man was sitting in half an office, marking a catalogue. 'Can I see the manager?' I said. Without a word, he turned, slouched to the office and spoke to the older man. After a minute or two the latter got up and came forward. He was, to the life, the elderly, dry-as-dust bookseller of fiction; spare, with a stoop, crabbed, peering over his spectacles, poking his head, less content with my company than he would have been with my room. 'Yes?' he said, testily. 'I've been here before,' I said. 'A year ago last May, in search of a volume of *Punch*. They hadn't got it then, but the manager suggested that I should come back later and that in the meantime – ' 'I remember you,' said the man. '*I took you up to the garage… No, it hasn't come in.*'

"I stared upon him in silence. He just peered back. I couldn't speak; but, as I put out my hand, he turned and went back to his office. In silence, I looked at the assistant. His eyes were upon the ground. So I turned, too, and made my way out of the shop."

"My God," said Daphne, closing her eyes. "Oh, my darling, how dreadful."

"It was devastating," said Berry. "I don't know how I got home. You see, I was unready. I was disappointed, for I thought the shop had changed hands. And then, without any warning, Tragedy threw down her mask and opened her cloak to show her nakedness." He put a hand to his head. "It was a most dreadful occasion. And the awful thing was that, by failing to recognize my poor friend, I had turned the knife in the wound… I sometimes wonder if I should have followed when he left me and said how shocked I was: but I think he had seen my hand before he turned, and wished for no intrusion on his adversity. Besides, I was greatly shaken."

"As," said Jonah, "anyone would have been. Oh, no. You were right to go. You couldn't have done any good. Whatever could have happened to wreak such a terrible change?"

"I dare not think," said Berry. "The poor fellow was transformed. He had shrunk in person and presence. His cast of countenance was quite different. In eighteen months he had aged, say, thirty-six years. He bore not the slightest resemblance to the man I had met before. What was, if possible, more painful, his infectious *joie de vivre* had been supplanted by a blank despondency. I can only suppose that he had become the prey of some shocking disease which had ravaged not only his body but also his soul. But I would give a very great deal not to have dealt that most unfortunate man yet another blow."

Jill was on her knees by his side.

"Darling," she said, "don't look at it like that. The same blow must have been dealt him again and again. And he was to blame – not you. He needn't have said who he was. You wouldn't have done such a thing. But suffering had made him bitter, and so he did. I expect he's dead long ago, and now he's happy again. Tragedy often splurges, because it knows it's got such a short time to go."

Berry picked up her hand, looked at it for a moment and then put it up to his lips.

"Can anyone tell me," he said, "where we should be – "

"No," said everyone.

Jill went quickly to Daphne and put an arm round her neck.

"You taught me," she said. "You've taught me everything."

"Honours are even," said Jonah. "I think that calls for a drink." He rose to fetch the decanter… When he had charged our glasses, he raised his own. "To our incomparable petticoats."

As, flushed with pleasure, Jill took her seat by my side –

"I feel," said Berry, " that your cask of legal reminiscence has not yet run dry."

I sighed.

"Its level is low," I said. "But I do remember a case of a death-bed Will."

"Come on. Let's have it," said Jonah.

"What's a death-bed Will, darling?"

"It's a Will that is made by someone who is actually ill in bed, whose illness is their last illness. Such Wills are naturally scrutinized.

"Now I was not in the case – in fact I was still at Oxford: but Coles Willing took me to hear it, because he knew that I was to go to the Bar. He was very good like that. It was thanks to him that I saw the old Old Bailey and much else to do with the Law that very few of my legal contemporaries have seen, because it had disappeared before they were 'called'. I can't remember when he first took me into the Courts, but I must have been still at Harrow, for all the 'silks' were then QCs – a KC had never been dreamed of for more than sixty years. I remember Willes, J and Lord Justice Rigby. The latter was too old to be there and his demeanour was painful to behold. He took no part in the proceedings, but just sat staring before him with a fallen jaw. And in the case of which I'm going to tell you, I saw two famous men, whom I never saw again.

"The queer thing was that it wasn't Coles Willing's case: but he knew a great deal about it – and more than some, for he had known the testatrix in other days, and he was a personal friend of one of her Trustees.

"What happened was this.

"A widow had died shortly after making a Will. The executors of a Will which she had made twenty years before were not satisfied that she was fit to make a new Will at the time at which the new Will was made, so they entered a *caveat*. This meant that the new Will could not be proved, until a Judge had pronounced in its favour. And the executors of the earlier Will were petitioning the Court to pronounce in favour of their Will, instead. So the case came to be tried.

"And now I must throw back a little.

"A good many years ago, a very nice couple, whose name, let us say, was Druce, were living in Devonshire. They had no children and next to no relatives. But they had many friends and they entertained a good deal. They lived in very good style, which they could well afford. When the wife was only forty, her husband died. This, to her lasting grief. She sold their home and moved to and fro about England, unable to settle down. In spite of her friends' entreaties, for thirty-five years she led this wretched existence, spending not a tenth of her income and preferring lodgings to hotels. Her friends diminished. She kept in fitful touch with a few, but they seldom knew where she was. As she grew older, rich as she was, she became obsessed with the idea that she must practise economy – that is a sad, but not uncommon, feature of cases like hers – and in the end she was staying in mean lodgings in Paddington, when she should have been the tenant of an agreeable suite at, say, the Kensington Palace Hotel.

"Now six months before she died she engaged a paid companion, for her sight was failing and she felt that she must have someone to help her to lead her life. I saw the companion in court and was unimpressed. Be that as it may, the two were installed in comfortless rooms in Paddington when Mrs Druce was taken seriously ill.

"The companion summoned the doctor whom the landlady employed and wired to her brother, who was a country solicitor. She did not inform Mrs Druce's Trustees or even her Bank, although their names and addresses were available. It was, in fact, by the merest chance that one of Mrs Druce's few friends came to the lodgings to see her two days before she died.

"The friend – we will call her Mrs Gascoigne – was received by the companion and her brother, to both of whom she took an instant dislike. In spite of their assurances and protests, she made her way into the sick-room... Horrified at the squalor prevailing, as well as the shocking fact that the patient was unattended, though clearly in danger of death, she took immediate action. She sought and found the addresses, she wired to the two Trustees and informed the Bank. What was better still, she called in her own doctor, a man of standing and an eminent GP. As a result, within a very short time two nurses arrived, as well as all the apparatus appropriate to an illness so far advanced. One Trustee arrived the following day. But all these measures were, of course, taken too late, and on the day after that the poor lady died. Late that night, Mrs Gascoigne's doctor informed the Trustees of the death and both arrived the next morning, after informing the deceased's solicitors. They were met by the companion and her brother, who inquired their business...

"One of the Trustees replied.

" 'I am not only Mrs Druce's Trustee. I am an executor of her Will.'

" 'I fear you're mistaken,' said the brother. 'My sister and I are the executors of her Will.'

" 'To what Will are you referring?'

" 'To one which I drew for her a day or two back.'

" 'Indeed. May I see this document?'

" 'When Probate has been granted, you will be at liberty to inspect it at Somerset House. And now perhaps you'll excuse us, for we have much to arrange.'

"So war was declared.

"The Trustees instructed the solicitors who had drawn the original Will: a *caveat* was entered: the new Will was duly inspected and copies were obtained.

"The new Will purported to have been signed by Mrs Druce on the day before she died, that is to say on the day after she had been visited by her efficient friend, Mrs Gascoigne. It was short, simple and straightforward; but its provisions were remarkable. By these, the doctor who had been summoned by the companion received five thousand pounds, while the companion and her brother shared the rest of Mrs Druce's considerable fortune."

"Good God!" said Berry.

"Exactly. The companion had certainly been with Mrs Druce for six months, but, looking upon the lady, I found it difficult to believe that in that short time she would have so endeared herself to any being that they would desire to enrich her to the extent of fifty thousand pounds. But that the companion's brother, a most unprepossessing individual, whom Mrs Druce had only known for the inside of a week, should have been similarly favoured, I found still harder to credit. A sinister reason for the most handsome remuneration of the doctor, who looked to me very hang-dog, whose professional advice I would rather have died than seek, immediately presented itself."

"He was to swear that she was perfectly capable of making a Will?"

"Well, it did look rather like it. Never mind. The signature of the deceased, which was undeniably shaky but did resemble her signature, had been witnessed by the two nurses who had been sent in."

"I never heard of anything so brazen," said Berry.

I shrugged my shoulders.

"Well, the usual procedure was followed, and the case was set down for trial. The Trustees would propound their Will, and the companion and her brother would propound theirs. And a special jury would decide between the two.

"The case was tried by Sir Francis Jeune, later Lord St Helier, President of the Court of Probate, Divorce and Admiralty. The executors of the old Will were represented by Sir Edward Clarke, Charles Gill and Priestley: the companion and her brother, by Bargrave Deane and Barnard, whom I have mentioned before.

"Before the case began, I was sitting with Coles Willing right in front, on the seat in front of that reserved for Queen's Counsel, waiting for the Judge to come in, when Sir George Lewis, the famous solicitor, appeared. He had a word with Coles and then passed on to speak with Sir Edward Clarke. 'You ought to win this case hands down,' he said. 'I mean to,' said Clarke. I heard the words myself."

"Was Sir George concerned in the case?"

"No. Lewis and Lewis were not concerned."

"Then how did he know about it?"

"Sir George Lewis knew everything. God knows how he was informed; but he always knew – everything. Somebody said of him once, 'From whom no secrets are hid.' A most remarkable man. Years afterwards I met Reginald Poole, who succeeded Sir George as head of the firm. He was such a very nice man, and a brilliant solicitor. I called him *Lacey* and put him in LOWER THAN VERMIN. They were a wonderful firm – for all I know, they're a wonderful firm today. But old Sir George was a legend. I'm glad to have seen him, you know. Of course Coles told me who he was. Few people know that he made Eldon Bankes when he was at the Bar."

"A remarkable achievement," said Berry.

I laughed.

"Bankes was a much better counsel than he was a Judge. And he had a very gentlemanly way, which made him valuable. Juries liked him.

"Here and now let me say that I didn't take to Clarke. He had for years, of course, been the leader of the Bar and he was undoubtedly a very eminent man. But I was disappointed. He'd a very forbidding expression and his manner was abrupt and autocratic. He was a small man and still wore the old-fashioned 'Piccadilly weepers', that is to say, long whiskers that hung down like twin beards on either side of his face. He always wore a grey frock-coat-suit and elastic-sided boots. Charles Gill, as you know, I came to know very well. He was already a distinguished 'silk' and a renowned cross-examiner. Priestley was one of the two leading juniors of the Divorce Court, and, as such, quite exceptional."

"A cryptic saying," said Berry.

"Well, those members of the Bar who practised in the Divorce Court, which was a very close borough, would seldom, if ever, have got on in the Queen's Bench Division. I'm speaking of my day, of course. Things may have changed; but in my day they were painfully undistinguished. Priestley, however, was out of another drawer. He was very able and he had an admirable address. Had he remained in practice, he would certainly have reached the Bench, for he was a head and shoulders above any of his fellows. I admit that to rise in the Divorce Court of my day was by no means difficult, but that does not alter the fact that Priestley was outstanding."

"Why ever did he give up?"

"I think he had a bad illness which was followed by a long convalescence. He then came back for a while, but again withdrew. I may be quite wrong, for it's such a long time ago, but my belief is that he had substantial private means, in which case it would have been idle to continue to jeopardize his health. And I don't think such a man can have enjoyed his work. Divorce work is easy enough to do, but it is hardly inspiring. And in any case of importance, such as the one which I am reporting, Common Lawyers were always brought in."

"But this wasn't a Divorce," said Daphne.

"It was a Probate matter – that is, to do with a Will. And Probate and Divorce belong to the same Division."

"How very confusing."

"I agree. Why Probate and Admiralty matters should have been linked with Divorce, I cannot conceive. Of course, when that was arranged, there weren't many Probate matters, few Admiralty cases and only about a hundred Divorces a year. Probate and Admiralty matters are still few, but Divorce cases have increased to thirty thousand a year. I believe those figures are accurate."

"Progress," said Jonah.

"I suppose so.

"To continue. I wasn't greatly impressed by Bargrave Deane. I think I am right in saying that he later became a Divorce Court Judge, but I may be wrong there. Barnard was the other leading junior of the Divorce Court. He was genial, but undistinguished. The Trustees certainly had very much the better team.

"Then Jeune entered and took his seat on the Bench. I can't say I liked his manner. I believe that he was accounted a good Judge, but his manner was by no means agreeable. I never heard him make a pleasant remark. That was the only occasion on which I saw him, and he may have been at his worst, for, as I shall show, there was feeling between him and Edward Clarke. Both knew, of course, that Clarke had been offered and had refused the Mastership of the Rolls. Had he accepted that great office, he would have taken precedence of Jeune, as President of the Divorce Court.

"Well, the proceedings began. The old Will was propounded and Clarke opened the Trustees' case. He disclosed that by the provisions of the old Will, every penny of Mrs Druce's considerable fortune was left to charities in which she had taken a lifelong interest; whereas, by the provisions of the new Will, not a penny was left to any charity, but the handsome legacy of five thousand pounds was left to an odd general practitioner who had attended her for five days and the whole of the rest of her fortune, more than one hundred thousand pounds, had been divided equally between a solicitor on whom she had never set eyes till four days before her death and the solicitor's sister who had acted as her companion for the last six months and was in receipt of a very humble salary. He declared that 'this infamous document' had been drawn without Mrs Druce's knowledge or consent, that when it was read to her, she was far too ill to understand its contents and that, when she affixed her signature – if, in fact, she did – she was moribund and quite incapable of knowing what she was doing. He submitted that it was a daring attempt – which, but for the fortuitous visit of Mrs Gascoigne, might well have succeeded – on the part of the

106

companion and her brother to steal the old lady's fortune and that the doctor whom they had summoned had been 'left' five thousand pounds to hold his tongue. Of course Clarke didn't put it so bluntly as that, but that was what he implied."

"As," said Berry, "he had every right to. I trust Jeune impounded the documents and that the wicked trio came by their rights. Sorry. Please go on."

"Well, then the witnesses were called.

"For some reason or other, Mrs Gascoigne did not give evidence. Looking back, I find that surprising; for her chance, but dramatic arrival and her description of what she found would have thrown a lurid glare on the events to come."

"You amaze me," said Jonah. "And she doesn't sound as if she would have made a bad witness. Why on earth wasn't she called?"

I shrugged my shoulders.

"I can't remember that Coles commented upon her absence, and I was too young and inexperienced to do anything but take things for granted. She may, of course, have begged to be excused; for particularly in those days ladies shrank from the idea of appearing in court. I think that's the most likely explanation. But it is quite possible that Clarke thought he could win the case without her evidence. As I've said, he was very autocratic, and, as being the leader, he had to have his way. The less time a case takes, the better – for any distinguished counsel whose services are in demand.

"Perhaps I ought to have said that the old Will was produced, I think by Mrs Druce's solicitors, and made an exhibit. I can't remember that happening, but I imagine that it was done.

"I think the eminent doctor, whom Mrs Gascoigne summoned, was the next witness. He said that he first saw Mrs Druce on the day before she was said to have signed the new Will and that she was even then so seriously ill that it was very doubtful whether she could have appreciated the contents of any document: that when he saw her the next morning she was worse and that on that same evening she was approaching a condition of coma. Bargrave Deane cross-examined him, but could not shake him on any material point.

"Then the two nurses were called. One was very definite. She said that she could not believe that the patient understood what was going on. She was too ill. Bargrave Deane, naturally, attacked her. 'Do you mean to tell the Court that you watched her sign her Will and then subscribed your name, when all the time you believed that she didn't know what she was doing? Why didn't you say, *But she's not fit to sign a Will?*' And so on. Still, he couldn't shake her. Gill re-examined very well and led her to say what was the undoubted truth – that she had felt that she ought to protest and decline to witness Mrs Druce's signature, but that she hadn't liked to. After all, she was quite a young girl, and the companion's brother was probably rather compelling.

"The second nurse, who had witnessed the ordeal which her comrade had just endured, was pardonably nervous. She was less definite than the other, but she did state that, when Mrs Druce signed the Will, she, the nurse, held the pen into the patient's hand and guided the pen over the paper, and that, had she not done this, the patient could not have affixed her signature. Coles told me later that in her statement to the solicitors she had said that Mrs Druce's signature had been written on the Will in pencil and that she had guided the pen to follow its shape. But she would not go so far in court; and, of course, Gill could not cross-examine her because she was his own witness."

"She'd been got at," said Berry.

"Possibly. And she was certainly scared of Bargrave Deane. He shook her to some extent, but she stuck to the fact that she had guided Mrs Druce's hand and that the companion's brother had told her to do so."

"What a shocking business," said Jonah.

"Yes, it was very dreadful. The poor, dying lady being used like a lay figure, to will her fortune away from the charities she had chosen to two people she hardly knew."

"I think it was awful," said Daphne. "How can people be so wicked?"

I shrugged my shoulders.

"I admit it smacks of the Old Bailey rather than the Law Courts, but there you are. And I don't think it's surprising that the case has stuck in my mind for fifty years.

"Well, so much for the evidence. Now for the Judge. For some astonishing reason, Jeune showed a definite bias in favour of the new Will."

"Impossible," cried Berry.

"It's a fact. He cross-examined the eminent doctor.

" 'You were not present when the Will was signed?'

" 'No, my lord.'

" 'Then you can't speak to her condition at that time?'

" 'No, my lord.'

" 'Are you going to tell me that it is impossible that her condition temporarily improved between the visit you paid that morning and the visit you paid that night?'

" 'It is not impossible, my lord. But it is improbable.'

" 'Why improbable?'

" 'Because her illness was taking a certain course.'

" 'Have you ever known cases in which patients who were dying suddenly rallied for a while?'

" 'I have known such cases, my lord. But I should be much surprised if this case was one of them.'

"Coles was outraged. I was too young to be outraged, but it seemed to me very surprising and most unfair."

"It was monstrous," said Berry. "Whatever was biting Jeune?"

"God knows," said I. "And he interrupted Clarke more than once, but favoured Bargrave Deane. The more I think upon it, the more inclined I am to the idea that Jeune's dislike of Clarke had much to do with his attitude. It's a very painful conclusion, but I can come to no other.

"Well, all this has taken a very short time to tell, but the examination, cross-examination and re-examination of witnesses is a slow business and the case for the Trustees was not concluded until the luncheon-adjournment on the second day. It remained for the companion and her brother to propound their Will and give their evidence and then for Clarke and Bargrave Deane to address the jury.

"As we left the Court, I remember that Coles touched my arm. I looked round. Then I followed his gaze to see Clarke and Bargrave Deane in close conversation, by themselves. 'The case will be settled,' said Coles. 'Let's go and lunch.' "

"Oh, I can't bear it," said Berry.

"He was perfectly right," I said. "When the Judge took his seat after luncheon, Sir Edward Clarke rose to his feet.

" 'I am happy to say,' he said, 'that your lordship will not be further troubled with this case. A settlement has been arranged agreeable to both parties.'

"There was a general rustle of astonishment, but Jeune just nodded.

" 'Very well,' he said.

"More was said, of course, because you couldn't have two Wills admitted to Probate. But I don't remember what was said and I really don't care. I believe the fortune was divided between the beneficiaries of the first Will and those of the second. But young as I was, I was wild. Bitterly disappointed and wild.

"Coles said very little, although of course I kept on asking him why the Trustees had thrown in their hand.

"As we walked back to his office, 'I shall learn the truth later,' he said. 'And I'll tell you then. I'm as upset as you are. I cannot bear to see a good case go wrong. The jury were certainly staggered, and I'm told that the betting in court was five to one on the Trustees.'

"I didn't see him again for three or four weeks.

"Then –

" 'D'you remember what Sir George Lewis said to Sir Edward Clarke?'

" 'I do indeed,' I said.

" 'What he said was perfectly true. Clarke should have won that case hands down. The Trustees' case was strong: but if the other side's case had been presented, you would have had the pleasure of hearing it pulverized. You see, Gill was brought in by the Trustees on purpose to cross-examine – that is his great forte. Imagine his cross-examination of the doctor, who had been left five thousand pounds. Or of the companion, or of her brother. Gill would have torn them in pieces. It was what he was there to do. And the jury would have found for the Trustees without leaving the box. Instead, the case was settled – before the other side had opened their mouths.

" 'You remember that Clarke and Bargrave Deane were in close conversation. Well, after we'd gone, Clarke saw the solicitor to the Trustees and said he wanted to see him and his clients in a consulting-room at a quarter to two.

" 'They duly appeared. Gill and Priestley were present. Then Clarke spoke. "In my opinion," he said, "you will be well-advised to settle this case. Things are not going well. The Judge is dead against us. Our most important witness, the nurse, failed to come up to her proof. What is worse, the Judge is going to protect the other side and to sum up dead against us. If you take my advice – and my experience of these matters is very wide – you'll settle, lest a worse thing befall. I mean, you don't want to lose – as you very well may. And you *can* settle now on very favourable terms."

" 'Well, the Trustees protested, of course. But Clarke snapped and bit and presently bore them down. Gill and Priestley never opened their mouths. So Clarke had his way.

" 'Now, why did Clarke force this course upon the Trustees? That is a matter of opinion, for Clarke alone knows the truth.

But I'll tell you what I believe. I think Bargrave Deane approached him, as he was leaving the court, and suggested that the case should be settled. Why did Bargrave Deane suggest that? I believe, in all honesty. He realized that he was on a loser and, though he can have had only a very faint hope that Clarke would agree, if he could get a settlement he would be doing his clients a very good turn, for half a loaf is better than no bread – especially when the half-loaf is worth fifty thousand pounds. So Bargrave Deane was perfectly right to try. I'll go so far as to say that he was doing his duty. Very well. But why did Clarke agree? I mean, Bargrave Deane's proposal was really ludicrous. Why then did Clarke virtually force the Trustees to accept it? Because he was sick and tired of Jeune's behaviour. Jeune was twisting his tail, and Clarke could do nothing about it. But a settlement, however monstrous, offered him a way of escape. And so he took it. He used his powerful personality to force the Trustees' hand.

" 'Mark you, I'm not going to say that the case could not have gone wrong. Any case *can* go wrong. But I simply cannot believe that, after Gill's cross-examination of the three supporters of the new Will, any jury, Judge or no Judge, could have returned a verdict in their favour. And if I can see that, so could Clarke – with a very much keener eye.

" 'Had Clarke been a lesser man, he would not have done as he did. But when a professional man attains great eminence, whether he's a lawyer or a doctor or anything else, unless he is very scrupulous, he sometimes subordinates his duty to his convenience.

" 'Of course, the Judge himself was greatly to blame. He took advantage of his high office to give Clarke offence, well knowing that Clarke could not hit back. A contemptible thing to do. But Clarke should have treated it with contempt – and gone on and won his case… That should have been his *riposte*.

" 'Now don't forget, Boy, that all of this is surmise. I may be quite wrong. But I don't think that I am wrong. I believe that what I have said is the very truth. I'm not sorry you've seen this side of the Bench and the Bar. I don't believe in disillusioning people, but it is just as well that you should know that Bench and Bar have their failings like everyone else. The etiquette of the Bar is very strict, but the members of the Bar are men, and you will sometimes encounter an opponent who is not too scrupulous. That is inevitable. But I know you'll always do your duty, whatever it costs.' "

"Most interesting," said Berry. "A clash between two great personalities – and Justice goes down the drain. I imagine it's often happened. Who'd ever go to law? Did you ever see the same sort of thing again?"

"Never," said I. "But what a wise man Coles Willing was. Take the case of the famous surgeon. How often does such a man put his convenience first?"

"Are you right?" said Jonah. "All the same, what a blasted scandal! The three of them should have done time."

"Indeed they should. It was a cruel and heartless crime, for which there was no excuse. If Jeune and Clarke had done their duty, the Trustees would have won their case and, as Berry said, the documents would have been impounded and sent to the Public Prosecutor. That he would have taken action, I have no doubt; and from what I remember of the doctor, my belief is that, to save his skin, he would have turned Queen's Evidence – with the happy result that the brother and sister would have gone heavily down."

"Why d'you think he would have turned Queen's Evidence?"

"Well, I've told you that he looked very hang-dog, and Gill in his cross-examination would simply have flayed him alive. And I think he'd have said to himself, 'Well, I'm not going through that again for anyone', and so he'd have thrown in his hand.

"And that is a perfect example of a good case going wrong. Mark you, you can't blame the Law any more than you can blame the apparatus when there's a railway smash. It is the human element that fails four times out of five. And you can't eliminate that."

*

Berry looked at me with a hand to his chin.

"I should simply hate," he said, "to speak out of turn; but in the last few days an unusual activity on your part and on that of your agreeable secretary has been apparent. I mean, as a rule she only comes twice a week: but lately she has appeared at odd times and the atmosphere of urgency has been unmistakable. I hope – we all hope that nothing untoward is afoot."

I began to laugh.

"It's all over now," I said. "But about ten days ago I suddenly learned that the title I had given my new book had been unwittingly taken by somebody else."

"Oh, my dear!" cried Daphne.

"But you'd passed the proofs," cried Berry. "The final proofs."

"The first edition had been printed," said Jill. "And the dust-cover, too."

"Good God!" said Jonah.

I nodded.

"It was most unfortunate. Mercifully, there was just enough time to change the title, yet keep to the publication date: but only just enough – for you can't drive the printer today. Only a few copies had been bound. Had we found out a week or so later, we should have been sunk."

"What a show!" said Jonah. "It's never happened before?"

"Never," said I. "Looking back, I think I've been lucky. Some of my titles have been unusual, but by no means all. *Cost Price* might well have been taken, and so might *Maiden Stakes*."

"No copyright in a title?"

"Oh, no," said I. "But – well, honour among thieves, you know. Dog mustn't eat dog."

"Supposing you'd only found out a week before your publication date?"

"Then it would have been too late to do anything. Thousands of copies would already have been distributed."

"Very worrying, darling," said Daphne.

"Just one of those things," I said. "But I hope it doesn't happen again."

"He was worn out," said Jill. "He was dictating straight on to the typewriter more than once. And cables too."

"Had I been younger," I said, "I shouldn't have been so tired. But, when I'm up against time, high concentration takes its toll today. I used to take things in my stride, but I can't any more."

"You rose to the occasion," said Jonah, refilling my glass.

"As you have done all your life."

"Supposing," said Berry, "supposing a book called *Wash Out* had a phenomenal success. That's just the sort of title that the public would fall for today. Well, there we are – *Wash Out*. And then, six months later somebody else calls a book they've written *Wash Out*. Can't the author of the original book do anything?"

I raised my eyebrows.

"I think he could," I said. "I think he could get an injunction, for that would be, to my mind, a clear case of plagiarism. And plagiarism is so contemptible and disgusting an exercise that any proved plagiarist would get a very short shrift."

"Have you ever suffered from it?"

"Once. But, if you'll forgive me, I'd rather not talk about that."

"Unheard of in the old days, of course."

"Exactly. But the world was more scrupulous then."

"*Florence* gets it in one. 'This patent-leather scum that wouldn't dream of stealing, but only lives by its wits.' "

"That," said Jonah, "was a brilliantly pungent remark."

"It's so damned true," said Berry. "*Florence* is among the godsends. No doubt about that."

"Ah," said I. "I wanted you to use that word."

"It's true," said Daphne. "Already I find myself thinking, 'What would *Florence* have said about this?' "

"That," said Jonah, "is because, besides being damned amusing, she's always right on the mark."

"What did I tell you?" said Jill, slipping her arm under mine.

"You're very good," I said. "But not everyone will get her. You see, she's a cook-housekeeper. And, as she herself proclaims, she knows her place. As such, today she's a blackleg, or unbelievable. Now listen to this. Not very long ago, some film company toyed with the idea of buying the rights of *Blind Corner*. But they turned it down, 'because', they wrote, 'it is felt that the audiences of today wouldn't understand the servants'. Those were the words used."

"God give me strength," said Berry.

There was a little silence. Then –

"And Bridget and Fitch and Carson," said Jonah. "And Carson, unless he's blown it, is worth two thousand a year."

There was another silence. Then –

"While we're on it," said Berry, "what films your romances would make."

"It has occurred to me that films made from them would be better than some I have seen. But the film people don't seem to think so."

"Have you approached them?"

I shook my head.

"It's for them to come to me."

"But take *Blood Royal*. My God, what a splendid picture!"

"Yes, it would film very well."

"All of them would – the romances, I mean. As they stand. The screen-writer would have nothing to do."

I shrugged my shoulders.

"It's just a matter of taste. After all, the film people are going to put up the money and take the risk. And they don't, apparently, think the risk is good enough. I don't agree with their decision, but I don't blame them at all."

"You're very good about it," said Daphne.

"My darling," I said, "I can't be anything else. My wares are for sale: if they don't attract purchasers – well, that's just too bad. After all, 'the customer is always right'."

"Well, I don't get it," said Jonah.

Something to my relief, they left it there.

"May I say," said Berry, "how very much I appreciate the fact that on the back of your dust-covers there always appears something from your own pen."

"That's very good of you. I can't remember how long I've been writing that. But I think the author's the obvious person to do it."

"How many authors do?"

"Not many, I think. I really don't know why. The idea is – or should be – not so much to commend the book, as to give the public an idea of what it's about. And the author is – or should be – best qualified to do this." I began to laugh. "To be honest, I believe the reviewer reads it more faithfully than the prospective purchaser. It helps the reviewer quite a lot, if he's pressed for time."

"Dedication and preface?" said Jonah.

"I don't think those are read by one per cent. They just get down to the book. Very natural, you know."

"One thing you've never told us," said Berry, "and that is – supposing one wants to get into some court when a case is being heard, how does one do it?"

"You mean, how does a layman do it, if he isn't concerned in the case?"

"Yes. Assume he finds himself near the Royal Courts of Justice or the Old Bailey, with an hour to waste and thinks he'll go in and sit down and listen to a case. How does he get in?"

"Well, in the Royal Courts of Justice, unless the court is crowded, it's easy enough – at least, it used to be. There'll be a tipstaff on the doors, but if you look respectable and you say you'd just like to go in or you're interested in the case, he'll make no difficulty. But you must be properly dressed. If the court is crowded, unless you happen to see some solicitor or counsel that you know, you probably won't get in. Of course, there's always the public gallery, but that's not a pleasant place and it's usually full.

"They're more strict at the Old Bailey. They have police on the doors there, and, unless he is vouched for, a layman won't get in."

"People of note seem to get in to hear murder trials."

"I know. The City Lands Committee have a right to certain seats in the Judge's Court, and if you know a Sheriff or someone, he'll give you a note or a pass to be admitted to them. In my time, to my way of thinking, this practice was sometimes abused. I've seen well-known actors and actresses in those seats at a murder trial. Well, that was just idle curiosity on their part, together with a desire for publicity. Myself, I think it was also very bad form. After all, the prisoner was on trial for his life and, if I had been he, I should have resented it bitterly."

"It was inexcusable," said Jonah.

"Things got better before I left the Bar. I rather think the Lord Chief had something to do with that."

"If you wanted to listen to a case at the Old Bailey today, what would you do?"

"I should go in by the private door which Judges and Counsel use and up in the lift. I should stop at the Court floor and have a word with the police-officer on the door of the Judge's Court. If I failed with him, I should send in my card to the Clerk of Arraigns, with a few words on it saying that I was an old hand."

"Dirty work," said Berry.

"Rubbish," said Daphne. "D'you mean to tell me that, after all the hours Boy's spent in that very court – "

"He'd be taking an unfair advantage."

"Yes, you wouldn't, would you?" said Jill.

"Certainly not. I should send for the Judge's clerk and say that his lordship would wish me to be given a seat on the bench."

Jonah began to shake with laughter.

"The silly thing is," he said, "I've no doubt you'd be given one – and asked to lunch afterwards."

"I should hope so," said Berry. "Why should I go empty away?"

No one of us felt equal to answering this question, so Daphne said 'Outrageous' and left it there.

"Idiosyncrasies," said Jonah. "Didn't Kipling always write with a very special ink?"

"Indeed, he did. And he used a special nib. And he wrote upon special paper, made up into special pads. But that was in no way a pose. Kipling had a master brain; and in order to comfort his genius and give it every chance, he found it best to humour its special demands."

"Your sub-conscious brain is less exacting?"

"Happily it is. All I ask is a pen or liquid pencil that writes easily and plenty of white quarto paper of good quality. Oh, and a typewriter, upon which I can roughly transcribe my longhand every now and then. But if I had a brain like Kipling's, I can't believe you'd consider any demand too high."

"I shouldn't," said Jonah. "He was a very great man."

"The last of the giants," I said. "His work will see out Time."

*

I looked at Berry.

"U and Non-U. I think you should deal with that."

Berry wrinkled his nose.

"A distasteful subject," he said. "I wonder what Samuel Johnson would have said. Never mind. The thing is this. Oh, and let me say, by way of preface, that *Noblesse Oblige* is probably the finest motto in the world, but it is worn in the heart alone…"

To my great regret, I must omit the remainder of his estimate, which was, I think, as valuable as it was severe. And when, in conclusion, he 'remembered' what Samuel Johnson would have said – 'Sir, a vulgarity of speech may be observed; but only the…' – it goes to my heart to suppress such pungency.

When he had finished –

"Admirable," said Jonah. "You are more articulate than our parents would have been. To my mind, the cheerful collection and promulgation of things which we were always most careful to leave unsaid shows almost more vividly than anything else how far we have come in the last fifty years. I still recall with acute embarrassment an incident which occurred when I was up at Oxford. I was in somebody's rooms when his scout came in quietly, to see to the fire. As, the job done, he stood up, 'Well, George,' said my host, 'did you get your partridges?' 'No, sir,' said the scout, smiling; 'but I did better than that. Mr Beechey gave me a nare.' To my horror, my host failed to get it. 'A nare?' he said. 'What the devil's a nare?' The servant grew slowly red and I could have sunk through the floor. Somehow I found my voice. 'George,' I said, 'you're very fortunate. Jugged hare is an excellent dish.' 'So it is, sir,' said George and left the room. When I looked at my host, his eyes were still tight shut. 'Oh, my God,' he wailed… You see, according to his lights, he had done the unspeakable thing." He sighed. "But there you are. Times change."

It seemed best to leave it there.

"Last night," said Berry, "you mentioned Lord Justice Rigby. I happen to know something about him, which I don't think you'll find in the books. Tell us what you know of him first."

"I know very little," I said, "except that he was a very fine lawyer and did very well at the Bar. This, in spite of the fact that he cared for no man and was always rather uncouth. He was unmarried and lived in considerable style. His two attractive nieces kept house for him. One of them, Ruth Rigby, married the Theobald Mathew of my day. I never met her, but I met her sister, Edith, once. I did hear it said that, when her sister had gone, her life was not too easy, for her uncle, who was never considerate, grew more exacting with age. She kept her eyes upon her duty, but she should and could have married long before she did. But I've little doubt that the Judge discouraged swains. And now you go on."

"It's a curious tale," said Berry. "But it is perfectly true.

"About the middle of the last century there was a curate of the name of Rigby at a little village in Kent. As was sometimes the way in those days, the Vicar was never there, so the curate acted as Vicar for year after year. He was a quiet, well-mannered man and was very much liked. He was *persona grata* with the Squire and his family and was a constant visitor at The Hall. That he should always lunch there on Sundays was an understood thing.

"Now the Squire had been called to the Bar, but, being wealthy and preferring the country to the town, he never practised, but did his duty in the village and minded his considerable estate. For all that, he was deeply interested in the Law and all to do with it. Before he reached middle age he was attacked by the illness called 'Poor Man's Gout', that is to say, a gout which he had inherited, but had himself neither promoted nor encouraged. Indeed, he was always a most abstemious man. So it was rather hard that he should be a victim of what proved to be a most painful, trying and, presently, fatal disease. As a result of this affliction he found himself forced to lead a very sedentary life, spending most of his time in his well-found library and less and less in his meadows and hop-gardens. So it came to pass that he devoted many hours to the study of law, reading the reports in *The Times* and watching the careers of members of the Bar who were his contemporaries.

"One Friday evening his wife received a note from the curate, saying that his younger brother was coming to spend the weekend with him and asking if he might bring him to luncheon on Sunday. Of course the lady said yes, and at the appropriate hour the two brothers arrived.

"To the family's great surprise, the young man's manners were as rough as his brother's were smooth. He was awkward and taciturn – by no means an easy guest. Mother and daughter on his right hand and on his left found entertaining him very uphill work. But from the opposite end of the table the Squire was watching the youth, and when the meal was over, he bade him follow him into the library.

"When they were seated –

" 'How old are you?' said the Squire.

"The youth replied – 'Nineteen.'

"It would have been more becoming to say, 'Nineteen, sir,' for his host was three times his age. But the Squire only smiled.

" 'And what are you proposing to do?'

" 'What can I do,' cried the youth, 'but take a post as a clerk?'

" 'Why d'you say that?'

" 'Because I've no money at all, and I've got to live.'

" 'What do you want to do?'

"The young man's eyes lighted.

" 'I want to go to the Bar. I'll get there somehow…one day.'

"The Squire considered his guest. Then he picked up *The Times*.

" 'You see that leader,' he said. 'Read it to me aloud.'

"The youth did as he said.

" 'Now give me the paper back.' The youth complied. " 'Now tell me what you remember of the leader you have just read.'

"The youth repeated the leader, *word for word*.

" 'Very good,' said the Squire. 'And now you shall go to the Bar. I'll pay your fees and allow you a hundred a year for the next five years.'

"And that was how Lord Justice Rigby came to go to the Bar."

"What a lovely tale," said Jill.

"It's perfectly true," said Berry. "I'm not going to say how I know, but I know it's the absolute truth."

"The Squire knew his world," said Jonah. "Nine men out of ten would have written John Rigby off. But the Squire saw the fire of genius glowing under the slack."

"I hope he was grateful," I said.

"He was indeed," said Berry. "He could never discharge such a debt, but to the day of his death he was one of the family's Trustees."

*

"One thing," said Daphne, "I've never understood is why reviewers persist in classing your work with Buchan's."

I smiled.

"I've never understood it, either."

Berry took up the running.

"I can see no resemblance whatever between any book that Buchan wrote and any book of yours. Now, if they said Anthony Hope…"

"I agree. There's far more resemblance there. He began with *The Dolly Dialogues* and I began with *The Brother of Daphne*. He went on to write that immortal book, *The Prisoner of Zenda*, followed by *Rupert of Hentzau*, and I wrote *Blood Royal*, followed by *Fire Below*. So there is a definite resemblance between his work and mine. But Buchan's books bear no resemblance to any of his or mine. At least, if they do, I can't see it."

"Criticism," said Berry. "How far can a reviewer go – and keep within the law?"

"The true answer is – all lengths."

"Are you speaking as a lawyer?"

"I am."

"But what about malice?"

"So long as the reviewer does not attack the character of the author, he can be as malicious as he likes – with impunity."

"D'you mean to say that, if some reviewer who, you knew, was your enemy, wrote of one of your books, 'I cannot advise my readers to buy this book. If they do, they will be wasting their money' – do you mean to say that you could do nothing?"

"Nothing."

"Even if you could prove that he had reason to hate you?"

"Not even then. The author is entirely defenceless."

"Supposing he said, 'Only a wash-out could have written this book'?"

"That would be an attack on the man. So an action against him would lie. But whether the author would win it is very questionable. You see, he would have to prove that, as a result of this statement, he had suffered damage, which would be very difficult. And, if he did win it, the damages he would receive – if they were ever paid – would in no way compensate him for the trouble, waste of time and expense which he had been caused."

"The law is at fault," said Jonah. "If an author can prove malice, he should be able to make a reviewer pay."

"I agree," said I. "But don't forget that malice is very hard to prove.

"I remember such a case. It was a long time ago and it attracted much attention. The book in question was the biography of an administrator of repute and it had been written by, I think, a soldier who had known him well and had for several years been a member of his staff. It was reviewed in a well-known periodical. And now mark this. The man who wrote the review was a permanent member of the periodical's staff; but he never, in the ordinary way, wrote the reviews.

"The review which he wrote was savage. He tore the book to shreds. More. It suggested that the book had been written by the author to glorify himself. Finally, it suggested that the author's personal record was not as creditable as it might have been.

"Well, this was too much, and the author of the book took proceedings. To my mind, he had a good case; and when it was proved that he and the reviewer were enemies of long standing – well, most people thought that it would only be a matter of what damages he was awarded.

"I was in court for a while and I saw the reviewer in the box, and a very poor figure he cut. For all that, he won his case, and the author had to pay all the costs."

"Never!" cried Daphne.

"It's a fact."

"How abominably unjust," said Jonah.

"But what happened?" said Berry.

"I cannot remember," I said. "I know there was a jury, all right. But I am inclined to think that the reviewer got home on a point of law. The author couldn't prove damage, or something."

"How the hell could he prove damage in such a case?"

"Exactly. But that's what I said just now. Of course he had suffered damage. A lot of people, probably, decided not to purchase the book. Others, as like as not, looked askance at him in his Club. But how could he prove these things? So you see."

"In fact, unless he could produce, for instance, a solicitor who would swear that, after reading that review, the author's godfather had cut him out of his Will, he could not possibly succeed?"

"I couldn't put it better," I said.

"What a blasted scandal!"

"I think it's wicked," said Jill.

"It really means," said Jonah, "that the author is at the mercy of any unscrupulous man?"

"That's what it amounts to." I sighed. "Malice can be trying: but I always bear in mind that reviews can seldom make or destroy a book."

"You're awfully good," said Daphne. "Some reviews you've shown me have sent the blood to my head."

"My sweet," I said, "you must remember, first, that the malicious review, which, I confess, I sometimes receive, is something I never received before the late war; and, secondly, that *some* – I repeat *some* – of those who review books today have neither the standing nor the background of the reviewers of other days. Such people allow their feelings to over-ride their duty, which is to review upon its merits every book that comes into their hands."

"But why should they feel malicious towards you? What harm have you done them?"

"My darling, I write of what used to be known as 'the upper class'. And the portraits I paint of them are true to life. Their servants, for instance, are devoted. They may be poor, as were *Coridon* and *Niobe*: but nothing can alter the fact that they were well bred. And that is what inflames such 'reviewers' against my work."

"Shocking," said Jonah. "Because today you present 'the upper class' in a good light, they regard your work as subversive propaganda and make every effort to discourage its perusal."

I nodded.

"Finally, let me refer to one review which I recently received. It was written by a distinguished man. Whether he reviewed books before the late war, I don't know: but that he was of 'the old school' is indisputable. It was a more handsome review than I think I deserved. But that is beside the point – which is that his review opened with these words –

That Dornford Yates has lost none of his old magic, no just man can deny; and that is the truth.

" 'No just man can deny.'

"Can you imagine such words being written before the late war? Why, then, did this reviewer write them?"

"Because he knew," said Berry. "Knew of and resented this malice."

126

"That's my belief."

"And he was of 'the old school'?"

"For that, I can vouch."

"Then why beat about the bush? It's the same old answer – with knobs on. You write so convincingly of 'the upper class' that your books give 'the new school' a violent inferiority complex. Well, you can't expect them to take that lying down, can you?"

When we had recovered from this broadside –

"That show on the wireless," said Jill.

"Yes, that was a funny business."

"It was an outrage, darling."

"I don't suppose it was – I really don't know."

"What do you mean?" said Berry.

"Something disparaging was said. But I don't know what it was or when it was said. Please let me leave it there."

"Well, I don't know," said Berry, "but from what you say the author seems to me to get a raw deal. If somebody wrote to the papers saying that such and such a grocer sold bad figs, the papers wouldn't publish the letter, and if they did, both they and the writer of the letter would be taken to court forthwith. But the wares which the author sells can be condemned, whether they deserve it or no, with impunity."

"That's perfectly true. But you must remember this – that the author invites the Press to review his book; but the grocer does not ask the Press to consider his figs."

"Yes, I see that," said Jonah. "But such an invitation does not confer a licence to be malicious."

"I know. But, as I have said before, I have really been very lucky. Taking it by and large, the Press have been very kind. I've had hundreds of handsome reviews: so it ill becomes me to complain if I get a few ugly ones. And you must remember that I'm getting out of date. Most of my work is today period stuff. To the present generation, the life we led at White Ladies seems almost mediaeval. And millions of them have been taught that such a life was as wrong as that which the Barons led in the time of Henry the First. Their teachers know that it wasn't, but that is beside the point. I think perhaps I'd better stop there."

"I think so, too, darling," said Daphne.

"After all," said Jonah, "many appear in *Who's Who*, but few – "

"I know," I said. "I'm very honoured."

*

"I have here," said Berry, "a little monograph which I have composed upon that romantic structure which was for many years the wonder of Europe, Old London Bridge. But it mustn't go into the memoir."

"Why not?" said Jill.

"Because it's too choice. That it should rub shoulders with the Old Bailey is unthinkable. A niche in the Poets' Corner would be more appropriate. I mean, you wait till you hear it."

"If it isn't any better," said Daphne, "than your stuff about Trustees, I entirely agree. Keep it for the Poets' Corner."

"Quite so," said Berry. "And when you've heard it, you'll go on your bended knees and beg for its inclusion in this most vulgar production, which may never see the light."

"Pray proceed," said Jonah. "Old London Bridge is part of the history of England, and it's stuffed so full of romance that I don't think you can have gone wrong."

Berry was bristling.

"Am I to interpret that statement as an assurance that, when I have cast before you my pearls, you will not turn and rend me?"

"Sorry," said Jonah, laughing. "What I really meant was that you are the very man to deal with this wonderful fabric as it deserves. There's never been anything like it in all the world."

Something mollified, Berry picked up his manuscript. After a moment or two, he began to read.

"Old London Bridge was the first stone bridge of importance built in the British Isles: it stood for more than six hundred years; and for more than five hundred of those years it was the only bridge over the Thames in the London district. Except at Lambeth, there was no recognized ferry – and that was avoided by the more prudent, for the ferry-boat frequently sank, on one occasion with the coach of his Grace the Lord Archbishop of Canterbury. It follows that for more than five centuries, virtually all the traffic to and from London, desirous of crossing the Thames, used Old London Bridge.

"The Bridge owed its being entirely to the devotion and energy of a determined priest, whose name deserves to be remembered. Peter de Colechurch was solely responsible for its conception, for obtaining the necessary funds and for its construction for twenty-nine years. Unhappily, that great man died four years before it was completed: but completed it was in the year 1209, in the reign of King John; and so well and truly was it built that, in spite of the occasional ravages of fire and water, it was never out of service for more than a few days for more than six centuries.

"When we consider the elaborate calculations which precede the construction of a comparatively minor bridge today, to build a stone bridge more than nine hundred feet long over a tidal river towards the end of the twelfth century was an astounding achievement; and when we remember that, through all those years, that bridge stood fast against the constant, angry thrust of a mighty head of water, a man may be forgiven for wondering whether the progress of which we are so proud, rests indeed upon foundations as sure.

"Now, lest I should be found guilty of the vulgar sin of exaggeration, before I proceed, I must justify two statements which I have just made. First, the width of the Thames at this point was nine hundred feet: but of this distance the nineteen piers of the bridge, with their protective armour, took up six hundred feet; so that when the bridge was completed, the river found itself deprived of two-thirds of the room which it was accustomed to take. With the result that it became no less than a ponderous weir, and the business of 'shooting the Bridge' in a wherry became well-known as a most hazardous exercise.

"Secondly, I must refer to the time-honoured ditty, *London Bridge is Broken Down*. Nobody knows the date of this Nursery Rhyme, which seems to give the lie to what I said a moment ago. But we are both right. In the reign of Edward the First, when the Bridge was only seventy-three years old, London was visited by a frost so hard that the Thames was frozen to a considerable depth. This frost was ended by a thaw so sudden that the ice broke up into great blocks which were swept down stream on to the Bridge. Before this fearful battery, no less than five of the twenty arches gave way: but repairs were soon set on foot, while the gaps were immediately closed by temporary structures, so that traffic over the Bridge should not be interrupted. Now it is interesting to learn that a still more severe frost nearly three hundred years later occasioned no damage at all. I find that strange – that a bridge should give way at the age of seventy-three, yet stand fast at the age of three hundred and fifty-six. Now there is a French proverb which says, *Cherchez la femme*. Let us obey it. When the Bridge was seven years old, King John died and was succeeded by his son Henry the Third. The latter's Queen was Eleanor of Provence, whose beauty was undeniable, whose insatiable avarice soon made her the most unpopular royal personage in Europe. On one occasion, when her barge was about to pass – presumably at slack water – beneath the Bridge, the citizens some thirty feet above were quite unable to ignore this glorious opportunity of indicating their impatience of her shortcomings, and Her Majesty was pelted with rotten eggs and other traditional emblems of disapproval. Piqued by these attentions, the lady bided her time, and, shortly before her husband's death, she induced him to award to her all the revenues and even the custody of Old London Bridge. As a result of this infamous transaction, for nearly ten years all the money which should have gone to the maintenance of the Bridge went into her privy purse: and, when the sudden thaw came in 1282, the Bridge was in no condition to withstand the pressure of the ice. Still, out of evil came good. On the collapse of the arches, the new King, Edward the First, immediately revoked the Queen Mother's grant, and, from that time on, the revenues of the Bridge always remained its personal property.

"And now for the surface of the bridge.

"It was the surface of Old London Bridge that made it the wonder of Europe, that would make it a wonder of the world today. For Old London Bridge was a street. It was a narrow street, for the roadway was only twelve feet wide, and there were no pavements. But on either hand there were houses – houses three storeys high, for the whole of its length. The ground floor was nothing but shops: above, were the parlours and kitchens; on the second floor were the bedrooms, while the servants slept in the attics, above again. And every house was as different as were the signboards that swung above the shops below. In the fourteenth century there were one hundred and thirty-eight shops on London Bridge. Now the whole width of the bridge was only twenty feet. Of these, as I have said, twelve were devoted to the roadway or street. It follows that there remained but four feet of the surface on either side to receive the houses and shops. Their builders rose to an occasion which would have defeated many less valiant souls. Every house was projected some ten feet beyond the flanks of the bridge, and these projections were supported by shores of timber which sprang from the bases of the piers. Upon the inside, the houses frequently overhung the street: and in some cases they were deliberately joined together by a chamber which was built on the second floor across the Street and was either shared by or divided between the occupants of the respective dwellings. In these two lines of houses, there were three breaks. One, near the middle of the bridge, was known as The Square: this was certainly the only spot at which two wagons, moving in opposite directions, could pass. The second break, nearer the Surrey side, was filled by a drawbridge, which could be raised to allow a small vessel to pass or to deny the passage of the Bridge itself to an enemy. The third break, almost at the end of the Bridge on the Surrey side, accommodated The Great Stone Gate, which was one of the gates of the City of London and was shut at night. It was above this gate that, for many years, the heads of traitors were exposed upon the ends of pikes, as an example of the wages of sin, to the discouragement of all those who might be contemplating high treason.

"The revenues of which I have spoken were, of course, provided by the rents of the houses and shops, which, for more than one reason, were much in demand. For one thing, life upon the Bridge was healthy, and its inhabitants were seldom the victims of the epidemics to which the City itself was often subject: for another, the fact that the Bridge had to be used by virtually everyone who crossed the Thames brought much custom to the shops; and, for another, Old London Bridge was continually the scene of the splendid passage of the great.

"I have no time to recite the many gorgeous spectacles seen at close quarters on the Bridge, or to name the Kings and Queens and Princes, the famous captains and statesmen, the prelates and embassies that passed in pomp and circumstance along its narrow street: enough that such as dwelled there lived cheek by jowl with great occasions.

"And now let us stroll the length of that wonderful thoroughfare: but we must walk very slowly, for we shall take five hundred years to cover those three hundred yards. Still, in our passage, we shall encounter four famous personages, each of whom must have used Old London Bridge. Two of them will need no introduction: of the others, one has stepped out of the pages of Chaucer and the other out of the paintings of William Hogarth.

"As we leave Fish Street Hill, three things strike us at once. The first is the swinging signboards on either side of the street, all bravely painted and every one declaring, usually by a symbol, the nature of the goods for sale in the shop below. I have not time to name them all – they were so many: but there were booksellers, haberdashers, linen-drapers, grocers, goldsmiths, glovers, butchers, hair-dressers, fishmongers, hosiers and, of course, taverners, all plying their trade on London Bridge. The second thing that strikes us is the steady roar of the water pouring through the archways beneath our feet. And the third thing is the colour of the busy street. This is afforded by the clothing of those who use it – reds and blues and greens and yellows, crimson and violet, scarlet and gold – some bright and some faded, but all filling the eye and making glad the heart of man.

"Here comes a pack-horse, laden with bales and led by a mounted servant, whose master, the merchant himself, is riding behind. Their faces are alight with relief, for Genoese velvet commands a high price and the country roads are dangerous. Next, with leisurely stride, comes a man-at-arms, fresh from the wars in France: a merry-faced, nut-brown man, in his coat of chain-mail and bright steel cap, a straight sword by his side and a painted long-bow on his back. He is bound for a house in the City where he is known and will be welcome. And here is a lady on horseback whom we have met before. And, as Kipling would say, she is a notable woman. She has just left Dan Chaucer, the poet, at *The Tabard Inn*, for she has ridden with him from Canterbury and, after a day or two in London, she will ride down to the West Country. Her servants, before and behind, have little duty to do, for the lady, though smiling, has a masterful air, and he would be a bold man that took an unwelcome liberty. Her magnificent wimple of fine linen is most elaborate, and, indeed, she is expensively dressed, with love-knots upon her frock, as becomes a lady who has buried five husbands. Indeed, it is quite clear that, as Chaucer says, the famous Wife of Bath could be excellent company.

"As we pass on, the colour grows more pronounced, but clothes are becoming fantastic and inconvenient. There goes a man with a liripipe three feet long: and here is a true dandy, in parti-coloured hose, with the toes of his long, soft shoes chained up to his knees. A few more paces, and the colour is fading again, and clothes are becoming more fashioned and more becoming. And there, a little way ahead, we see the first ruff...

"How many scores of times must Shakespeare have crossed the Bridge? For the Globe Theatre was at Southwark, and his favourite tavern, *The Mermaid*, stood in Cheapside. Coming slowly towards us is the quietly dressed figure, with the fresh, linen collar and the unmistakable face – high forehead, straight nose, delicately pointed beard and those magnificent eyes. Here is no dreamer. Intensely human himself, all mankind is his study, and, as he walks, how vigilant is his gaze. He misses nothing in that crowded street, for all is fish that comes to Shakespeare's net. We have rubbed shoulders with one of the very best fellows that ever called for wine, who is modest to a fault, whose wisdom and understanding are not of this world, whose ear is tuned to catch the music of the spheres, whose name liveth for evermore.

"Time presses, and we must hasten.

"Colours are becoming more delicate and a true style is creeping into habiliments. The tailor and cutter are coming into their own. And wigs are on the way. 'God willing,' writes Samuel Pepys, 'I shall begin next week to wear my new periwig.'

"Talk of the devil, here comes the rogue – the man who made the Royal Navy, in his well-cut, close-bodied coat, with a gold edge, silk breeches and stockings and well-fitting shoes. True, he had a wide heart, but, as like as not, he will stop to buy his wife some silk for a new petticoat. Pepys worked very hard, but he knew how to play. His cheerful demeanour is infectious, his merry eye meets us more than halfway, and he looks the man of the world he always was. And what a world to be a man of! The tyranny of the Puritan regime over, England has let herself go. Because Cromwell was virtuous, there had been no cakes and ale. But now the case is altered, and The Merry Monarch is on the throne. See the smiles and hear the laughter on every side. But Pepys has gone. He's seen a pretty girl at that window, and has stepped in to ask her name.

"I fear we have no time to follow him, if we are to reach The Stone Gate. So we pass through the reigns of the ill-fated James the Second, William and Mary, Queen Anne and George the First. All the time apparel is growing more handsome and the great wigs are dying hard. And here before us is a sedan-chair, whose door and top are open, for a lady of fashion is about to come out of a shop. And, as we hang on our heel, here she comes. Her, too, we have met before, for it is none other than the Countess, of Hogarth's famous pictures, *Marriage à la Mode*. She has been to see her mother in Southwark, and, on her way home, she has stopped to choose some silk stockings at Mr Bennett's, a hosier of London Bridge. As might be expected, her garments are very fine. Her bodice is tight-laced, and the flowered silk panniers over the hoop skirt mean that she must pass sideways into her chair. A jaunty, little, round straw hat is perched on her head, and her skirt is daringly short, to display her excellent ankles and dainty, high-heeled shoes. Poor spoiled lady, her airs and graces sit ill upon her: spoiled as the only child of a rich, self-made man, spoiled as the wife of a foolish nobleman, and soon to come to a sad end, little does she imagine that six portraits of her will hang for ever hard by Trafalgar Square."

As Berry laid his manuscript down –

"Quite lovely, darling," said Daphne.

"I entirely agree," said I. "It's much the best thing you've done. Please let it distinguish the book."

My brother-in-law frowned.

"And give up the Poets' Corner?"

"Well, you know how sticky they are. And we don't want this to be lost."

"If you slipped the Dean a fiver…"

"I may predecease you," I said.

"So you may," said Berry. "So you may. Oh, well… After all, what's sacrilege today?"

*

"Sorry," said Berry, "to keep on returning to the Law, but what about etiquette?"

"Etiquette of the Bar?"

"Yes. I don't know if that's the right word: but you probably know what I mean."

"I think it's a very good word. More than any other profession, the Bar has been ruled by etiquette, some of it very ancient. No rules were ever drawn up; but there were certain understandings which counsel were expected to honour."

"A pregnant phrase," said Jonah. "You mean that some members of the Bar were less, shall we say, scrupulous than others?"

"I'm afraid so. But I think that on the whole the rules were faithfully observed. If they were not, except in an outrageous case, no action was taken: but the man who continually broke them soon got a very bad name. But please remember that I am speaking of the Bar as I knew it, nearly fifty years ago.

"I think the most ancient matter of etiquette is shewn forth by the appearance on the back of the gown worn by the Junior Bar of a tiny triangular pouch, into which you might inveigle a threepenny bit. This is a survival of the purse which was worn on the back of the gown, into which counsel's clients were supposed to slip the fee, the idea being that counsel was above taking money and, if he were to be paid, must know nothing about it. That custom, in another form, survives today, for counsel's fee is always arranged by his clerk and never by counsel himself. Naturally, the private discussions between counsel and his clerk are nobody's business but in point of fact I never knew what I was to be paid till I saw the fee in writing upon the brief. Of course the clerks were pretty hot, for the more their master earned, the more they received. When I was Travers Humphreys' pupil, I remember overhearing his clerk, Hollis, speaking on the telephone. 'I can't let you 'ave Travers for that: you can 'ave Boyd if you like – 'e'll do it quite well.' Boyd was in Humphreys' chambers. And the clerk, of course, kept the fee-book. Naturally, the cheques were made out to counsel himself, I don't think we gave receipts. Oh, yes: stamps were put on the back-sheet of the brief, and we signed across them. And, as you probably know, if the client didn't pay up, we could take no action. Counsel may not sue for his fees. But the clerk was careful. If he wasn't sure of his man, he demanded the fee with the brief.

"Another most important matter of etiquette is that counsel must always be instructed by a solicitor and never by the client direct. Only if you took what was called a 'dock brief', or the Judge asked you to defend some prisoner, could the solicitor be omitted."

"What," said Daphne, "is a 'dock brief'?"

"This, my sweet. If, when he is arraigned – "

"Sorry. What do you mean by 'arraigned'?"

"The arraignment consists of calling the prisoner to the bar by name, telling him what he is charged with and then asking him whether he is guilty or no. The Clerk of Assize (at the Old Bailey, the Clerk of Arraigns) does that.

"Well, if, when he is arraigned, he speaks up and asks the Court for permission to be legally represented and shows that he has a guinea, he can choose one of the counsel in court to represent him. I never saw it happen, but I know that it did."

"What, any barrister?" said Berry. "Supposing he picked a QC?"

"Well, he was told that he couldn't have him, because he was otherwise engaged. So he tried again. He always got someone, you know. And now let's get back to the rule that counsel must always be instructed by a solicitor.

"Some counsel, particularly 'thieves' lawyers', did break that rule. The Judges spotted it, of course, and did what they could. I remember a fellow who appeared in the High Court for one of the militant suffragists, without a solicitor behind him. And I heard the Lord Chief ask him who was instructing him, and I heard him admit that there was no solicitor in the case. The bleak look the Lord Chief gave him made me feel cold. I imagine he reported the case to the Bar Council. I don't think anything was done in the case of 'thieves' lawyers'. You see, they were case-hardened and the only way to stop them would have been to disbar them. But all were pariahs.

"Then again it was an unwritten law that members of the Bar should not tout for work. Again the 'thieves' lawyers' broke that rule – I've seen them doing it. And so did other members of the Bar *through their clerks*. I knew one very bad case – and the man was a QC. His clerk touted right and left. Of course it soon got known, and the Bench and the Bar didn't like it. His chambers got a bad name, and his work began to fall off. (I met him at a private house soon after he'd taken silk; and that very slight acquaintance convinced me that he did not deserve that honour. His promotion had gone to his head and his manner was insufferable. And he didn't spare his wife, who was really very lovely and very sweet. She left him a year or two later, and God knows I didn't blame her. Years afterwards I met her again, when, I'm glad to say, she was very happily married to somebody else.) Soon he came to be employed only by firms of solicitors which were not above reproach, and that was the beginning of the end: but he had a powerful friend who got him a very good job. So he left the Bar.

"Then, again, there was a popular fellow who did a lot of work in the country. He was a member of the Junior Bar, but he ran a damned fine car – and he made a practice of giving solicitors lifts... Well, you know, that Rolls paid dividends. Solicitors much preferred a luxurious ride to and from some country court to a couple of train journeys, especially in the winter and when trains didn't fit. But he was within the law and he was a jolly rogue, so people turned a blind eye and most of us wished him well.

"Then there was another unwritten law governing the 'devil's' fees. If a 'devil' did a case for the Head of his Chambers in the country, then he was entitled to receive half the fee which was marked on the brief. I'm afraid he didn't always get it – particularly if the fee was a big one. Still, that was the rule."

"You say 'in the country'. What about London?"

"Any case the 'devil' did in London, he did for nothing at all."

"That seems rather hard."

I shrugged my shoulders.

"Some masters were generous, I know. But they need not have been. That was the recognized rule. After all, the 'devil' was gaining valuable experience."

"What about that case you did in the Court of Chancery?"

I shook my head.

"Oh, I got nothing, of course. I never expected a fee. But the experience I got was very well worth having. You see, the 'devil' was really an apprentice, and he learned his profession by doing his master's work. He was given half the fee in the country because it cost him a lot to get to and from the court. I seldom made a penny, but that was my fault."

"How was that?"

"Well, the Bar wasn't allowed to travel third class – etiquette again – but the Junior Bar was supposed to travel second class and the 'silks' first. But I liked being comfortable, so I always travelled first. And if my case was at Brighton, as it sometimes was, I travelled to and fro by 'The Southern Belle', or whatever the train was called: so there wasn't much left out of my half-fee."

"Comfort first," said Jonah. "You put up a better show."

"I think I probably did.

"Another piece of etiquette has just occurred to me. No member of the Bar, however young and inexperienced, ever called any other member of the Bar, however exalted, by any name other than that by which he usually went: and he used that name *tout court*. I found this embarrassing, but I knew that I had to conform. Shortly after I had been called, I often had to speak to Denman, the famous Clerk of Assize. He was twice my age and a most distinguished and important man. But if I had called him anything but 'Denman', he would have come down upon me like a ton of bricks. And before I had been at the Bar for six months, I was Dickens' junior – Henry Fielding Dickens QC. Well, I had to call him 'Dickens'. When I was junior to Marshall Hall, I had to call him 'Marshall ' – and that was that. And the same with Charles Gill, though that was easier, for we were both members of the same Club. My instinct was, of course, to call each of them 'Sir', but, if I had, they would have instantly corrected me."

"That," said Berry, "was valuable. The brotherhood of the Bar."

"I agree. But to take the plunge was most embarrassing."

"If you'd been Rufus Isaacs' junior, would you have called him 'Rufus'?"

"I suppose I should have tried to; but the thought of it makes me feel weak."

"And F E Smith?"

"I think I could have managed 'F E.' And now I have remembered a very curious point of etiquette, which prevailed in my time. I had to observe it once – and it lost me the case."

"Proceed," said Berry.

"Well you probably know that Agreements which have been reduced to writing and signed have to be stamped. That is to say they have to be taken to Somerset House or some local government office, where for a trifling sum they will be officially impressed with a kind of red seal. I think they have to be stamped within fourteen days of being signed. You can get them stamped later on, but if you are out of time you have to pay a fine. And for every month that you are out of date, the fine is increased; so that if you forget all about the matter for two or three years, to have them stamped may cost a considerable sum.

"Well, if you want to produce an Agreement in court, it's got to be stamped. Otherwise, the Court will not accept it. Without its stamp, in the eyes of the Law it is a valueless document. But sometimes the Court is nodding, and an unstamped Agreement is produced and accepted, because neither the Judge nor his Registrar or Associate has noticed the omission."

"But surely," said Daphne, "surely – "

"I know, my sweet. Speaking for myself, the stamp would have been the first thing I looked for; but, as you will hear, its absence was sometimes unnoticed.

"Now it was a matter of etiquette that the counsel against whom the Agreement would militate should never draw the attention of the court to the fact that it was not stamped."

"Well, that's a good one," said Berry. "Because a couple of doddering old fools can't use their eyes, you're to sit still and watch your case go down the drain."

"You're telling me," I said. "I once had that devastating experience, when I was against a very nice fellow called Whitely, in some County Court. He was rather older than I was. He produced his Agreement and, as he put it in – that is to say, tendered it as evidence – he gave me an old-fashioned look; and that, of course, told me that the rotten thing wasn't stamped. Well, the Court had a look at it, and then, as usual, I asked if I might see it, too. Counsel, of course, has a right to inspect any document produced by the other side. Sure enough, the Agreement wasn't stamped. Hoping against hope, I handed it back; for if the Court didn't notice the omission, my cake was dough. You may imagine how fervently I prayed that one of the two would use his blasted eyes. But my prayers were not heard. I remember that the Judge looked at me and smiled very pleasantly – he was a very nice man. 'In the face of this Agreement, Mr Pleydell, what do you expect me to do?' I tell you, I could have screamed. Instead, 'Sir,' I said, 'I'm afraid I have nothing to say.' So judgment was given against me. Sheer misfortune, of course; but there you are. Afterwards, in the robing-room, Whitely came to me and set his hand on my shoulder. 'Pleydell,' he said, 'I have much to thank you for.' 'I don't think you have,' I said, laughing. 'I think it's a poisonous custom, but customs must be observed.' 'I know,' he said, 'I know. But when you inspected the Agreement, the Judge was watching you, and it would have been so easy for you to have raised your eyebrows or put your head on one side. But you did nothing.' I smiled. 'I can't see you doing that.' 'No,' he said. 'But – well, it's nice to know that there are one or two of us who didn't forget everything when we were called to the Bar.' "

"Well, I'm damned," said Jonah.

"It's true," I said. "You see how it's stuck in my mind."

"One moment," said Berry. "What about your unfortunate client? But for your damned etiquette, he'd have won his case."

"I know," I said. "To my mind, it was an outrage. But, to be honest, it's not as bad as it looks. This particular matter of etiquette arose in this way. If an Agreement was produced in Court and the other side pointed out that it was unstamped, the case was adjourned and the fellow who produced the Agreement went off, paid his fine and got it stamped before the next hearing. Well, that helped nobody except the Revenue. And so it became the custom not to point out that the Agreement was not stamped. The snag was that, if the Agreement was an old one, the fine that the man who produced it would have to pay would be so heavy that, rather than pay it, he would throw in his hand and consent to judgment: in which case, of course, as in mine, his opponent lost his case by holding his tongue."

"Well, I call it wicked," said Daphne. "If the Judge had been wearing glasses, you would have won your case. But because of this rubbishy custom, you had to sit still and smile and be disqualified."

"I know. It was very trying. To this day I can see the Judge's gentle smile and Whitely sitting there with a hand to his mouth. I daresay things have changed. I hope they have."

Berry expired.

"Would it be too much to suggest that your luckless client hadn't the faintest idea that his case was really in the bag, when his highly scrupulous counsel opened the mouth of the bag and damned well shook it out?"

"I hope he hadn't," I said.

"And you talk of etiquette. If you called it rank chicanery, you would be nearer the mark. All I can say is that if anyone who is considering going to law in the mistaken hope of obtaining justice reads this book, I should think it will probably stop him from paying handsomely for the privilege of entering what I can only describe as a den of thieves."

"That's nonsense," I said, "and you know it. Taking it by and large the client does very well. He gets a very fair deal. For one thing only, if his counsel is inexperienced, the Judge will always help him, so that he's not weighted out. And if he appears in person, he's given great latitude. I've given you one or two instances of misfortune or even dereliction of duty; but I have said nothing of the scores of cases I saw, with some of which I had to do, which were admirably conducted and most fairly tried. In my day the Bar was probably the most honest of the professions and I have no doubt that the same can be said today. Indeed, you may take it from me that British justice most truly deserves its name."

*

Jonah looked at me.

"Not very long ago," he said, "I read two obituaries. Both caused me some surprise, for I had not thought that the men about whom they were written were so distinguished. I drew your attention to them. But you only smiled and said, 'Some maxims should be amended'. Would you care to elaborate that statement?"

"There is," I said, "a tendency today – there has been a tendency for some years for those who decide what should be said in obituary notices to make out that the deceased was much more eminent than in fact he was. This may be because those who are responsible for such notices are misinformed. In any event it is unfortunate, for such tributes are not only misleading, but, for those who know better, they bring the memory of the dead into contempt.

"Here perhaps I should say that, since there are always plenty of people ready to misrepresent the written word, I am well aware that many men die and are commended who deserve to the full the praise and commendation which their obituaries accord them. Some of them are done scant justice. But I am dealing with the cases of those men who, when they are dead, are represented to have been far more distinguished and brilliant than in fact they were. I have no desire to deprive the blessed dead of their laurels; but it is, I think, a very great mistake to proclaim that so-and-so was a very much more talented member of society than he was. Myself, I believe this to be nothing less than the result of what is called publicity. Some of those thus dealt with have courted and gained publicity, while alive, and are still borne on the bosom of that meretricious flood for a week or so after their death.

"Of course the old Latin maxim, 'Speak nothing but good of the dead' – that is the accurate translation – has much to answer for. Years ago someone suggested that it should be amended and that it should run, 'Speak nothing but the truth of the dead'. But such an amendment is, perhaps, too drastic; for there is no reason why a dead man's offences should be remembered. Indeed, they are better forgotten. But to declare that a man was a greater man than he was is provocative and manifestly undesirable.

"Three cases come to my mind.

"In the first case, I knew all about the man – as did many others – although I am glad to say that I never made his acquaintance. In the second, I only knew the man's work. In the third, I was once able to study the man at close quarters, and the impression I formed has, as you will see, stayed with me to this day.

"Now for the first. Soon after I became a solicitor's pupil, there was pointed out to me at the Old Bailey a 'thieves' lawyer'. In that and the following year I had many opportunities of observing him. He was, I should say, the leader of that disreputable cult. He was a man of little education and frequently dropped his h's, when addressing the Court. Often enough, he appeared with no solicitor behind him and I have seen him myself in the hall of the Old Bailey touting for work. I have seen and heard him bullying his unfortunate witnesses and treating them as though they were dirt – not, of course, in court. What was, to my mind, worse than anything, in spite of the fact that he was a barrister of many years' standing, he was grossly ignorant of some of the most elementary rules of law. His name was Abrahams: but this, no doubt for a very good reason, he changed early on by deed poll to that of – well, I'm not going to say what name he took, but it was a very honourable and distinguished old English name. He looked the rogue he was: but he had quite a good practice, because he always attacked the witnesses for the Crown, whether or no he had reason so to do. And that was what his clients wanted. If the 'busy' who had 'shopped' them was severely handled in the box, even if they were convicted, they felt they had had their money's worth. So Abrahams prospered.

"Now in the nineteen-thirties he died, and I read his obituary in *The Times*. Who wrote it or authorized it, I have no idea. But it took up half a column and it made out that he was a most distinguished figure of the Criminal Bar. It mentioned several of the cases in which he was engaged and announced that he had led for the defence of —, for whose conviction he was solely responsible: it spoke in glowing terms of his great ability as an advocate and his excellence as a Criminal lawyer. Any layman reading it would have sighed for the passing of a great man. And in fact he was a disgrace to his profession, and he spent his life obtaining poor men's money by false pretences.

"My second illustration is less valuable. I never knew the man, but he wrote one book which I greatly admired, which has always stood on my shelf. I have every reason to believe that he was a very nice man and he was, without doubt, accomplished. When he died, he was given an obituary notice, which occupied nearly a column. I have no doubt the praise which it bestowed upon him was richly deserved. But in the course of this tribute, the article declared that he was the inventor of a certain kind of jingle, something resembling a Limerick, which had been called after him. This interested me, for I had never heard one before. The writer of the notice quoted two of these jingles, to which he referred as 'gems of wit'; he also used the word 'brilliant'. Now for the Limerick, particularly the original Limericks written by Lear, I have always had a certain admiration. I think they are most entertaining, frequently very witty and always very well done. But these two jingles which were quoted and commended so handsomely were the most arrant rubbish. They certainly rhymed, but no attempt had been made to make them scan and that anyone with a sense of humour could have found them funny is more than I can believe. Wondering whether there was in them some virtue which had escaped me, I memorized them and tried them on three or four reasonably intelligent people, with quite painful results. I mean, they heard me out, and then stared upon me as though they thought that I had gone round the bend. I need hardly add that I never got the flicker of a smile."

"I can bear you out," said Berry. "I was one of your 'reasonably intelligent' guinea-pigs."

"I beg," I said, "that you won't repeat your comments. They certainly satisfied me that my estimate of the jingles was good, but they were rather forcible. The point is that in that obituary notice they were hailed as brilliant and unforgettable flashes of the genius of a great man at play.

"Now what effect did this obituary notice have upon me – a very ordinary member of the reading public? Some of the admiration I had always had for the deceased evaporated. And I felt that, if whoever had written that notice was seeking to glorify the dead man's memory, he had more than failed. Indeed, I am inclined to believe that, for many people, he brought it into contempt.

"The third case is rather different. I shall have to be careful here, for I have no desire to shatter any illusions. After all, these are only examples of misrepresentation of the truth by those who probably know no better. I mean that they approach the wrong sources of information. But this is – or was – an outrageous case. And I think publicity was to blame here. Be that as it may, I cannot declare the whole truth. If I did, you'd go through the roof: but the man would be immediately identified.

"Not long before the first War, I was invited to attend some rehearsals of an important Shakespearian production in the West End. I had come to know the Actor-Manager concerned, when I was President of the OUDS, and he knew that it would interest me to watch the building-up of the play. And so I did attend – and found the exercise extremely interesting. Naturally enough, I went to the first night…

"Now on that night, after the first act I left my seat in the stalls and when the curtain rose on the second act I stood for some minutes at the back of the dress-circle, to see how the performance looked and sounded from there. I was just about to return to my seat below, when the Business Manager, who was passing, asked me to have a drink. So we entered the bar, which led out of the promenade at the back of the dress-circle. There I saw five men, all in evening dress. One of the four was seated upon a high stool, up against the bar: the other four seemed to be his admirers, for they were standing about him, hanging, so to speak, upon his lips and behaving as sycophants behave. Them, I cannot remember at all: for I had eyes, as they had, only for the man on the stool. So vivid was the impression that, though nearly fifty years have passed, I can see him now. Fat, pasty-faced, languid, he resembled a white slug. He was most elegant. He was exquisitely dressed – in full evening dress, of course – from his perfectly ironed silk hat to his patent-leather shoes. His pudgy hands were white and manicured: his button-hole was a dream: his ebony cane belonged to the books. His demeanour was that of languid contempt. He never smiled; occasionally vouchsafed a word, which was received with rapturous laughter by his squires; sipped his drink.

" 'My God,' I whispered, 'what's that?'

"The Business Manager looked at me and smiled.

" 'Don't you know who that is?' he said.

" 'I've no idea,' I said. 'I've never seen it before and I hope to God I never see it again.'

"The Business Manager laughed softly. Then he breathed the name in my ear.

"It was that of a very well-known critic – who had been appointed by the periodical that paid him to attend the first night and criticize the play. And there he was in the bar, exuding his loathsome airs and graces, playing to his contemptible gallery, a revolting sight. He reminded me irresistibly of Coles Willing's description of Oscar Wilde – fat, pasty-faced, languid…

"Not long after I saw him on that first night, he left England…

"And now mark this. When that man died and was gathered, I suppose, to his fathers, article after article appeared in the Press, all speaking of his 'charm', his 'perfect demeanour' and 'gentle modesty'. One paper said that he was shy. And that man was a fat, white slug, preferring to sleek himself in the adulation of his decadent disciples to doing his duty and earning the money which he was presently paid."

"How revolting!" said Daphne.

"I'm with you," said Jonah. "I find it most offensive. God knows I desire to think no ill of the dead: but misrepresentation of fact like that makes the gorge rise."

"I know. It shouldn't, of course. I think what gets us under the ribs is that so many really fine men, whose names deserve to be remembered, are often dismissed with half a dozen lines."

Berry lifted his head.

" 'Sweet are the uses of *advertisement*.' "

"Yes, that is the truth. These fellows advertise themselves and have their reward. But the man who does not pose, who shuns advertisement, who does his duty – well, he, too, has his reward: but I fancy it is of more value than a write-up in the public prints. And allow me to say that of this particular case, I haven't told you the half – because I wish to suppress the man's identity. And when I say the half, I mean it."

"Oscar Wilde," said Jonah. "We know the sordid story; but he was before our time."

"Coles Willing saw him," I said. "With another man, he went to one of his lectures – to have a look at him. He told me that Wilde was a perfectly beastly sight – in a word, he looked what he was. Beginning his lecture, he spoke these memorable words. *If I were not beautiful, I should die.* When he said that, with one consent Coles Willing and his companion rose and left the hall. I remember Coles saying, 'I thought I was going to be sick.' "

"Am I right in saying that he was given a chance to clear out?"

149

"I've heard that he was. I've heard that, when the warrant for his arrest had been issued, he was told that if he left England within twenty-four hours, the warrant would stay on the file. That is to say, that unless he returned to England, it would not be executed. The idea, of course, was to avoid the hideous scandal which the case provoked."

"But he wouldn't go?"

I shook my head.

"He had the effrontery to maintain that he had done no wrong. During his trial, he lounged in the dock, reading – or pretending to read – a book of poems, and ignoring – or pretending to ignore – the irrefutable and revolting evidence which was being given against him."

"And that poisonous blackguard," said Berry, "will have his statue yet."

"I can't believe it," said Daphne.

"He will," said Berry. "You see."

"To be honest," said I, "I'm not sure he isn't right."

*

"Darling," said Jill. "I know QCs are called 'silks', because they're said to wear a silk gown. But are their gowns really silk?"

"I'm sure they aren't today: I don't think they were in my time – as a rule, at any rate. Probably a QC had a silk gown which he kept to wear on special occasions. Any way, his gown was cut differently to that worn by the Junior Bar, but the great difference was that the QC wore a special coat. For some strange reason, I can't remember this very well, but I think it resembled the coat worn with Court Dress. And if ever the Court was in mourning, the QC always wore lawn cuffs on the sleeves of his coat, and mourning bands, instead of the ordinary bands. I think the Junior Bar used to wear mourning bands, too: I know that I did.

"As I expect you know, the original band, which was worn by Henry the Eighth, was a linen collar and the forerunner of the ruff. It presently gave its name to the band-box, in which varieties of such collars were carried and kept. Naturally, with the coming of the ruff, the band-box became very large and, to a well-dressed man, a most important piece of baggage. But some of the collars were 'falling collars' and the bands worn by the Bar are derived from them."

"A few nights ago," said Berry, "you mentioned a barrister called Boyd as being in Travers Humphreys' chambers. Didn't he become a Metropolitan Police Magistrate?"

"Yes, he did. I think it was what he wanted, and I was very glad. He was a very nice, quiet, earnest man, rather soldierly in appearance, for he had a clipped moustache."

"Surely that's wrong for Counsel?"

"Well, I think it's a mistake. It doesn't look well with a wig. But there's no rule about it. Phillimore J had one."

"He would," said Berry.

I laughed.

"He was rather trying," I said. "He was a cold-blooded Puritan – and that was that. But Ellis Hume-Williams QC wore a moustache. So, I think, did Shearman J. And Fletcher-Moulton LJ. But, personally, I never thought it looked right."

"Didn't Scrutton have a beard?"

"You're perfectly right. He did; and so did Ridley. But somehow a beard didn't look as wrong as a moustache by itself. But I can't commend it. Bench and Bar should be clean-shaven. At least, that's my idea."

"Last night," said Jonah, "you mentioned a case of a fellow whose name was Abrahams, changing his name. Anybody can do that I believe."

"Any British subject can. He executes what is called a Deed Poll and advertises the fact in the *Gazette*. That's all."

"And he can take any name he likes?"

I nodded.

"Which," said Berry, "is iniquitous. Everyone knows that such licence is constantly abused. There are genuine cases, such as where the last male of his line doesn't want the name to die out and stipulates that, if his daughter is to inherit his property, her husband must change his name to that which she bore before she married him. But how often does that happen? Yet names are being changed all the time, simply because men think it will benefit them financially to sail under false colours. And they are usually right. I mean, if your true name is Stunkenstein, provided you are a naturalized British subject, you can change it to Howard or Cavendish by a stroke of the pen: and nobody can deny that, for most people, 'Messrs. Howard and Cavendish' will inspire more confidence than 'Messrs Bahnhof and Stunkenstein'."

"Outrageous," said Daphne.

"So it is," said Jonah. "The law should clearly be changed. What does Boy say?"

"I've felt that for many years: and I've never understood why the point has never been raised by some private member. I mean, it's extremely simple. Anyone who desires to change his name should have to appear before some Court and present his case for so doing. If the Court considers that his reasons for so doing are good, then permission will be granted. The Court would, of course, have the right to approve or disapprove the name which he proposed to take. And he would have to pay the costs of such procedure. It is as simple as that. In plain language, for many years a privilege has been abused and it is high time that such an abuse was abated."

"Would you have stayed in Travers Humphreys' chambers had there been room?"

"Not on your life. Nothing would have induced me to practise at the Criminal Bar."

"That's rather severe."

"I don't mean to be severe. It's a question of taste. Many better men than I have stuck to the Criminal Bar until they retired or were promoted. But for two full years I had a close-up of the work, and to spend the best years of one's life in such an atmosphere was to my mind unthinkable. I've related some sordid cases, but, believe me, they were the cream. The depths of iniquity to which man can sink are unbelievable.

"Well, somebody's got to do it, and somebody thinks it worth while. But it wasn't down my street. You must have a special outlook to practise at the Criminal Bar. How Bodkin contrived to do it, I never knew, for he was a sensitive man. The experience I had was very valuable. It opened my eyes and it made me very careful. But that was more than enough. In a word, I was glad to get out."

"Is money the attraction?"

"Oh dear, no! The Criminal Bar is very badly paid. At least, it was in my time. If you had the good fortune to be appointed Counsel to the Treasury at the Old Bailey – well, you had a safe job: but the Treasury is notoriously stingy and the fees were by no means high. Still, Treasury Counsel were allowed to accept some briefs for the defence. Not all, of course. They would not, for instance, have been allowed to defend Crippen. And they had to obtain permission in every case. A Treasury Counsel who had shown himself really able, such as Bodkin, did do a certain amount of private work. And that reminds me of a little case which I had forgotten.

"In the spring or early summer of 1909, a well-known peer of the realm came down the steps of the Carlton Club and asked the Commissionaire to call a taxi. The Commissionaire signalled to the cab-rank and a taxi drew up at once to the foot of the steps. This meant, of course, that the taxi was facing West, for the Canton Club used to stand on the South side of Pall Mall. The Commissionaire opened the door: as the peer was about to enter the cab, he hung on his heel, as usual, and gave the driver the address.

" 'Fifteen Berkeley Square.'

"Well, that was easy enough. Straight on along Pall Mall, up St James's Street, in and out of Piccadilly and up Berkeley Street. But, instead of taking this direct and obvious way, the driver turned his cab round and began to drive East instead of West.

"For a moment the peer didn't notice what the driver had done: but when he saw Regent Street on his left and Waterloo Place on his right, he leapt to his feet and put his head out of the window.

" 'Where are you going?' he cried. 'I said Berkeley Square.'

" 'What if you did?' said the driver. 'I know my way.'

" 'Damn it, man,' cried the peer. 'You're driving East!"

"The driver brought his cab to the kerb and pulled down his flag.

" 'You can get out,' he said. 'If you think you can swear at me, you're – well wrong.'

"In a silence big with emotion, the peer got out. Then he slammed the door and looked round for another cab.

"As he signalled to one to stop, he found his late driver by his side.

" 'What about my fare?'

" 'I'm not paying you any fare,' said the peer.

" 'I'll see about that,' said the driver. 'What's your name?'

"The peer handed him his card. As he entered the second taxi –

" 'I'll summons you,' shouted the other.

"He was as good as his word. He applied for a summons at Marlborough Street. This was duly served at the Carlton Club. The peer instructed Wontner and Sons and they briefed Bodkin for the defence. The magistrate who heard the case was Denman, a very nice man.

"Well, the result may be imagined.

"The taxi-driver said his piece, and Bodkin rose to cross-examine. The driver was truculent. When asked why, when he was told to drive to Berkeley Square, he drove in the opposite

154

direction, he replied, 'That's my business.' When asked whether, in such circumstances, he was surprised that his fare should emphatically protest, he replied that if a man, just because he was a lord, thought he had a right to swear at everyone else, he was mistaken. The peer gave evidence. The driver, in cross-examination, asked him whether he thought it right to refuse to pay his fare. The peer replied that, when a fare, who was being driven the wrong way, was ordered out of a cab, he thought only a fool would pay the fare on the clock. It was proved that no streets were up and that the way from the Carlton Club to Berkeley Square was as I have said.

"In the circumstances, it is not surprising that the summons was dismissed with costs. These, the peer did not demand. But Bodkin's fee, I remember, was twenty guineas."

"What a monstrous show!" said Berry.

"The taxi-driver," said Jonah, "was before his time. If this affair had taken place forty years later, he would probably have won his case."

"I give," said Daphne, "full marks to the peer for going through with it."

"I agree," said I. "It was most unpleasant for him and very expensive. That little flurry cost him the best part of thirty pounds. But he felt that to submit to such abominable behaviour was all wrong."

"What," said Berry, "were your impressions?"

"Myself," said I, "I think that the taxi-driver was a communist. I think he decided to offend a member of the Carlton Club. For that reason he went on that rank. For that reason he drove in the opposite direction to Berkeley Square. For that reason he applied for his summons. Indeed, I can see no other explanation. Denman, who was very gentle with everyone, dressed him down properly."

"He should," said Berry, "have lost his licence."

"I daresay he did. The police were very particular in those days. And taxi-drivers were almost invariably very civil. Which reminds me of the case of a fellow in the Grenadier Guards. When war broke out in 1914, he was afraid that he might be killed and his widow left badly off. So he bought a couple of taxis and gave them to her. I was told that they brought her in twelve hundred pounds a year. Of course by no means all drivers had their own cabs: but they got a good percentage and people were generous with their tips. And if a driver was obliging, it paid him hand over fist."

"To return to what we were saying – I take it the biggest money was made at the Common Law Bar?"

"Curiously enough," said I, "it wasn't. I don't say that Rufus Isaacs and F E Smith, who were both Common Lawyers, didn't head the list in their time; but, on the whole, the biggest fortunes were made at the Parliamentary Bar. This was a very close borough, and its citizens, being jealous, were very few. Their names were seldom heard and they argued before Committees of the House of Lords. Their work was devastatingly dull, which is, perhaps, why they were so well paid. They never appeared for individuals but only for 'bodies', so that their clients were not paying them out of their own pockets. Let me give you an instance. If some Town Council wanted to scrap its trams and use trolley buses instead, some other body of standing might oppose this idea and prefer to stick to the trams. Then counsel of the Parliamentary Bar were instructed and they had it out before a Committee of the House of Lords. For some reason or other, on one occasion, Harker was given a junior brief in one such case, and, as it went on for ages, more than once I devilled for him. I had nothing to do but listen, and I found it terribly hard to stay awake. I don't think witnesses were ever called: all the evidence was by affidavit. I may be wrong there. I can't remember the name of the leader of the Parliamentary Bar in my time, but he was briefed in this particular case and I heard him speak. I didn't think he was particularly brilliant, but his tongue was that of a ready talker and it was obvious that he was *persona grata* in their lordships' eyes. He was certainly very convincing and occasionally humorous. It was clear that he and the Chairman – I think, Lord Newton – got on very well. Well, it's a great thing to be liked by the Bench before which you are appearing. I don't suggest for one moment that any favouritism was shown, but if I could see that he was popular, so could solicitors. So far as I can remember, there were only two or three other 'silks' at the Parliamentary Bar and as time never seemed to be an object, there was plenty of work for all. And I always understood that the fees were very high.

"At the Common Law bar, the really big money came from commercial cases – two companies, or very big firms, at variance, and money no object at all. Those were the cases in which the inimitable Rufus Isaacs, with his magnificent brain and memory and his astounding flair for figures, came into his own. Some of those cases used to go on for three weeks – and Isaacs would be in two or three at the same time. And that was the way to make ten thousand a month."

"Terrific," said Jonah.

"But, mark you, Rufus Isaacs earned his money. Think of passing from court to court, each time leaving behind you all the figures and dates and intricate circumstances of one case and immediately assimilating a precisely similar mass of particulars relating to another. Only a giant's brain could do a thing like that."

"It makes my brain reel," said Daphne.

"At least," said Jonah, "no machine could do that."

"Am I right in saying," said Berry, "that counsel would sometimes undertake never to leave a case?"

"Yes. The fee had to be substantially increased in the case of a busy man, for it might well mean that he had to refuse other briefs. And it would never happen if the case was to last for some time. I don't suppose that Isaacs ever did it; but lesser men would. I mean, if you wanted Rufus Isaacs, you had to take him on his own terms. And people thought themselves lucky to get him on those. And so they were. I'm proud to have seen him at work. He was a very great barrister."

"You spoke of cases that lasted for three weeks. How long did The Tichborne Case last?"

"That was phenomenal. The civil case lasted more than a hundred days and the criminal case about a hundred and fifty. The plaintiff was in the box for twenty-two days and the Lord Chief Justice took nearly a month to sum up."

"Good God," said Jonah.

"Sorry," said Jill. "What was The Tichborne Case?"

"There you are," said Berry. "The most famous case that has ever come to be tried, and the younger generation doesn't even know its name."

I smiled.

"My darling," I said, "Berry does you an injustice. The Tichborne Case took place thirty years before you were born. Its story has been told very often and books have been written about it, so I'll only summarize it here. But it was a most sensational case and the British public ate it from beginning to end. Coles Willing told me that people talked of nothing else. Sides were taken and heated arguments were conducted in Clubs, at dinner parties and in the public house. It was headline news for years – and when I say 'years', I mean it, for civil proceedings began in 1871 and the criminal proceedings, which followed straight on, finished in 1874."

"Refresh our memories," said Berry.

"Well, it was a most romantic and sensational affair. A young man, whose Christian name was Roger, who was the eldest son and heir of a baronet, Sir James Tichborne, was on the way from South America to Australia, when his ship foundered and was never seen again. He had been in the Army, but had retired. Had he succeeded his father, his income would have been some twenty thousand a year. The ship foundered in 1854 when he was twenty-five years old. His mother refused to accept the fact that he was dead. His father presently died and his second son succeeded to the title and the estates. This drove the poor mother frantic, for Roger was her favourite son, and in 1865, although eleven years had passed since his ship had foundered, she began to advertise for him. Her advertisements bore fruit. A firm of solicitors wrote saying that they were happy to inform her that they had found her son: that he had escaped with some members of the crew from the sinking ship, had reached Australia and had been living there ever since under the name of Castro. Poor Lady Tichborne was overjoyed, sent the money necessary for him to come home and went to Paris to meet him. There she fell upon his neck, but, when he reached England, the rest of the family refused to believe that he was Roger Tichborne indeed. Some of his brother officers said he was: some said he wasn't. After all thirteen years had gone by, since his ship went down.

"Well, he set up his claim to the baronetcy and the income. This was resisted by his 'nephew', for his 'brother,' the baronet, had died, and his son was reigning in his stead. After long Chancery proceedings, the case came to be tried by a Judge and jury.

"As I have said, it lasted for more than one hundred days. In the middle of it came the long vacation, when of course, it was adjourned. While it was on, the defendant and his advisers kept seeking and finding fresh evidence to prove the plaintiff's claim false; and at last they discovered the truth, which, of course, the plaintiff denied. But the jury believed it and, after listening to a speech by Coleridge, who led for the defence, which lasted for twenty-six days, they found in favour of the defendant.

"As he left the court, the plaintiff was arrested on charges of perjury and forgery and cast into Newgate jail. Shortly afterwards he was tried before the Lord Chief Justice and two other Judges, when it was proved that he was, in fact, one Arthur Orton, a butcher, who had plied his trade in Wapping, had later emigrated to Australia and had there been groomed to impersonate the dead Roger Titchborne. After a trial, which began in April and ended in the following February, he was found guilty and sentenced to fourteen years' hard labour. Ten years later he was released on ticket-of-leave and ten years after that he confessed his guilt.

"And that was the end of a business which had been head-line news for nearly three years, the cost of which to the Tichborne family and the British public must have approached one hundred and fifty thousand pounds. It was probably the boldest and most determined attempt to steal away another man's birthright that ever was made, and but for the tireless efforts made by Sir Henry Tichborne's advisers it would undoubtedly have succeeded. It made the name of Henry Hawkins, the famous Judge, for he led for the Crown in the criminal proceedings, and it was the end of Dr Kenealy, who led for the defence, for he afterwards attacked the Judges with such violence that he was disbarred."

"Astounding," said Jonah.

"That," I said, "is the word. That a Wapping butcher could have put up such a show is amazing. But he had been wonderfully coached. Sir Roger Tichborne, whom he pretended to be, had been, I think, at Eton and had had a classical education: the claimant, Arthur Orton, was accordingly cross-examined on what he had learned at school. And he got a lot of it right. The names of masters and boys, and things like that. Of course he made mistakes: but always then he blamed his memory. Coles Willing told me that he heard him asked to translate *Laus Dei*, when he at once replied, 'The laws of God'. Well, that was forgivable, but it made an educated man think. Mercifully, his poor, deluded 'mother', who started the ball rolling by her advertisement, died before the criminal proceedings began: she was therefore spared the anguish of seeing her 'son' go down."

"Well, I'm much obliged," said Berry. "Your summary has interested me no end – and told me quite a lot that I didn't know. I suppose you couldn't do the same with the loss of the *Titanic*?"

I hesitated. Then –

"How you jump about," said Daphne. "Why should Boy be able to give you the low-down on the *Titanic*?"

"You never know," said her husband. He got up and filled my glass. "He has a knack of picking up bits and pieces, which never appear in print."

"As a matter of fact," I said, "I do know one or two things about that dreadful occurrence. For I happened to meet one of the officers who had served under Captain Smith, who was in command of the *Titanic*, shortly after the disaster. He was not on the ill-fated ship. He had served regularly under Smith on the *Olympic*, but, just before the *Titanic* had completed her trials, he had had a difference with Smith and it had been amicably arranged that he should leave Smith's command for two or three months. So he stayed with the *Olympic*, instead of going with Smith to the *Titanic*.

"Not long before the *Titanic*'s first and last voyage, I saw Captain Smith in court, in the witness-box. So I was able to size him up.

"He was a bluff sailor – rough, downright, with no party manners at all. He looked about fifty-five. His hair was grey, going white."

"How," said Jonah, "did he happen to be there?"

"You'll remember when I remind you. Not very long before the loss of the *Titanic*, HMS *Hawke*, a cruiser, collided with the *Olympic* at Southampton or just outside. As a result, The White Star Line claimed damages from the Admiralty and the Admiralty counterclaimed. Smith gave evidence for his Company. The Admiralty won the case. They maintained that, such was the size of the *Olympic*, she sucked the *Hawke* into her side and that the Commander of the *Hawke* was powerless to avoid the collision. This theory, the jury accepted. Their finding was widely discussed and criticized: but never was a verdict so handsomely vindicated. A few months later, as the *Titanic* was leaving Southampton on her maiden voyage, she passed an American ship which was tied up to the quay: as she drew level with this, the American ship snapped her cables as if they were threads and began to move towards the *Titanic* as though drawn by invisible cords: a collision was only just averted."

"I remember now," said Jonah. "A most remarkable thing. Sorry. Please go on."

"Well, we all know what happened. At a quarter to twelve on a Sunday night in April 1912, the *Titanic* struck an iceberg in mid-Atlantic and presently sank with a loss of nearly two thousand lives. That Sunday afternoon her Captain had been warned by wireless that if he held on his course he would encounter icebergs. The ship's course was not altered.

"When I met the officer to whom I have referred, I asked him to what he attributed the disaster. Without hesitation he replied, 'To the speed the *Titanic* was going.' I said, 'When the iceberg was sighted, it was some way off. How was it that they couldn't avoid it or pull the *Titanic* up?' He smiled. 'When the iceberg was seen it was almost certainly less than a hundred yards away. An iceberg is black at night, and as the sea was dead calm, there was no line of surf. And when a ship of sixty thousand tons is doing twenty-three knots or more you can stop her engines and put them into reverse, but you won't stop that ship in less than three miles.' "

"God bless my soul," said Berry.

"Three miles," I repeated. "To tell you the truth, I'm not sure he didn't say four. But I don't want to exaggerate. I believe the order was given to put the helm hard over, but it was, of course, too late."

"Smith went down with his ship?"

"Yes." I hesitated. "But here is a curious thing. On Sunday at luncheon, ten or eleven hours before she struck, the *Titanic* had a definite list to port. To this, passengers at his table called the purser's attention. He replied, 'Probably coal has been taken mostly from the starboard side.' I make no comment, but that is what he said. When she struck, she was holed on the starboard side. She did not sink for two and a half hours. During this time she listed heavily to port. Finally, she went down by the head. These facts may mean nothing at all. But there they are."

"They seem strange to me," said Jonah: "but, as a landsman, I have nothing to say."

"Nor I," said Berry. "She was an ill-fated ship."

"They boasted that she was unsinkable. So Nature stretched out an arm."

"It does look like that," said Jonah…

"Before the *Titanic* sailed, it had been announced that the White Star Line was having a sister ship built and that she was to be called the *Gigantic*. But if the ship was built, the name was changed."

My sister shuddered.

"Give us something less dreadful, darling, before we turn in."

"I know," said Jonah. "Books. How and when did books begin?"

I put a hand to my head.

"Well, the very first books, I believe, were written on tablets of lead."

"That must have been fun," said Berry. "I wonder how many tons *The Odyssey* weighed?"

"Be quiet," said everyone.

"But about 500 BC papyrus came in. Papyrus was a reed, and strips of it were soaked and pasted together to make a sort of paper. This was rolled round a stick. Still, books which were so made were inconvenient to handle and easily damaged. And then at last somebody thought of sheepskin or parchment. This was a great step forward, for parchment is indestructible and you can write on both sides: and leaves of parchment were cut and stitched together, just as is done with the books of today."

"Was there any publishing?"

"In Cicero's time there was – say about 50 BC. Cicero went to a publisher called Atticus, and Atticus paid Cicero a royalty on every copy of his books which he sold."

"Every copy," said Berry, thoughtfully.

I smiled.

"Yes, they really were copies then. When the author had delivered his manuscript the publisher dictated it to a whole army of scribes. If the edition consisted of a thousand copies, as it sometimes did, this was an exhausting procedure for all concerned: and I need hardly say that the copies produced were often full of mistakes. This used to infuriate Cicero, who felt unable to read and correct one thousand copies himself: but he did sometimes revise copies which his friends had bought."

"Booksellers?" said Jonah.

"Yes, there were booksellers then. They used to hang up a list of the books they had for sale outside their doors. And there were libraries, too."

"And all books were hand-written?" said Jill.

"Yes, indeed. Printing didn't come in till the fifteenth century – into Europe, any way. I always find it strange that some monk who was fed up with copying didn't get the idea before."

"Quite so," said Berry, thoughtfully. "All the same, it might be argued today that the discovery of printing was not altogether for the good of the human race."

*

"One incident, I remember," said Berry, "which shows forth with remarkable accuracy the outlook of the Boche."

"Oh dear," said Daphne.

"It's not revolting," said Berry. "It's not even bestial. But it shows the infinite pains which the Boche will take – the very great inconvenience to which he will put himself in order to achieve something, which cannot possibly advance his interests, so long as its achievement will cause another being distress.

"The incident belongs to the very last days of the first great war. The Boche was on the run, being hounded out of France: and we were hard on his heels. What had been his old front-line was miles away, and German units which had been comfortably housed for years had to clear out of their 'homes' and run for their lives.

"One such unit – some headquarters, of course – had been installed in a pleasant country-house – a *château*, the French would have called it. Any way, it was a handsome residence of some importance and many years old. It had all the amenities of an agreeable country home, and I have little doubt that the Boches who lived there were very comfortable.

"Now they had to leave in some haste, and so, no doubt to their annoyance, they were prevented from ruining the residence. A few minutes after they had gone, the new tenants, British troops, took possession. First on the scene was a British cavalry regiment: and there this was ordered to stay for twenty-four hours. They had been going all out, and the horses needed a rest.

"Now it happened that the French liaison officer attached to that particular regiment had known the *château* well in other and better days and he was delighted to find that little irreparable damage had been done. The house had been fouled, of course, and would have to be cleaned, fumigated and redecorated from bottom to top. And the furniture would have to be scrapped. But it was not a ruin, for the Boche had been pressed for time.

"A feature of the property was the English kitchen-garden. This was an acre in size and was comfortably walled all round: and even on that November morning it made an agreeable pleasance. The liaison officer strolled round it with the second-in-command. The latter was enthusiastic. 'This is superb,' he said, 'and by Jove, they've kept it well.' The other shrugged his shoulders. 'It suited their stomachs,' he said. 'But what espaliers!' cried the second-in-command, pointing to the great fruit-trees splayed out upon the walls. 'Never in my life have I seen such magnificent trees.' 'Aren't they superb?' said the other. 'The Count was most proud of them. How old would you say they were?' 'Heaven knows,' said the other. 'I'm no authority. But what magnificence!' 'The fruit they bore was far too much for the house, and the Count used to send his neighbours baskets full day after day.' 'I can well believe it,' said the other. His brows drew into a frown. 'That one doesn't look too good.'

"It was the first to die. That very morning, before the Boche cleared out, the last thing he did was to saw through every espalier three inches above the ground."

My sister covered her face and Jill cried out.

"Well there you are," said Berry. "For the truth of that tale, I can vouch, for the liaison officer told it me with tears in his eyes. It shews forth the outlook of the Boche. When an army is in retreat – not to say flight – with the enemy close behind, there are, as you may imagine, a thousand things to be done, and every single soldier is either on the move or working all out. Yet, pressed for time as they were, with the British hard on their heels, men were detailed to commit that cruel, abominable waste. It served no military purpose. It was done in hatred and malice, to injure the innocent man they had forced to be their host for more than four years. But that is the Boche. More. It will always be the Boche. That cruel and beastly outlook is bred in the bone: and it is ineradicable.

"I don't suppose that everyone who reads it will believe this tale. A young man I met, who had seen the Belsen film, assured me that it was faked, 'to put the Germans in a bad light'. And some, who do believe, will maintain that the outlook of the Boche has changed. But we know better."

"But what is the matter with them?" said Daphne.

"It's inherent vice," said Jonah. "The blood is dangerous. And Berry is perfectly right. Those who read these words will say that they are untrue. But they are not untrue. People are unable to believe them because such wickedness is 'not dreamed of in *their* philosophy'."

There was a little silence. Then –

"Oh, I know," said Berry. "Curtis Bennett. Or would you rather not?"

I raised my eyebrows.

"I can tell you as much as I know – for what that is worth."

"If you please."

"Derek Curtis Bennett, QC, who died in 1956, was the son of Henry Curtis Bennett, QC, who was at the Bar with me, and the grandson of Curtis Bennett, who was for some years the third magistrate at Bow Street and later Chief Magistrate for a little while.

"I'll deal with the grandfather, first.

"When I was a solicitor's pupil, I was frequently before him, so I had many opportunities of observing him as a magistrate and as a man. As a magistrate, he was adequate, but undistinguished. He was disliked by his colleagues – that I know for a fact."

"Who were his colleagues?" said Jonah.

"Sir Albert de Rutzen, the Chief Magistrate, and Marsham, the second magistrate at Bow Street. Curtis Bennett was certainly in a different class to them. He was never natural on the bench, as they were: he seemed to be striving for effect: and he loved publicity. Not very grave faults, perhaps, but ill becoming a magistrate. And Muskett never cared about appearing before him. He often had to, of course – nearly all the militant suffragist cases seemed, to Curtis Bennett's delight, to come his way. But if a summons had to be applied for, and Muskett was to do the case, the police always applied to Sir Albert or Marsham, so that the case would be heard by one of them. Mead of Marlborough Street was another magistrate before whom Muskett would never appear, if he could help it. He was a remarkable man – Mead; and an efficient magistrate. But he was most damnably rude. And Cluer was rude, too. But they were the only three that Muskett disliked."

"If I may say so," said Jonah, "Mead was much more than rude: he was deliberately offensive. And, with respect, I don't agree that he was efficient."

I laughed.

"I'd forgotten," I said, "that you had suffered at his hands."

"Once only," said Jonah, "but that was more than enough."

"Let's have it," said Berry.

"I was only one of many," said Jonah, "for I know that Mead's name was a byword just after the first great war. Be that as it may, early one afternoon I was stopped by keepers in Regent's Park for exceeding twenty miles an hour. They said I was going twenty-five, as I think I was. It was just about one o'clock. The broad road was empty – mine was the only car in sight. The pavements were empty, too: only three pedestrians were in sight. I pointed out these facts to the keepers, who admitted that they were true. I asked them to acquaint the magistrate with them, if they got the chance. This, they promised to do.

"Well, I was summoned to appear at Marylebone Police Court. I went blithely enough. As I came to the door, I asked one of the police who was sitting. When I heard his reply, I got the shock of my life.

" 'Mr Mead, sir,' he said. 'But he sits at Marlborough Street,' I said. 'That's right, sir. But he's taking the duty here today.' Sheer misfortune, of course: but there you are.

"There were about six of us – all charged with exceeding the speed-limit in Regent's Park. The case of a nice-looking fellow was taken first. I can't remember his name; but we'd had a word together, before Mead took his seat. 'D'you think he'd believe me if I said I was a chauffeur?' he said. 'I don't think I should,' I said, 'but you never know. Why do you ask?' 'You'll soon see,' he said. Here Mead took his seat. After one or two applications, my friend's name was called and he stood in front of the dock. The charge was read out. 'Guilty or not guilty?' snapped Mead. 'Guilty,' said my friend. A park-keeper entered the box and stated the facts. He was said to have been doing twenty-four miles an hour. 'Owner-driver or chauffeur?' snapped Mead. 'Owner-driver,' said my friend. 'Fined four pounds,' said Mead. 'Next.'

"Now the next offender was a chauffeur. More. He happened to be the chauffeur of some people I knew. More. Less than a fortnight before, on my way with them to the theatre, he had driven us down Park Road at seventy miles an hour. And I had protested to my hostess. 'He'll smash you up one day,' I said. 'I know he will,' she replied. 'But, except for this failing, he's really terribly good. He's summoned once a week, but he'll never learn.'

"Well, he pleaded guilty, looking the while the picture of innocence. He had been driving in the park at thirty-two miles an hour. 'Chauffeur, aren't you?' says Mead. 'Yes, sir.' 'Which means, of course, that you have to do as you're told. Fined fifteen shillings. Next.'

"That was me. I pleaded guilty and the park-keeper said his piece. He didn't say that the park was empty and, as he was about to step down, I asked if I might ask a question. 'No,' snapped Mead. 'You've pleaded guilty. Owner-driver or chauffeur?' 'Owner-driver,' I said. 'Fined four pounds,' said Mead. And that was that.

"Well, comparing those three sentences, I decline to agree that Mead was efficient. In the first place, I find it impossible to believe that he did not realize that a chauffeur's fine was always paid by his employer. In the second place, my friend and I were each fined more than five times as much as the chauffeur, although our speed was considerably less than his. Thirdly, I think I had a clear right to ask the park-keeper a question, provided I was not disputing my guilt."

"You certainly had," I said.

"Fourthly," said Jonah, "I think the fines Mead imposed upon my friend and myself were out of all proportion to the offence."

"I entirely agree."

"Fifthly, to ask us whether we were owner-drivers or chauffeurs was meant to be rude."

"Undoubtedly," I said.

"Finally, if you can give me a finer example of 'one law for the rich and another for the poor', I'd like to hear it."

"Jonah," I said, "you have all my sympathy. At Marlborough Street, summonses were always applied for when Denman was sitting, because Muskett couldn't bear Mead. We were only before him two or three times, and Mead always improved the occasion by being intolerably rude. Still, rudeness is not incompatible with efficiency. And he did deal with his work with commendable dispatch. And I don't think he was ever taken to the Divisional Court. According to his lights, he did his duty for very many years: and that is the kindest way in which to remember him.

"Wait a moment. Something else about Mead has just occurred to me. I was before him, I suppose, five or six times in all: but never once was I able to see his eyes. Even sitting with Muskett at the solicitors' table, which was well below the bench yet very close, and looking up, I never saw his eyes. I don't think anyone ever did: for they were always hooded. I will swear that there was never more than an eighth of an inch – if that – of the eyes themselves to be seen."

"Quite right," said Jonah. "Now that you mention that, I remember it well. Looking upon him, you might have thought he was blind."

"Yes indeed. I have never seen any other man, who was not blind, so hood his eyes. It was, I suppose, a mannerism, for I never saw him use glasses, even to read. But that mannerism and the fact that he never smiled did lend him, let us say, an unsympathetic air.

"Which reminds me of Horace Smith who sat at Westminster Police Court. He was benevolence itself. He was very cheerful, invariably wore a frock-coat and had a white beard. He always made me think of Father Christmas.

"And now let's get back to Bow Street. All the courts, except Bow Street, have two magistrates: but Bow Street has (or had) three, because of the amount of work at that, the principal Police Court of the Metropolis. I can't remember the days upon which each sat; but I do remember that Curtis Bennett sat on Saturdays and Sir Albert on Mondays. And now please bear in mind that I said that Curtis Bennett had a weakness for publicity or advertisement.

"As you know, from the word 'go', the Crippen case was headline news. Well, Crippen was arrested in Canadian waters and presently brought back to England on board a liner whose name I forget. Extradition cases are always taken at Bow Street. Now when a prisoner has been extradited, he is brought directly to Bow Street and, if the Court is sitting, is immediately brought before the Magistrate, who hears evidence of arrest and then orders a remand. And once having been before that Magistrate, his case can be dealt with by no other Magistrate: in other words, the Magistrate before whom he first appears must deal with his case. If the Court is not sitting, then the prisoner is held, I think in the cells at Bow Street, until the next sitting of the Court.

"Well, it seemed pretty clear that Curtis Bennett, who was mad to get the case, would have his heart's desire; for the liner was due to reach Liverpool on Saturday morning and the boat-train would almost certainly reach London before the Court at Bow Street rose. On Saturdays the Court usually rose earlier than usual, for there was not so much work as on ordinary days. All the same, unless the liner was delayed, Crippen would certainly reach Bow Street while Curtis Bennett was there. (This, I may say, to our disgust, for we would much have preferred that Sir Albert or Marsham should take the case.)

"Well, the liner *was* delayed – by fog in the Mersey. Not for very long: but the boat-train left Liverpool very late… Sitting at Bow Street, Curtis Bennett was beside himself. His list was almost finished, but Crippen had not arrived. And he knew that he *should* have arrived, if the train was running to time. I wasn't there, of course, but I was afterwards told that Bennett wasted time in the most barefaced way. He did everything he could think of to keep the Court in session. The Chief Clerk, the ushers and the police were simply wild: but until the Magistrate rose, they had to stay where they were. And then at last Curtis Bennett threw in his hand and left the bench. Half an hour later Crippen reached Bow Street, was held over the weekend and brought up on Monday morning before Sir Albert de Rutzen.

"Now that reminiscence is true. And it is, I think, revealing: for the office of a Bow Street Magistrate is an office of great importance and responsibility: but such behaviour was beneath the dignity of the youngest Justice of the Peace."

Berry spoke with some warmth.

"I entirely agree."

"With such an example before him, it is not surprising that his son, Henry Curtis Bennett, should have displayed the same weakness. And thanks to the publicity he courted, he did obtain a reputation, among laymen, which I don't think he truly deserved. He was quite a good fellow, but by no means in the front rank. He never, for instance, approached Marshall Hall – still less Charles Gill. He was capable; but no more than that. His ability was limited. His manner was bluff and hearty and he was popular. He did a lot of work for the AA – that was how he made his name. The fact that he bore the same name as his father helped him, of course. He was eventually appointed Chairman of – well, they used to be known as the Newington Sessions: but I think they're called something else now.

"His son, Derek Curtis Bennett, I never set eyes on. I have seen it stated that he always felt overshadowed by his father's great reputation. I find that rather difficult to believe. He certainly figured in several sensational cases. What sort of a show he put up, I have no idea."

"Did you ever meet the Magistrate?"

"Once. At least, I was introduced to him. It was past ten o'clock at night, and Muskett and I had been in court at Bow Street all day, appearing for the Crown against militant suffragists. About a hundred arrests had been made the evening before, and every single woman pleaded not guilty and called evidence on her behalf. Such behaviour was intended to hold up the ordinary business of the Court and so, by God, it did. That was why Curtis Bennett was sitting to all hours. He was quite right to do so, for somehow or other the cases had to be heard. I remember that he adjourned for a quarter of an hour at ten o'clock. Muskett and I had, of course, no time to go out for a drink, even if there had been anywhere to go; so the Chief Clerk very kindly invited us to his private room, where someone – an usher, I think – was making tea. (The Chief Clerk at Bow Street was an exceptionally nice man and very able. I'm afraid I can't remember his name. The senior usher's name was, I think, Wade.) We were gratefully drinking the tea, when the door opened and Curtis Bennett came in. I don't think he knew we were there. We all rose and Muskett said 'Good evening, sir,' and then introduced me. Curtis Bennett gave me the slightest nod. Then he took his stand, back to the fire. Nobody said anything. After a minute or two, 'How long,' said Curtis Bennett, 'is this business going on?' He didn't address himself to anyone in particular, so after a moment or two Muskett replied. 'I can only suppose, sir, for as long as any cases remain to be heard.' I don't think anything else was said, but Muskett and I drank up our tea and then bowed ourselves out. Muskett never said anything, but he was obviously ruffled."

"I'm damned if I blame him," said Berry. "After all, Muskett was a pretty big man and for half the day he'd been on his feet, so it was very bad manners not to tell him to sit down and to say, 'I'm afraid you must be very tired,' or something."

I shrugged my shoulders.

"Well, there you are. That was Curtis Bennett, then third Magistrate at Bow Street and later Chief Magistrate. He was only Chief Magistrate for a little while, and died suddenly, I think while attending some function at the Mansion House. Curiously, his son, Henry, died suddenly, too, not long after he had been appointed Chairman of the Sessions."

"How late did he sit on that particular night?"

"I think till eleven o'clock. That meant that we had been at it for over eleven hours, for we'd started at ten in the morning and the breaks for food had been short. Mark you, he was right to go on and right to adjourn at eleven, for everyone was dead beat."

"Was he good on the bench?"

"He was quite all right, but always gave me the impression of being unsure of himself. He wasn't nearly firm enough with the militant suffragists. Each defendant was charged with obstructing the police in the execution of their duty. The witnesses they called almost invariably gave evidence which was entirely irrelevant to that charge. Curtis Bennett should have stopped them instantly. He never did. Several times, to my mind, he should have ordered the court to be cleared. The women's supporters gave him ample excuse. And then we should have got on much faster. Then again, on another occasion, when Mrs Pankhurst and one of her daughters and, I think, a third woman were in the dock all day and witness after witness for the defence was being called, I looked round once to see the Pankhursts and their companion having tea."

"What? Not in the dock?" said Berry.

"In the dock. Thermoses, packets of bread and butter and sandwiches, mouths full, 'After you, dear', and all the rest."

"And Bennett did nothing?"

"Nothing."

"Words fail me," said Berry.

"As a Justice of the Peace," said Jonah, "what would you have done?"

"I should have told the jailer to take the prisoners out of court, take away their victuals and put them in some safe place, and then bring the prisoners back."

"That," said I, "is what he should have done. For his own dignity, I mean. But there you are. Still, on one occasion I did hear him speak very kindly to a poor old man who stood in the dock charged, I think, with begging, who was completely destitute. It was nothing to do with us: Muskett and I were there on some other case. But I was impressed by his very kindly words and the pains he took to arrange that the poor old fellow was cared for."

"Charity," said Berry. "That outweighs many failings."

Which is undeniable.

*

"When I was a child," said Berry, "the daily paper was very different to the daily paper of today. It was dignified: it reported matters of moment: its circulation was small. The only illustrated daily paper was *The Daily Graphic* – I think I remember its birth. The vast majority of Englishmen read the news once a week. That was, I believe, a very good thing. Today we are told far more than is good for us and, to serve some political end, there is much *suppressio veri* and *suggestio falsi* – to put it mildly – in the public prints. Of the sensational tripe with which some papers regale their customers, the less said the better. Enough that it degrades the soul. It's too late to do anything now, but that the Press should wield so much power is a terrible thing: and I firmly believe that if every daily paper was washed out and an official news bulletin was issued and broadcast every day, the world would be a very much happier place."

"A dream," said Jonah. "But you are perfectly right. And please continue to cast back. Your first impressions of London would interest me no end."

"Straw down in the street," said Berry. "Opposite and on either side of a house in which someone lay seriously ill. Or tan. It made an astonishing difference. The passing traffic was silenced. There were then no engines or horns or gears: only iron tyres and the horses' shoes. But they were noisy.

"Then hatchments. These were black-boards about four feet square, with coats-of-arms painted on them, and were hung over the front door of a mansion in which someone of consequence had died. They hung there, I think, for a year, and were then hung for ever in the church which the deceased had attended.

"I remember the pantomime at Drury Lane. I simply loved that. It started at half past seven and went on till midnight or later. The matinées started at half past one and went on till past six. And they had a matinée every day. The pantomime itself was followed by the harlequinade which young people of today have never seen. It was a street scene, with a barrow on which strings of sausages were displayed. There was a real clown, wearing the red and blue doublet and trunks, white hose and rosetted shoes: there was Harlequin, with his sword, wearing half a mask and elegant and lithe in black and silver: there was Columbine, all glorious in her ballet skirt: there was Pantaloon, worthy of his name, to whose seat Clown always applied a red-hot poker: and finally the policeman who arrested Clown for stealing a string of sausages. The clown was always called Joey and always bounded on to the stage, crying 'Here we are again'. Very childish, of course; but in the tradition: and the immense audience ate it.

"Then 'cab runners'. These were rough men who waited outside stations, marked down a four-wheeler with luggage on its roof and ran behind it to its destination. There they desired to be permitted to carry the luggage upstairs. Whether their services were accepted or not, they could usually be sure of a shilling, for people were sorry for them. Now some of those who read what I have just said may declare that it was a monstrous scandal and typical of the era that poor men should be reduced to such an ignominious way of earning their bread. So let me say here and now that among my first impressions of London were the notice-boards invariably nailed to the hoardings where building was being done. These bore two words – HANDS WANTED.

"Then fogs. When I was of tender years, the London fogs really were fogs. I've never seen fogs like those we used to have before the first war. As a child, I thought they were marvellous; and, as nobody seemed to be in a hurry in those days, I don't think people minded them so much as they do today. I remember the link-boys, with their torches or flares, guiding carriages home: and hundreds of people walked, because it seemed quicker and safer than going by cab or by bus. I remember hearing an old fellow who lived in Kensington relate that he had walked from Hyde Park Corner to High Street Kensington, holding his stick against the park railings all the way, because he feared that if once he lost them he might not find them again. How he got through Knightsbridge, I can't remember. All traffic, of course, proceeded at a walk. Years later, I remember crossing Shaftesbury Avenue, only to discover, after several minutes of bewilderment, that I hadn't crossed it at all, but was on a large island in the middle of the street. By the time I had found that out, I no longer knew in which direction lay the pavement from which I had come. So far as I could make out I had the island to myself; but if there had been anyone to ask, they wouldn't have known which side of the street was which. So I chanced it – and made the wrong choice… I spent about half an hour in that blasted street.

"And now to return to my childhood. One of the most exciting sounds was that of a fire-engine's bell. No matter how heavy the traffic or crowded the thoroughfare, the press of vehicles seemed to shrink. With one accord, carriages, cabs, buses, all got to the side of the street – somehow, anyhow, in any order, leaving a clear run for the fire-engine. And then this came by – a most inspiring sight. The greys – they usually seemed to be greys – at full gallop, and the brass-helmeted firemen clinging to the rails, with one of them ringing the bell like fury, and the driver leaning forward with a rein in either hand. And then at once the river of traffic seemed to re-enter its bed, and everything was as before. I never saw the Tooley Street fire, but I was about eight when it occurred and I remember the sensation it caused. The wharves and warehouses burned for twenty days.

"Then crossing-sweepers. These certainly plied their trade up to the first great war. Dickens has labelled them for all time: but, as a matter of hard fact, they were a cheerful, prosperous crowd – so far as I saw. They did a most excellent job and I very much doubt if they would have exchanged their work for any other. One got to know them and was always happy to give them a trifle for the clean lane they kept swept from pavement to pavement, across a side-street. They must have earned good money, for very few passengers failed to give them something."

"I remember the fellow," said I, "at Bennet Street. A cheerful bloke, with one leg."

"I remember him well," said Berry. "That was a very good pitch. Taking it at its lowest, I should say that he made between two and three hundred a year."

"You amaze me," said Daphne.

"I'm sure he must have." said I. "Not every pitch was so good; and not every crossing-sweeper was so civil and cheerful. I think most people always kept some pence in the ticket-pocket of their overcoat for the crossing-sweepers, but if I'd run out and began to feel in my trousers' pocket, he'd always stop me. 'That's all right, sir, thank you. Next time.' Well, that made you want to give him half a crown. But taking them by and large, I should say that the crossing-sweeper was more than content with his lot."

"Cries of London," said Jonah.

Berry raised his eyebrows.

"I can only remember two – hearing them used, I mean. *Milk below* – which we must all remember – and *Knives, Scissors to grind*. I know people say they remember *Sweet Lavender* and others: but I don't. Still, there was the muffin-man, always very correct – with his bell and his tray on his head; and, of course, the lamp-lighter, who certainly did walk very fast and so justified the saying. I confess I regret their passing, for both belonged to a contented and comfortable age.

"The old 'Underground' was awful, for locomotives were used. These continually vomited clouds of most filthy smoke of which, unless their windows were kept shut, the compartments of the coaches were necessarily full. And when windows were shut in hot weather, you damned near died. But people endured it, because they could do nothing else. You see, the tunnels were very low and there were many trains. When you were standing on a platform, waiting for a train, smoke was continually billowing out of the tunnels on either side.

"I can't honestly say I remember Astley's Circus in Westminster Bridge Road, but I know that when I was very small I made one of a distinguished audience. On that occasion, as part of the entertainment, *Red Riding Hood* was presented. If those in charge of me may be believed, my wrath and indignation were deeply provoked by the sinister appearance of the wolf, and, to the delight of the house and the performers, I rose to my small feet and called upon the beast to withdraw. Unhappily, I was not yet able to pronounce the consonant 'g', so my roars of 'Do away' aroused more sympathetic amusement than anything else."

"How sweet," said Jill.

Berry shrugged his shoulders.

"Naturally," he said. "I was a most charming child. And talking of circuses, Piccadilly Circus was always known as Regent Circus in the old days. I mean, that was – and still is, I believe – its true name. I remember the Lowther Arcade: that was in the Strand: it was a paradise for children, for it was full of toy-shops. The volume of traffic in the streets was always very great; but its sound in the old days was not unpleasant to the ear, for it roared as gently as Bottom's sucking-dove. Only in Piccadilly or Regent Circus do I remember any setts: and there, between the iron tyres and shoes, and the uneven granite, the uproar was shattering. There were no doubt many streets still paved with setts, particularly in the City, but, when I first visited London, I don't suppose I used them.

"I don't seem to be able to remember anything more which belonged to London alone; but I can speak generally about one thing, and that is the wearing of mourning. There is no doubt that in this respect we have improved a great deal in the last sixty or seventy years.

"Never, since mediaeval times, have we been as bad as the French: but when I was a child we did carry the display of mourning too far. The funeral was really dreadful, but the aftermath was unnecessarily painful. Six months after his loss, I've seen a man with so deep a band on his hat that you could hardly see the silk."

"I don't understand," said Jill.

"Well, in those days in London everyone always wore a silk top-hat – I mean, every day. The same headgear was worn to Church in the country on Sundays – always: and in many country towns – every day. Now when the hat was sold to you, it always had a very narrow silk band round it just above the brim: but that didn't look at all smart, so you always had a cloth or, really, a mourning band put on it, instead. I should say that that was about an inch and a half in depth. And that gave the hat an air. It set it off, as it does a grey top hat. But if you went into mourning, you had a deeper band put on in its place. Two and a half and three-inch bands were quite common: but, as I say, I have often seen a cloth band so deep that only an inch of the silk crown appeared above it. That was the mourning worn by a bereaved husband sixty years ago – with unrelieved black suits for months on end. I've worn dress trousers at a funeral myself – and not that of a relative. Which reminds me that I was in France when His Majesty King George the Fifth died. And the French servants were shocked when the next day I wore my ordinary country clothes and confined my mourning to the wearing of a black tie. And that was in 1936. People sometimes remark upon the fact that the country women in France are always dressed in black. The reason for that is that they are virtually never out of mourning. And so it's no good buying coloured frocks. A parent dies – that means unrelieved black for a year: before the year's out, an uncle dies – that means unrelieved black for six months: before that time is up, a grandmother dies... And so on. That is why the French peasant is always clad in black."

"Weepers," said Jonah.

"I was spared them," said Berry. "I think they must have gone out just before I was born, or very soon after. I never saw them, anyway."

"What were weepers?" said Jill.

"They were broad crape scarves – oh, about five feet long. They were worn only at the funeral. They were wound round the top-hat once and loosely knotted at the back: their ends hung down the man's back. A shocking sight. If the French affected the top hat, they'd be wearing them to this day. As I've said, they're much worse than us. I remember once, when I was in Paris, seeing The Madeleine hung in black cloth. When you entered the famous church, except for the roof and the pavement, you couldn't see any stone. It was completely lined with black cloth.

"To return for a moment to the top-hat – there was much to be said for this headgear. It was becoming and it was a great protection to the head, which is why, of course, it is worn in the hunting-field. Then again you could pray into it."

"What ever d'you mean?" said Daphne.

"Praying into the hat was an admirable fashion, now gone by the board. I have seen it done. I have seen an old gentleman follow his wife into Church: when they had entered their pew, she fell on her knees to pray, but he stood erect by her side, with his top hat up to his face, praying into it."

"Is that really true?" said Jill.

"Certainly," said Berry. "It was an old Admiral that I remember. I think his name was Burdett. He always did it – and did it very well. It used to fascinate me. About 1889, when I was five years old."

Jill looked at me.

"You put it into *The Stolen March*," she said.

"I did," said I. "At *The Peck of Pepper*, Snuffle prays into his hat."

"And I never knew that it was really done."

"I don't suppose, my sweet, that one in a thousand readers did. But it was an old English custom: and if you remember, they were very old-fashioned in 'The Pail'."

Jonah addressed himself to Berry.

"Try and think of some more. I love these old-fashioned ways."

Berry raised his eyebrows.

"At the moment, I can't remember anything else. What about Boy?"

I shook my head.

"But there is," I said. "one thing which I seldom see referred to, and that is the immense change in the lighting of private houses. When you and I were children Cholmondeley Street and White Ladies were lighted by candles and lamps. (In cities and towns you could have gas, but I don't think we did.) It seems strange to think of a lady of fashion dressing for dinner by the light of half a dozen candles. But so she did – and never gave the matter a thought. Nobody found the system inconvenient, because nobody had ever known anything else. Yet, today, if the light fails, the household is sunk."

"I agree," said Berry. "The change was fantastic. It was more than a change: it was a transformation. The private house was transformed, when electric light came in."

"Ices at Gunter's?" said Jonah.

"I know what you mean," said Berry, "but I can't remember it."

"What does he mean?" said Jill.

"In the old days, my sweet – in the seventies and eighties, I mean, it was the fashion in the summer to drive in the Park – Hyde Park, in the afternoon. That fashion prevailed till at least 1910. But in the old days, if the weather was hot, after a drive the coachman would be told to proceed to Gunter's in Berkeley Square. There he would berth the carriage as close to Gunter's as was convenient under the trees and a waitress from Gunter's would bring his ladies ices which they devoured where they were. I always think it must have been a pretty picture: all the fine equipages, the attractive surroundings, the bright sunshine and the frocks and parasols, the grooms standing to their horses and the waitresses flitting to and fro." He sighed. "You can't get away from the fact that the most beautiful Rolls cannot compare with a handsome barouche or landau and a pair of well-matched, good-looking horses. That was a sight for sore eyes. And there's another thing I never saw, but which constantly happened in London when I was very young. That was Her Majesty Queen Victoria driving down Rotten Row. Hers was, of course, the only carriage permitted to use it."

"Didn't she have postilions?"

"Indeed, she did. Four horses, two outriders in front and two grooms behind, and an equerry riding on either side. And her people loved it. That was always her way in London, if ever she wished to go out. Myself, I think it was very right and proper, in those great days."

*

"The price of the novel," said Jonah.

I shook my head.

"Prohibitive," I said, "is the only word. Before the first war the price of a new novel, whether it was written by Kipling or written by me, was four and six. Between the wars the price was seven and six. Today it is fifteen shillings. So much for the new novel. As for what is called the Library edition – that is to say, reprints of the original in a cheaper form – I've watched the price from three and six in 1944 to eight and six in 1956.

"Well, people can't afford to pay such prices for fiction. That's why my books will very shortly be published in paper-backed form."

"No!" cried everyone.

"It's a fact. I never thought I should see it, but it's a fact. They'll be well turned out, you know. Nice print and the rest. And that will bring them within the reach of the very many people who simply cannot afford eight and sixpence today."

"But this book – "

"Oh, no. Only such books as appear in the Library edition will be published as paper-backs. And the Library edition will always be obtainable. But here is a prophecy. It's my belief that within a very few years, even new novels will cease to be published in cloth."

"As in France?" said Daphne.

"Yes. Of course they'll be better turned out. Larger print, better paper, nicer covers. And they will cost more – perhaps about seven and six. But, if things go on as they have, I'm sure it'll come."

"All your books are in print?"

"Oh, yes. Owing to a shortage of paper, I think one or two ran out just after the war. But only for two or three months. But thousands of people can't afford them today – not even some libraries. Only the other day I got a letter from a fan, telling me of a retired Colonel who had been advised to read my books. So off he went to a public library."

"Oh dear," said Jill.

"Yes, my darling, it hurts. A distinguished soldier couldn't afford eight and six. And when he got to the library all my books were out, except a very worn copy of RED IN THE MORNING – and that was due to be rebound, but not replaced. You see, the library couldn't afford eight and six, either."

"Heart-breaking," said Daphne.

"Yes," I said, "it's tragic. I don't say my books are any good, but they take people out of themselves. Some of my books make them laugh. And they can be re-read. But thousands of people can't read them, because of their price.

"So the paper-backed edition will do something: at least, I hope it will. Mark you, it's not all philanthropy. We're out to maintain the sales as best we can."

"My memory," said Berry, "is growing more and more capricious. I can only suppose it's old age. Still, I've just remembered one thing that I've always meant to ask you. The incomparable Fowler of *Modern English Usage*. When did he die?"

"In 1933, at the age of seventy-four." I hesitated. " 'There was a man.' Despite his wonderful contribution to English Literature – for he also wrote *The King's English* and *The Concise Oxford Dictionary*, a truly brilliant achievement – he lived and died a very, very poor man. So poor that his life was tragic; but he refused to see it that way. Though he couldn't afford many of what most people would consider the necessaries of life, he was always cheerful and glad to be alive.

"When the first great war broke out, he was fifty-five. He enlisted instantly, and before October was old he was not only

185

out in France, but in the front line. There he presently attracted the attention of some senior officer, who gave orders that he was to leave the line and stay with the transport. A day or two later he was back in the trenches again. Once more he was discovered; and this time he was transferred to a labour battalion which was miles behind the lines. He fought to get back to the trenches, but all in vain. So at last he wrote in and said that he had enlisted to kill Germans, but that if all they were going to let him do was to make roads, he felt that he had better return to his work as a lexicographer. Accordingly, he was discharged. But you've got to hand it to Fowler – at fifty-five."

"A lion-heart," said Berry, "that deserved the Order of Merit, if ever a man did."

"I couldn't agree with you more. But I don't think he got as much as an MBE."

"I think, when he died," said Jill quietly, "he was given the GFS."

We all looked at her.

"What's the GFS, darling?" said Daphne.

"It's not given on earth," said Jill. "It's always pos – , pos – What's the word I want, Boy?"

"Posthumous?" I said.

"That's right. Posthumous. 'Well done, good and faithful servant'."

There was a little silence. Then –

"Good for you, darling," said Berry, uncertainly.

*

"Jewellery," said Daphne

"Ah," said Berry. "A fascinating theme. Reminiscent of *Safe Custody* and *Cost Price*." He looked at me. "Your descriptions of the jewels were superb. I admit that they carried me away. But when I came down to earth, I found myself gasping at my credulity. I could just swallow the dimple – a very charming conceit: but the diamond head of Hermes was rather hard to digest. You did spread yourself rather, you know. I confess that I wallowed in the contemplation of such magnificence: and, with the exception of the head of Hermes, given the stone and the craftsmen, the thing was possible. And you were very cunning. 'Pope Alexander the Sixth just swept the board. By hook or by crook he garnered what sculptured jewels there were.' That silenced criticism."

"I loved it," said Jill. "And nobody said he was wrong."

"They couldn't," said Berry. "Because he might have been right. But that's not the only reason. In fact the main reason was because the ignorance of the average English man and woman about jewels is quite remarkable. And they are such lovely things.

"And when I say ignorance, I mean it. The Frenchwoman knows to a franc the value of the jewels which she wears. The American woman runs her pretty close. But very few Englishwomen have any idea at all of the value of the jewels they possess. Now that's a very attractive quality: but in these unhappy days I venture to think it a mistake. For jewels are valuable, and times are hard.

"Often enough, it's like this. A woman inherits a ring which she has always admired. She values it for its associations. And she thinks – is perfectly sure that it's a very good ring. But that is the sum of her knowledge. Possibly, that is enough. And yet, I think it's a pity that she shouldn't know rather more of the stones which she likes so much, which she is so pleased to wear."

"But how can she do that?" said Daphne.

"Well," said Berry, "her best way would be to buy this book. Another way would be to ask a reputable jeweller to value the jewel for insurance and to give her a signed valuation. But then she'd only know its value. Whereas if she were to read what I am about to say…

"There are only four precious stones – the diamond, the emerald, the ruby and the sapphire. Others, such as the opal, garnet and amethyst are near-precious. And others are semi-precious, such as the topaz and aquamarine. Not everyone will agree with that classification: but I think it's accurate today. Before the first war, the stones I have called near-precious were called semi-precious stones. But, in all that I say this evening I'm dealing with precious stones.

"First, as regards their shape...

"The oldest style of cutting is the Cabochon style: that is to say the stone is so cut that it stands up out of its setting in the shape of a polished hump. I can't believe that a diamond so cut could be attractive; but emeralds, rubies and sapphires are sold *en cabochon* today. (In the very old days garnets were almost invariably cut like that, and the red garnet, so cut, was known for years as a carbuncle; from which, of course, the affliction takes its name.) Myself, I admire them greatly. One of my earliest recollections is that of an old lady one of whose rings was a star-sapphire *en cabochon*: she would lay her fingers in mine and tell me to find the star, for you couldn't see it from every angle; and I would peer until I could see it – a lovely sight. It was a flaw, of course, and I don't suppose the stone was particularly valuable: but it gave me infinite pleasure, as it did her.

"Then came the Table style of cutting. This was very unenterprising and did nothing to show off the stones.

"Then came the Rose style of Cutting. This still survives in the case of very small diamonds which are of little value. Indeed, they are always known as Rose diamonds.

"Finally came the Brilliant style of cutting, which truly deserves its name. This rapidly became so general that, as we all know, the word 'brilliant' is often used as a synonym for a diamond today. It displays a stone – particularly a diamond – as can no other style; and quite five-sixths of all precious stones are now so cut.

"Still, there is now the Step style of cutting, which we all know, for which I have never cared. It's more often used in the case of coloured stones than that of diamonds. Flat top, square or oblong. When large and square, sometimes vulgarly compared to a postage stamp.

"So much for the different styles of cutting. Now for the size and weight...

"An easy thing to remember is that a brilliant-cut diamond, weighing ten carats, is almost exactly the size of a threepenny bit. (It looks considerably larger, but that is its actual size.) The trouble is that you very rarely see a diamond as large as that. It is, in fact, enormous and, if a fine stone, of immense value. So far as I can remember, I've only been able to consider one once: and that was in the window of Van Cleef and Arples' shop in the *Place Vendôme*. It really was a most magnificent sight. Still, if you bear in mind that a threepenny bit means ten carats, it does give you something to go on. A stone of five carats makes a superb solitaire. In fact, solitaires of one or two carats are more usually seen today."

I feel that perhaps I should insist that the Brilliant style of cutting makes a stone look larger than it is, and that a stone of five carats looks just about as large as a threepenny bit and a stone of ten carats much larger. It isn't really; but it looks as if it was. So if you see a stone which you are ready to swear is the size of a threepenny bit, its weight is probably five carats. And that in all conscience is rare enough today."

"What is a carat?" said Jill.

"Well, the ancients used to weigh precious stones against seeds; and that, I believe, is the origin of the word. A carat's about the weight of a grain of corn.

"For many years the diamond has taken pride of place. Myself, I think that's as it should be. A white or blue-white diamond is, to my mind, incomparable: but the slightest tinge of yellow will spoil the stone. Its value is determined by its colour and its size. Such value rises very steeply indeed. I mean, if you have two stones of equal quality – one weighing one carat and the other two carats, the second may be worth twenty times as much as the first.

"Next, I think, comes the emerald – a lovely stone. But its colour must be deep and rich. Flawless emeralds are rare.

"Then comes the ruby. The Burmese or 'pigeon's blood' ruby is the best. A very beautiful stone: but really large ones are rare.

"And then the sapphire, which can be very lovely, but is, I believe, difficult so to set that the stone looks its best. Myself, I prefer the dark sapphire; but the light are popular. Like emeralds, sapphires are very often flawed."

"Imitations," said Jonah.

"The coloured precious stone can be imitated with success. The imitation ruby is, I believe, the easiest to produce, and the emerald the most difficult. I know that before the first war thousands of imitation rubies were shipped from England to the East, where they were sold to eager tourists as the real thing. But to imitate the diamond with success is quite impossible. A very little practice or comparison of the diamond with paste will enable anyone to tell the real from the false almost at a glance." He hesitated. "Here perhaps I may say that some ladies who possess and wear fine jewels never seem to think about keeping them clean. Indeed, I have seen a diamond necklace so dirty that, if I hadn't known it was real, I might have been uncertain. Jewels, like everything else, get dirty. But all that is needed to clean them are a little surgical spirit, a very fine soft brush and a little cedar-wood dust. As for settings, platinum is now very expensive, but is always worth paying for. There is nothing to compare with it."

"You've said nothing of pearls," said Jill, pouting.

(By Piers' expressed desire, my wife was to hold and to wear the famous Padua pearls for so long as she lived.)

"My sweet, they are not precious stones. They stand entirely alone. They are not comparable with other jewellery. And a glorious rope like yours will diminish anything. There is a purity

– a refinement about pearls, with which no stone can compete. At least, that's my idea."

"Imitation pearls," said Jonah.

"Easy," said Berry, "as we have reason to know. I mean, to tell at a glance is very difficult. And no one on earth – not even the finest expert – can tell you which is a natural and which a cultured pearl. The only thing to do is to have the necklace X-rayed.

"When the cultured pearl really got going, after the first great war, the market value of the ordinary true pearl necklace came down with a run. Since then, it has climbed again, though I really don't know why.

"To go back to where I began...

"I remember an instance of natural ignorance." He looked at Daphne. "D'you remember Lady Bagot?"

"Very faintly," said my sister. "She must have died about 1906."

"In 1905," said Berry. "And she had named me as one of her executors. She had little jewellery of her own: the Bagot sapphires, of course, were family jewels. What she had, she left to Derry. I had to see it, of course. There was a nice pearl necklet, which Sir Anthony had valued at eighty pounds.

"I remember that I looked at Derry, who was showing me the stuff.

" 'Where d'you get that figure from?' I said.

" 'That's what they're insured for,' he said.

" 'Good enough,' I said.

"So it was – for probate.

"That figure was duly accepted and the Will was presently proved.

"Then I advised Derry to go to —'s and ask them to value that necklet. 'Don't say anything. Just ask for a valuation.'

"He took my advice.

"—'s valued that necklet at more than nine hundred pounds.

"So you see…I'm perfectly sure there are hundreds of elderly people in England today, whose jewellery is worth a great deal more than they think. If they were to take it to a first-class London jeweller and ask him to value it 'for insurance', they would get a true idea of what it was worth. And then, if they wanted to sell it, they wouldn't be done down. But I may be imagining things."

"I don't think you are," said Daphne. "But you haven't said how they should sell them. That's what most people don't know."

"Well, anything that is valued at over fifty pounds can quite well be sold at Christie's. The commission they charge is not high; and as it's an open market, nobody can be done down. If it's valued at less than fifty, they can choose a smaller firm. But they should never sell except in an open market; for a jeweller, as he would put it, 'has got to live'. Yes, but you've got to live too, haven't you? And seventy pounds goes further than forty-five."

*

Berry looked at me.

"Have you thought of a title yet?"

"For this book of ours? Not yet. It presents difficulty – as our last one did."

"The title must be striking," said Berry. "What about *The Rising Gorge*?"

Jonah and I were laughing, but Daphne and Jill, who were outraged, protested violently.

As the explosion died down –

"That's a good selling title," said Berry. "Right out of the ruck."

"Don't be absurd," said Daphne. "Fancy going into a bookshop and asking for *The Rising Gorge*…"

"It's certainly arresting," I said, "but I fear it would be asking for trouble. The reviewers would simply eat it. I mean, we might as well call the book *Stinking Fish* and have done with it."

"That," said Berry, "would be vulgar. Now *The Rising Gorge* – "

"There's nothing doing," I said. "You must have another think."

"Well whatever we choose has got to arrest and invite. What about *The Capricious Toadstool*? Or *What the Sundial Saw*?"

Jill put a hand to her head.

"But – but what do they mean?" she said.

"There you are," said Berry. "You buy the book to find out."

"But you won't find out even then."

"That doesn't matter," said Berry. "You've bought the book."

"I'm sorry," I said, laughing, "but the prospect of receiving about five hundred letters all asking me to justify the title is too dreadful. If I'm to buy trouble, it's got to be worthwhile."

"The trouble with you," said Berry, "is that you're too old-fashioned. If only you'd move with the times, we should call the book *The Careless Nunnery* and sell about two hundred thousand before people knew where they were."

Even Daphne went down before that.

When order had been restored –

"As an old-fashioned author," I said, "I think we ought to suggest that this book is what it is – that is to say, a sort or kind of sequel to *As Berry and I Were Saying*. I mean, one must be fair. I don't want people to buy it in the belief that it is, say, a romance. Which reminds me that one fellow who'd read *As Berry and I Were Saying* wrote and said that he had enjoyed it very much but that the title had suggested that it was 'a Berry book', and that he was surprised that I should have yielded to the temptation to swell its sales in such a questionable way."

"He *didn't*!" – incredulously, and Daphne and Jill cried out.

"He did indeed," I said.

"Whatever did you reply?"

"I said I was surprised, too. For I'd had thousands of letters in my time, but that his was the first to accuse me of attempting to obtain money by false pretences."

"Very mild," said Jonah. "As a matter of fact, that was a very good title. And your note on the back of the cover made everything plain."

"I agree. But you see how very careful one has to be."

"I know," said Jill, bubbling. "I know. *B-Berry and I Look Back*."

"Very good," said everyone.

All things considered, I don't think it is too bad.

*

"Oh, and here's another thing," said Berry. "More than once I've seen it stated – possibly by way of being humorous – that if ever an author is particularly proud of something which he has written, he may be sure that it is bad and will be well advised to strike it out or tear it up. Do you endorse that statement?"

"Certainly not as it stands. Let me demolish it in a sentence. Don't you think Kipling was proud of *The Recessional*?"

"Thank you," said Berry. "If that isn't an answer, I don't know what is."

"Was he to tear that up, because he was pleased with it? Don't you think Paul Lamerie was pleased with some of his lovely salvers? Because he was proud of them, was he to cast them into the melting-pot? No. It all depends on what is meant by the word 'author'. Anyone who writes a book is an author. Well, there are all sorts of authors. Many never have their work published. Many ought not to have had their work published."

"There," said Berry, "I cordially agree."

"Some show signs of promise – sometimes great promise, but need experience. And some have learned by experience and have become craftsmen."

"Few enough today," said Jonah.

"Yes, I'm afraid that's true. Well, to some of those in the first three classes of authors, the statement Berry's seen may apply. I can't be sure. There's certainly more than one passage in my earlier books that I don't think much of today. But I don't remember that I was particularly proud of them. I thought they were all right, or I shouldn't have let them stand. But I don't think I was ever proud of anything I had written, until I became a craftsman."

"And then you were?"

"And then I was. And I say so without any shame. Wasn't the experienced silversmith proud of the tankard he'd made? He kept his pride to himself, as a craftsman does; but, because he knew it was good, it warmed his heart. And don't forget – he's the best judge. He knows if his tankard's a good one, and just how good it is. But where the embryo author is concerned, there may be something in the statement which Berry has read."

"But you can't bear it out?"

I shook my head.

"I can remember being pleased with – I don't say 'proud of' – two or three passages I wrote thirty-six years ago: but I couldn't better them today."

"Well, I'm much obliged," said Berry. "I always felt that the statement was too facile, too facetious and too contrary. You know. After Bernard Shaw."

"Your *bête noire*."

"I'm afraid so. I shall always consider him a most over-rated man. Now be honest."

"I'm bound to admit," I said, "that in my humble opinion, not much of his work will live."

"Meiosis," said Berry, "Shaw was a charlatan."

I raised my eyebrows.

"I don't think you can say that. But he got away with a lot, because, as he would have said, most people are fools."

"I'm a heretic," said Berry. "And a lot I care. Barrie was over-rated."

"I'm inclined to think he was. He was terribly good, Barrie. In a different class to Shaw. But he was not always as good as he was made out to be."

"And Hardy?"

"Hardy achieved greatness. If today some of his work seems dull, that is the fault of those who find it so; for they are too impatient to give such passages the consideration they deserve. And no one has ever approached Hardy at his best – in his own line."

"And Conrad?"

"Conrad was a wonderful writer. Remember that he was a Pole and that he learned his English before the mast. But I am bound to confess that some of his work is dull. *Typhoon*, on the other hand, will see out time. I don't believe anyone else could ever have written such a book. It stands entirely alone. And *The Mirror of the Sea* is incomparable."

"Kipling?"

"Even Homer nods. Some of his last work was not so good. To the average man some of *Debits and Credits* and *Limits and Renewals* is virtually unintelligible. I'm being terribly outspoken; but that is the plain truth. I believe Kipling went on writing after he should have stopped, because writing was his great resource: because, once in his study, he could forget an unkind world and live in one of his own. I may be mistaken, but I don't believe I am. *Thy Servant a Dog* – his last book but one – may seem to prove me wrong, but that's rather in a class by itself and I'm inclined to think that it had been in his mind for years. But this is all surmise, and I may be entirely wrong. But he did drive his wonderful brain extremely hard for more than fifty years."

*

The reading of 'the news' ended, and Jill turned the wireless off. Then she resumed her seat and picked up the piece of linen from which she was drawing some threads.

Nobody said anything. There was really nothing to be said.

Presently Berry looked round.

Then –

"When," he said, "wherever you look, what are called 'world affairs' are not so much disturbing to the mind as devastating to the senses, I find it a relief to consider some thing or some habit or manner which belonged to happier days. The pictures which such things conjure up can be very restful and the contemplation which they inspire can minister to the mind."

"I quite agree," said Jonah. "What, er, relic have you in mind tonight?"

"Well," said Berry, "I was thinking of that curious appendage – that *vade-mecum* of every English schoolboy for more than two hundred years, the hornbook.

"Now the hornbook has much to commend it. In the first place, it was essentially English: in the second place, it was a very simple and sensible piece of work: in the third place, it must be the only gadget which served its purpose so well that nobody sought to improve it in all its very long life. But what I shall always find remarkable is that, though hundreds of thousands of hornbooks were made and distributed between about 1570 and 1800, hardly any have survived. Yet it was by no means fragile: indeed, it was made for hard wear. Such hornbooks as have survived are naturally very much prized. There's one in The Bodleian Library."

I nodded.

"Their almost complete disappearance is very strange and rather pitiful. That Shakespeare learned to read from his hornbook, there can be no doubt."

"Dare I ask," said Daphne, "what a hornbook was?"

"It was a primer," said Berry: "an elementary school-book for teaching children to read. But, although it was called a hornbook, it wasn't a book. It was a small sheet of stout paper or parchment, stuck on to a bat."

"A bat?" cried Jill.

"Well, it was almost exactly like those things, which were sold in pairs, that pats of butter used to be made with."

"We used to call them the butter-pats," said Daphne. "Like table-tennis bats, only oblong instead of round. And, of course, they were grooved."

"Well, the hornbook was rather bigger, but it was the same shape. And the paper or parchment was stuck on to the blade. On the paper were written or printed the alphabet in small letters and capitals, the vowels, a few simple combinations of letters, the Invocation of the Trinity (which is always used today by a priest before his sermon), and, finally The Lord's Prayer. To preserve the paper, a framed sheet of transparent horn was laid over it and the frame was fastened to the bat with studs. And the horn, of course, gave it its name.

"Now every English school-boy had his own hornbook, which he always took with him to and from school. And from that, he learned to read for more than two centuries. As far as I know, its text was never altered and I am quite sure that it could not have been improved. For what was more proper than that the first thing the child learned to read should be The Lord's Prayer?"

"If," said Jonah, "they learned it properly, as I've no doubt they did, they could give points to some clerks in holy orders today. I'm tired of hearing 'who art' for 'which art' and 'on earth' for 'in earth'.

"Am I with you?" said Berry. "I find such 'improvements' offensive beyond belief. But let it go.

"The hornbook was a great institution. It was thanks to the hornbook that one summer's day Samuel Pepys found a little child reading the Bible to an old shepherd whilst he was watching his sheep."

"What a charming picture," said Daphne.

"So Pepys found it, my darling, three hundred years ago."

"When you say 'horn'," said Jill…

"I mean horn," said Berry. "The horns of animals. When cattle were slaughtered, the horns and hooves were sold to a bloke called a horner, who melted them down and produced sheets of horn of various thicknesses. Before glass came into England, windows were made of horn. And lanterns were furnished with horn to protect the candle's flame. People even wore horn spectacles, though whether these helped their eyes, I beg leave to doubt.

"Well, there we are. The hornbook had a great run. It was the urchin's text-book from the time of Elizabeth to that of George the Third. It is part of the history of England. And it was so English, so homely and so personal that nothing that I can think of recalls for me more vividly those old and handsome days. Little boys used it, hit one another over the head with it and lost it while Naseby was being fought: mothers found it and washed it and dried it during the battle of the Nile: fathers, who could not read, stared with awe at its symbols on the days on which the Spanish Armada was smashed. Human nature being what it is, perhaps I should value it less if more had survived."

"Well, I did enjoy that," said Daphne.

"My sweet, you're easy to please."

"Not at all. I found it most refreshing."

"I loved it," said Jill. "And I'll bet no other country can show a thing like that."

"Only the English," said Berry, "could have produced and adopted so precious a document. 'Train up a child,' you know."

*

"If," I said, "I may comment upon the excellent monograph on hornbooks which you gave us last night, I can't help feeling that the 'horn spectacles' to which you referred must have been glasses framed in horn. I mean, the magnifying-glass was known in the thirteenth century, and we do speak of 'steel spectacles', when we are referring to lenses framed in steel. Mark you, I'm by no means sure that you're not right. But Pepys tells us that he was using green spectacles in the hope of helping his eyes. Well, they were clearly of glass, and, on reflection, I think it quite likely that they were framed in horn."

"What about silver?" said Jonah.

"I admit that that's equally likely. But, looking the facts in the face, surely lenses of horn could only embarrass the eyes. And glass was made in England in the sixteenth century – and imported much earlier. However, I'm only groping."

"I think," said Berry, "that you must be right. I mean, I know that the world is much more than half full of fools, but that anyone who felt that his eyes required assistance should deliberately purchase and employ spectacles whose lenses were made of horn is almost incredible. I mean, such behaviour belongs to *The Stolen March*. *Pouch* would never have been without them."

"Well, that's what gets me," I said, laughing. "All the same, it is curious that, after rejecting horn frames in favour of gold or silver or steel, we should have returned to horn, in the shape of tortoise-shell."

The thing was too hard for us, and we left it there.

*

"You say," said Berry, "you allege that the cask of your legal memories has run dry. I hope and believe you're wrong. Any way, I feel that if we were to ask you some questions relating to legal affairs, one or more questions might get the cask going again."

"I agree," said Jonah. "Let Daphne begin."

"There's one thing," said my sister, "I've always wanted to know. Supposing an engagement is broken off: in the ordinary

way, the girl returns the ring. Supposing she doesn't return it...
Can the man demand it by law?"

"I believe the answer is that he can, if it was she that broke
the engagement off. But not otherwise."

"How would he proceed?"

"He would bring an action for recovery – I think that's right."

"Supposing he broke it off, but the ring was an heirloom."

"I don't know what the procedure would be in such a case.
The man would have to offer to buy it back; and if she refused
to sell, then he'd have to take her to court in some other way.
Possession's nine points of the law, but if the compensation was
fair, I think he'd find some way of making her give it back."

"Breach of promise," said Berry. "Were you ever concerned
in such a case?"

"I'm glad to say that I wasn't."

"Why d'you say 'glad'?"

"Oh, I don't know. But such actions have been brought by
way of blackmail. I mentioned one in *As Berry and I Were
Saying*. The most impudent one I remember was brought by a
beautiful, but notorious divorcée. Unhappily for her, she was
unable to deny that at the time at which the promise was made
the man in question was married to somebody else. Which
meant, of course, that the promise was bad in law."

"Libel," said Jonah. "If a man thinks that he has been libelled,
he can bring an action against the culprit, can't he? Very well.
But in certain cases, he can prosecute instead. Am I right?"

"Yes, indeed," I said. "I can't remember off-hand in what
cases he can prosecute: but I can tell you this – that to an action
for libel, truth is an absolute defence: but to a prosecution for
libel, it is not. That, I believe, is the origin of the cryptic saying,
'The greater the truth, the greater the libel.'"

"Sorry," said Daphne, "but I can't follow that."

"I shouldn't think anyone could," said Berry. "And if that's
the sort of wash you talked when you were up on your feet, I

don't wonder you never got a red bag. A brown-paper one full of gooseberries would have been more appropriate."

"You wicked liar," cried Jill. "Boy never talks wash. And I'll bet you wouldn't have got a red bag. Someone might have sent you a sack."

As the laughter died down –

"Good for you, sweetheart," said Berry. "I take it all back. But the points he makes are usually very clear, and so I've got spoiled. Perhaps, if you asked him nicely, he'd give it to us with a spoon."

"It's very confusing," I said. "And that cursed motto troubled me for years."

"I'm glad to hear that," said Berry.

"Look at it this way," I said. "X writes a letter to the papers in which he declares that ten years ago Y was sent to prison for obtaining money by false pretences. Well, Y brings an action against X, claiming heavy damages. Now, if X can prove that in fact ten years ago Y *was* sent down for fraud – well, there's an end of the case. Y's action will be dismissed with costs. What Y should have done was to prosecute X. Then the fact that what X wrote was true is no defence: and unless X can satisfy the jury that it was in the public interest that Y should be exposed as an ex-convict, X will go down. One can conceive cases in which so to expose Y would have served no purpose at all and only have been a very cruel thing to do. And then the motto comes in – 'The greater (or more bitter) the truth, the greater (or more savage) the libel'. And X may well go to prison as a result."

"I'm much obliged," said Berry. "But such prosecutions are rare."

"They used to be. I do remember one. I wasn't concerned in it, but I was in court for part of the time. I was then a solicitor's pupil and, as such, as I sometimes did, I got wind of what was afoot. And when I told Muskett, he kindly gave me leave for two or three hours. I was very lucky, for the court was not at all crowded: if people had known what was going to happen, it would have been packed out."

"How did you get to hear?"

"As that of the Solicitors to the Commissioner of Police, the office was always well-informed."

"Very interesting. Please go on."

"A man called Crossland, a poet and the Editor of some highbrow periodical, had published a libel or what was alleged to be a libel on a man of whose name I can't be certain, so I'd better call him John Doe. And John Doe was prosecuting him. The trial was to take place before the Common Serjeant at the Old Bailey. But what made the case stand out – and what nobody seemed to know – was that Crossland proposed to call Lord Alfred Douglas to give evidence on his behalf.

"I don't have to tell you that Alfred Douglas was a stormy petrel. He had been a devoted friend of Oscar Wilde and had stuck to him to the end. I don't believe for one moment that he was concerned in any of Wilde's abominable practices; but he greatly admired Wilde's undoubted ability and thought him an ill-used man."

"Alfred Douglas," said Berry, "was born before his time. In those dark days decent feeling ran so high that a man who was convicted of a crime which is sometimes described as 'not to be mentioned among Christians', had to leave the country when he emerged from jail. The humblest inn would have turned him from its doors."

"Wasn't it on Douglas' account," said Jonah, "that his father, Queensberry, thrashed Wilde in St James's Street?"

"Yes. Alfred Douglas was then very young, and his father was justified. As the indirect result of that assault, Wilde's case was investigated and he was charged and sent down. But, so perverse are some natures, these things seemed only to stiffen Alfred Douglas' resolve to champion his dreadful friend. Mercifully, the latter only lived for three years after his release from jail, and those he spent abroad. But Douglas looked after him, cared for him when he was dying and stood by his grave. Always remembering that he was not in any way concerned with Wilde's misconduct – for that is my firm belief – such devotion to an outcast must command some respect; but in all the circumstances it was a most unfortunate association and Douglas, who was extremely able, not to say brilliant, was simply written off. So he ran with people like Crossland, for whom, I believe, he wrote provocative articles.

"I seem to have strayed a long way from the Old Bailey, but now I'll go back.

"All I knew of the case was that George Elliot had been briefed for the prosecution, but that when it was learned that Alfred Douglas was to be called for the defence, Marshall Hall was brought in to lead George Elliot, who was himself a 'silk'. And I thought it certain that two such powerful personalities as those of Lord Alfred and Marshall Hall would not so much clash as collide.

"My luck was in, for, when I entered the court, Lord Alfred was giving his evidence-in-chief…

"He was a handsome man and looked astonishingly young for his age. And he gave his evidence with clarity and vigour. His way was compelling and he held the Court. Bosanquet was on the Bench. He was a sound lawyer, a very good judge and a very nice man. He should have been a Justice of the Queen's Bench. As Common Sergeant, he was, to my mind, thrown away."

"Didn't he succeed Forest Fulton?"

"Yes. And that was all wrong. If he wasn't to be a High Court Judge, he should have been made Recorder, in Fulton's stead. He was a far better man. But that is the way things go.

"And now let's get back.

"Lord Alfred's evidence-in-chief was concluded, and Marshall Hall rose to cross-examine.

"You could see the two men measuring one another. Then –

" 'I think,' said Marshall Hall, 'I think that you were a friend of Oscar Wilde.'

"In a ringing voice –

" 'You know that I was,' said Douglas. 'And let me tell you this – that it was because Mr George Elliot refused to consent to question me about that association that you were hired to come here and do it.' "

"O-o-oh," said everyone.

"Yes. Talk about a broadside. Well, that was the beginning. And as Alfred Douglas began, so he went on. To say that he wiped the floor with Marshall Hall is no more than the truth. I never saw counsel so used in all my life. And this was no sucking barrister. This was Marshall Hall. Before my eyes, that famous man was reduced. Again and again Alfred Douglas hit him for six. Twice Marshall Hall turned to Bosanquet and asked for 'the protection of the Court'. And each time Bosanquet only said grimly, 'Go on'. I think he felt that the questions should not have been put and that, if the witness liked to lash out, he was not going to interfere. I may say I entirely agreed with him. George Elliot was right and Marshall Hall was wrong. More. He was extremely foolish to consent to endeavour to discredit a witness in such a way.

"After about twenty minutes, Marshall had had enough and resumed his seat. But of course the case was over. Douglas had won it hands down. No jury that ever was foaled would have found Crossland guilty after that. It's the only time I ever saw counsel drawn and quartered. And this was Marshall Hall, who knew how to brow-beat men.

"It was a most astonishing show, and most dramatic. I'm only so very sorry that I can't remember more of the questions and answers: but after fifty years, one tends to forget. But I can see the two now – Marshall Hall in his splendour (for he had a magnificent presence) leaning forward to put his question and then recoiling before Lord Alfred's riposte, and Douglas, his eyes alight, whipping out these bitter answers, always perfectly phrased and soused with contempt.

"I remember feeling very sorry for George Elliot, who looked ready to sink through the floor. And I couldn't help feeling sorry for Marshall Hall. Never was so famous a counsel so hoist with his own petard. However, there were very few there to see it.

"Whether Crossland deserved to get off, I really can't say. I have an idea that he didn't, but as I'm not quite sure what the libel was, I'd better leave it there. I don't think the result really mattered very much, for the libel was presumably true or Crossland would have been sued. And the prosecutor was a man of substance. Crossland was tall and dark and rather a strange-looking man. He could have sat down in the dock, but he never did. He stood the whole time, continually tapping his heart, as if he were afraid of its stopping. I don't think he did this for effect. I think he was genuinely nervous about his state of health. And old Bosanquet sat there like an image, as always he did."

"Douglas was certainly a loyal friend."

"He was indeed. His loyalty was unhappily misplaced. Which shows the damage that a blackguard like Wilde could do. 'The evil that men do lives after them.' I shall always believe that Lord Alfred Douglas could have had a brilliant career. He had one of the most striking personalities I've ever seen."

"Well, I'm much obliged," said Jonah. "Our idea of asking you questions has brought forth most excellent fruit. We shall have to do it again."

*

"Darling," said Daphne, "you've remembered so very well so many things: but wasn't Muriel G— mixed up in some shoplifting case?"

"Well done indeed," said I. And then, "You're perfectly right. It had gone clean out of my mind. Give me a minute or two to marshal the facts."

"When you're ready," said Jonah…

For a minute we sat in silence. Then Berry addressed himself to Daphne, speaking low.

"Who was Muriel G— ?"

"You might not remember her. She was very sweet – the only child of the L—s. Very fond of Boy, whom she'd known as a child. But happily married and ten years older than him."

"I've got her," said Berry. "Very fair and quick in the uptake. Her father was a 'back-woods' peer."

"That's right," I said. "And I've got it straight now.

"She rang me up one evening and asked if I was in court the following day. If not, would I help her out? I asked what it was she wanted. She said she wanted me to take her to Marlborough Street Police Court. 'That,' I said, 'I will never do. No Metropolitan Police Court is a fit place for you.' And then she was off.

"A friend of hers had been charged with shoplifting. And she wanted to be in court, to hold her hand. 'It's a hideous mistake, of course.'

"In the end I promised that if there was nothing in Chambers to prevent me, I would be at the court at eleven o'clock – but only on the condition that she stayed outside in her car.

" 'I promise,' she said at last. 'But come at a quarter to, and I'll put you wise.'

"There was no question of my appearing. Bodkin had been instructed for the defence. But the woman and her husband were friends of Muriel's and had turned to her in their extremity.

"Well, I arrived on time: and there the three were in her car. I was greeted and introduced. The woman was much older than Muriel – just about fifty, I'd say: but young for her age. Her husband was a soldier, retired. They were obviously well-bred people – quiet, perfectly dressed, of impeccable demeanour. The husband was a very nice-looking man. They didn't look rich. I studied them carefully. The woman was gay and seemed to regard the affair almost as a jest. 'I'm sure, Mr Pleydell, you've never been put in a cell… Then I'm one up on you. Not that the police weren't nice. They were perfectly charming to me. And they gave me such excellent tea. I was really quite sorry to leave, when they came and bailed me out.' Her husband subscribed to her mood – but I saw the strained look in his eyes.

"After a little, he and I took a short turn.

" 'Must she stand in the dock?' he said.

" 'I'm afraid she'll have to,' I said. 'But I'll have a word with the jailer, and you shall stand – not in the dock, but just by her side.'

" 'That's very good of you. Er, is Bodkin any good?'

" 'The best man you could have,' I said. 'If you had asked me who to have, I should have put him first.'

" 'He advises that she should reserve her defence and be committed for trial. Would you have said the same?'

" 'I haven't seen the papers,' I said. 'But I hope I should.'

" 'Why d'you say that?'

" 'Because Bodkin's brain is a far better brain than mine.'

"There was a little silence. Then –

" 'Things do go wrong,' he said.

" 'I'd lay you fifty to one that this one won't.'

"He stared.

" 'But you haven't seen the papers,' he said.

" 'I've seen the accused. Do as Bodkin says, and you'll find I'm right.'

"I shall always be glad to remember that he seemed more or less relieved.

"I saw the jailer, with the result that, when the case was called on, he was allowed to stand just beside the dock, with his hand on the rail. I also saw Bodkin – before the case was called on. When I told him why I was there, he gave me a whimsical look. 'We shall go for trial,' he said. 'I think even you would have given that advice.' 'As bad as that?' I said, laughing. 'You listen to the evidence,' said Bodkin.

"This was damning. Selfridge's. The woman had had a portfolio. She had been seen to pick up two baby's garments, open the portfolio and drop them in. When she was taken to a manager's room and the portfolio was opened, the garments were there. She denied all knowledge of them.

"She duly reserved her defence and was committed for trial. And when she was tried, she got off, as I knew she would. Wallace was then Chairman of the Sessions and I really don't believe he ever sent a shoplifter down.

"When it was all over, Muriel asked me to dine.

" 'What do you think?' she said.

" 'I imagine,' I said, 'she's a kleptomaniac. She's no children and, therefore, no grandchildren. The garments were useless to her. But she had an impulse to steal them; and so she did. And her husband knew she was guilty. I'll lay any money you like she'd done it before. The moment I saw his face, I knew there was something wrong. And when I heard that she was to go for trial, I knew that Bodkin knew that that was the only way to save her skin. They all get off at the Sessions. But she wouldn't have stood an earthly at Marlborough Street.'

" 'D'you know,' said Muriel, 'I did begin to wonder. She was so very bright. I mean, I should have been devastated.'

" 'Of course you would.'

" 'You think there's no doubt, Boy?'

" 'I haven't the slightest doubt that she stole the things. But in view of the things she stole, I don't think she's a shoplifter. I think she's a kleptomaniac. Have you missed anything?'

"Muriel shook her head.

" 'But I shan't have her here any more.'

" 'I'm glad of that,' I said. 'For I don't think kleptomania knows any law.'

"Well, there's the sordid story, for what it is worth. A shocking thing for a husband to have a thief for a wife. And they were – well, distinguished people. No doubt about that."

"What a terrible thing," said Daphne.

"It was indeed, my sweet. But the man was the one to be pitied. I felt damned sorry for him."

"Didn't you bring shoplifting into one of your tales?"

"Yes. Into *Period Stuff*. A girl is arrested by mistake. That can happen, of course: but I think it's rare."

"Weren't the goods being passed?"

"That's right. The girl was wearing a squirrel coat: so was 'the receiver': and the thief slipped her spoil into the girl's cuff by mistake. Fortunately a stranger was there, and he saw the whole thing."

"In such a case," said Jonah, "an action could have been brought."

"Yes. For the girl was detained. An action for false imprisonment. You may remember the manager's relief when, in response to his apology, the girl said, 'I don't think it's anyone's fault.' "

"Such actions have been brought?"

"Oh, several. And won. It's very hard lines on the stores. They lose – or used to lose – thousands of pounds a year, thanks to the activity of shoplifters. Naturally, they do what they can to catch the thieves out: but mistakes – or alleged mistakes – are easy to make. When you consider the crowds of people – all potential customers – continually on the move on every floor, to me the wonder is that more mistakes are not made.

"One such action, I remember, was brought against Selfridge's not very long after that famous store had opened its doors, while it was still the wonder of London and its name was still in everyone's mouth. A woman had been detained and was presently charged with stealing three or four of those little, fluffy chickens – toys, of course – that used to be sold."

"I used to love them," said Jill. "They really looked alive."

"So they did," said I. "Well, her defence was that she had bought the chickens off a street-vendor, before entering the store. They used to be sold in the streets by fellows with trays. The magistrate gave her the benefit of the doubt and she was discharged. Whereupon she issued a writ and claimed damages for false imprisonment and, I think, malicious prosecution.

"The case was heard by Darling J. I can't remember which way it went, though I was in court part of the time. But I do remember that when the plaintiff's counsel, who was opening her case, stated that she was taken to Marylebone or Marlborough Street, Darling looked up. Then, with the most innocent of airs, 'Isn't there a resident magistrate at Selfridge's?' he said.

"It mayn't seem very funny at this distance of time, but I can still hear the roar of delighted laughter which greeted his remark."

"I think it was brilliant," said Berry. "And very typical."

"Yes, it was typical of Darling. He had a very pretty wit."

*

"In *The Pickwick Papers*," said Berry, "one of the drawings by Phiz (whose name, I believe, was Hablot Browne) shows *Pickwick* in *Serjeant Snubbin*'s chambers. On the table there is a wig-block, and on the block there is a wig. I believe that wig-blocks have been out of fashion for years. Did ever you see one, except in a robe-maker's shop?"

"Only once. I was very young – I mean, I was still at school – when Coles Willing took me with him to Lincoln's Inn. He wanted a word with a Chancery counsel he knew – John E Harman, by name, whose son is now on the Bench. He was a first-rate lawyer and a most charming man. Coles Willing took me that I might see a barrister at work in his chambers. The fact that he knew that Harman wouldn't mind shows, I think, what a very nice fellow he was. Of course I only sat still and used my eyes. And the first thing I saw was a wig-block and, on the wig-block, a wig. I don't remember much else. I expect I looked round the room, but I always came back to the wig-block and its burden. Harman must have observed my fascination, for when the conference was over, he got up, took the wig from the block and fitted it on my head."

"How very sweet of him," said Jill.

I nodded.

"You may imagine my rapture... But that was the only wig-block I ever saw in use except, as Berry said, in a shop-window. In fact, I think the wig-box – a japanned case, always used in my time – was much better; for if the wig was left out, it got dusty."

Daphne looked up.

"Tell me, darling, have you ever regretted that, after the war, you didn't go back to the Bar?"

"Never for one moment, my sweet. Mark you, I wouldn't have missed the five years I had at the Bar for anything. I enjoyed them enormously and the experience I gained has been invaluable. But until, if at all, he becomes a big shot at the Bar, a barrister's life is seldom as good as many people believe. I think I've said that before, but here is one reason, to which I don't think I've referred, why it may not appeal to a sensitive man. And that is the everlasting competition.

"I don't mean the battles in court: they're almost always friendly and rather fun. I mean the competition in the market of the Bar. This is unavoidable, for the Bar is a personal profession. A brief is delivered at your chambers with your name on it. That means that you have been selected out of quite a number of counsel who are equally available. You can't conceal this good fortune. It's known in your chambers and your clerk mentions it to other clerks. In the end you have to advertise it by carrying your brief in your hand and, of course, appearing in court. Well, your fellows at the Bar are human and quite a lot of them feel that they ought to have had that brief and that they would have done it better than you will. As like as not, they're right: but you were selected. Sometimes the feeling is very thinly veiled. Well, you can call that the dust of the arena and say that it should be ignored. But, while I entirely agree, all

I know is that I was heartily glad to see the last of it. Of course this only happens when you're trying to build up a practice at the Bar. But that may well take ten years."

"You speak feelingly," said Jonah.

"Well, I did meet it once or twice and I found it extremely distasteful. Notably in the Crippen case. There was no question of a brief there; but to act as Travers Humphreys' junior throughout, to work on the case with him in chambers and appear with him first in the Coroner's Court, then at Bow Street and, finally, at the Old Bailey was, of course, a great privilege. And there was a great deal of feeling in his chambers about it. Still, I had come back from my holiday ten days before anyone else, and I was well down in the saddle when they did appear. Besides, it was a matter of etiquette that the 'devil' who first got his hands on the brief should see that case through. So there was nothing to be said or done – although an attempt to supplant me was actually made. But Humphreys rejected it."

"How very unpleasant," said Daphne.

"Well, there you are," I said. "When one comes up against that, one's impulse is to withdraw: but if you want to get on, you mustn't do that. I expect there are other professions which have the same disadvantage for a sensitive man: but I can't think of one – except, perhaps, the stage. A solicitor's position is quite different. He is usually a member of a firm. And in any event he doesn't have to parade the fact that he has been instructed, as the barrister must. And so there is no feeling, except perhaps in the case of rival firms in a country town.

"You mustn't think I don't know that a lot of eyebrows were raised – to put it mildly – when, as a novelist, I began to make my name: but I never saw them raised. And that is everything. The writer who keeps to himself and leads his own quiet life is very fortunate. He is competing, of course; but he doesn't meet his competitors: then again there's plenty of room for all; and because A's book is a success, it doesn't follow that B's book won't be bought. And A doesn't know how B's doing – I mean, what his income is: but at the Bar there's no such secrecy, and everyone knows very well how his fellow is getting on.

"Finally, let me say this. Remembering what a steep ladder success at the Bar is to climb, there is very little jealousy. At least, there was very little in my day. My fellows were on the whole very generous. But when you did meet it, it set your teeth on edge."

"What," said Berry, "what about promotion to the Bench?"

"You mean that one day fellow 'silks' are calling John Doe 'Johnnie' and the next day they have to call him 'My lord'?"

"That," said Berry, "is exactly what I mean."

"Well, I never moved in those circles, but it is my belief that the change in estate was perfectly accepted. After all, big men were concerned, and it would have been very bad form to have revealed any feeling they might have had. Still, there were cases in which such behaviour did them great credit, for I know of more than one appointment which was deeply resented."

"Darling," said Daphne, "I know you've had one thing in *Punch*. I think you might have had many, if you had pleased."

"I don't know about that," I said. "I'm proud to be able to say that I once contributed to *Punch* and that my contribution appeared before the first war. It was a very slight sketch. But soon after that war I offered *Punch* a very much better one – which *Punch* turned down."

"Why?" said Berry.

I shrugged my shoulders.

"The painful presumption is that *Punch* thought less of it than I did." I hesitated. "As a matter of fact, when it had been returned, I offered it to the Editor of *The Windsor Magazine*. I offered it to him with some diffidence, for I had written it for *Punch* and it wasn't the sort of contribution that a magazine prints. Still, when next I saw the Editor, he said he would be glad to use it if we could agree a fee.

" 'Well, now that you've said that,' I said, 'before we go any further, I think you ought to know that I offered this to *Punch* and they turned it down.'

"Arthur Hutchinson inclined his head.

" 'Thank you,' he said. 'But that doesn't affect me at all. May I know who turned it down?'

" 'E V Lucas,' I said. 'As of course you know, Owen Seaman is sick and Lucas is editing *Punch* until his return.'

"The Editor laughed.

" 'As well for us,' he said. 'Owen Seaman would never have turned this down. But Lucas has no sense of humour.' "

"Very interesting," said Jonah. "Did you offer *Punch* anything else?"

I shook my head.

"By that time, you see, I was writing full length books; and any short tales which I wrote I wrote with a view to their collection into a volume. But *Punch* could only use a very short sketch."

"Was *Punch* a close borough?"

"In the old days it was. That was natural enough. *Punch* had its own permanent staff; and if a paper has that, then that staff must be employed. Still, *Punch* did accept contributions if they were really worth while."

"I imagine," said Berry, "that *Punch* must have received no end of 'voluntary contributions' in its day. Most of them, of course, completely valueless."

"I imagine so, too. Which reminds me… W S Gilbert is said to have encountered Burnand, then Editor of *Punch*. 'Tell me, Burnand,' he said, 'don't you get a lot of jokes sent to the *Punch* Office?' 'Any number,' said Burnand. 'Then,' said Gilbert, 'why don't you put them in?' "

"Oh, very nice," said Jonah. "And Gilbert all over."

"And whenever I feel, as I sometimes do, that the *Punch* of today is less attractive than was the *Punch* of yesterday, I always remember Burnand's reply to someone who expressed that view. 'You know, Burnand,' said someone, '*Punch* isn't what it used to be.' Quick as a flash, 'It never was,' said Burnand."

"There's a lot in that," said Jonah.

My sister looked at me.

"Wouldn't you have liked to be on the staff of *Punch*?"

"Once upon a time, perhaps. It used to be a great honour to sit at *The Punch Table*. But it was an honour for which I could never have qualified. You see, I am not a journalist. I have never been able to write to order, as a journalist must: and to render a humorous trifle once a week without fail would have been beyond my power. I simply couldn't have done it."

"You never let *The Windsor Magazine* down."

"I know. Still, that only appeared once a month. All the same… The first chapter of *Anthony Lyveden* appeared in print before I had finished the third. When I think of that now, it makes me go hot all over. But I never thought about it then. I think the truth is that the Editor, Arthur Hutchinson, knew me better than I knew myself. Never once in our long association did he so much as hint that he would be glad to receive my next chapter or short tale. With the happy result that I never thought about writing to time, which might easily have been fatal. I owe a great deal to that good man. I often feel that I must have been a sore trial to him; for, though I didn't realize it at the time, he was as wise as I was foolish."

*

"Last night," I said, "I was speaking of competition at the Bar and of the fact that the dust of the arena is, on occasion, er, noticeable. So it is – or was. But it is right and proper to observe that many members of the Bar were very kind and helpful to younger men. Of such kindness I have, I'm glad to say, remembered a notable example which heartily deserves to be recorded – and I'm ready to lay any money that this particular story has never been told. I'm sorry to say I didn't witness what happened myself, but it was reported to me by a member of the Bar who was in court at the time.

"The Divisional Court was sitting. Danckwerts the Great had just disposed of one case. (I use the word 'dispose', for it is appropriate to the man. In the ordinary way, the Bench 'disposes' of such cases as come before it. But Danckwerts QC was the finest lawyer of Bench or Bar and he did 'dispose' of those cases in which he was engaged.) As he was due to appear in the next case but one, he did not leave the court, but sat where he was: for the Divisional Court, which consists of two Judges, deals with points of law which don't, as a rule, take long. And so it came to pass that Danckwerts was sitting in court, when a very young counsel was speaking and doing his very best: but he had a 'silk' against him and the Bench was not treating him well. He was standing just behind Danckwerts, who turned and regarded him. That probably made him more nervous, for to argue in the presence of so tremendous a personality was embarrassing. Then Danckwerts looked at an usher, and the usher came to his side. Danckwerts pointed to the shelves of Reports with which the court was lined and told the usher to bring him one of the books. The usher hastened to obey. The great lawyer opened the volume, found the case he desired, slewed himself round on his seat, handed the book to the youth and pointed to certain lines. With an apologetic look at the Bench, the young man stopped speaking and applied himself to the words... After a moment, Law Report in hand, he raised a confident face. 'If I may remind your lordships of the decision in...' *It was a case on all fours with his*. The volume was passed to the Bench, and Danckwerts sat smiling grimly, as the two Judges studied the ruling which they were bound to observe. So, thanks to that timely assistance, the young man won hands down.

"Now that was a very kind gesture, made by a giant to a pygmy, for which I can vouch. And please spare a thought for the brain that not only remembered the case, but remembered the very year in which it had been decided, and so was able to indicate the requisite volume of all those hundreds with which the court was lined."

"Magnificent," said Jonah. "Superb. What a very great lawyer he was."

"A head and shoulders," said I, "above anyone else."

"Who were the Judges who were putting it across the young counsel?"

"I've no idea. I've no doubt my informant told me, but I have forgotten now. In that respect, I was fortunate, for the Bench was almost always very kind to me. I remember one occasion when I had to do a case for the head of my chambers at very short notice in the Mayor's Court. This is a very ancient civil court and sits at Guildhall. Its procedure is peculiar, the pleadings are antique, and, as I'd never been there before, I was clean out of my depth. Talk about floundering... But Judge Rentoul was sitting. As a friend of his son, I'd more than once dined at his house and he recognized me. To my immense relief and the fury of my opponent, he took the case out of my hands, just giving me cues now and then which I couldn't mistake, and eventually decided in my favour. Of course I didn't dare thank him, but I hope he saw the look of dog-like devotion which inhabited my eyes. He was very human, Rentoul: I know that he had his faults, but he did very well on the Bench and he never forgot a friend."

"Quite so," said Berry, "quite so. You'll forgive me for saying that I have some sympathy for your opponent. No doubt it's misplaced, but I know how I should have felt. I suppose you'd call that 'the dust of the arena'. All I can say is I should think he was damned near choked."

"I confess that I didn't feel too easy. But I've no doubt justice was done. Rentoul saw that I was weighted out and, er, put things right. As did Danckwerts."

Berry regarded me.

"You've shut my mouth," he said.

*

"Hallmarks," said Daphne.

"Fascinating things," said Berry. "And most romantic. They're rather faint sometimes. Been polished away."

"I never can read them," said Jill. "I get as far as the Lion and then I'm done."

"No one but an expert," said Berry, "can read the date which they tell without consulting a book – unless, of course, he's got a very old-fashioned memory. I mean, how many ordinary human beings, who are interested in old silver, could tell you the date-letter for 1782? Not one in a thousand. But, so far as Georgian silver is concerned, if you can remember two dates, you'll get a long way. Only two dates."

"Please go on," said everyone.

"Well, up to the end of the year 1784, all Georgian silver bore only four hallmarks. These were the Leopard's Head, the Lion Passant, the Date Letter and the Maker's Mark. But in 1785 another hallmark was added – namely the King's Head. So that after 1784 the number of hallmarks on Georgian silver is five. And that is the first date to remember – 1784.

"The second date to remember is 1823, for after 1823 the Leopard's Head was uncrowned. Till then, it had always worn a crown. So that the appearance of the Leopard's Head uncrowned shows that that particular piece of silver was assayed after 1823.

"Manifestly, if you can remember those two dates, you can get quite a long way. Five marks means 'later than 1784': the Leopard's Head uncrowned means 'later than 1823'."

"I take it," said I, "that what you have said applies to silver assayed in London."

"Yes," said Berry. "To silver assayed in the provinces, I cannot speak. But as five-sixths of the silver assayed seems to have been assayed in London, it's near enough."

"I entirely agree."

My sister was regarding my wife.

"What a good thing, darling," she said, "we didn't buy that skewer."

Berry looked up.

"What skewer?" he said.

"It was in the Red Cross sale we went to today. Two of the hallmarks were clear, but the others were worn. But I know there were only four."

"*Only four?*" screamed Berry. "How much did they want for it?"

"Thirty shillings," said Daphne. "But you said – "

"I said that if there were only four marks, that meant that the silver was assayed before 1785."

Daphne's hand flew to her lip.

"Oh dear," she said. "I've got it the wrong way round. I was mixing it up with the Leopard."

Jonah and I were laughing, but Berry had his hands to his head.

"God give me strength," he wailed. "I've done more harm than good. What was the skewer's condition?"

"Lovely," said Jill. "It wanted cleaning, of course."

"What were the marks you could see?"

"Well, the Lion was clear. That's how we knew it was silver." Berry covered his eyes. "And it had two initials together."

"That's right," said Daphne. "They were beautifully clear. Would that be the Maker's Mark?"

"Yes," said Berry, "it would. Er, what were the initials?"

Daphne regarded Jill.

"T C," said my wife.

Berry stifled a scream.

"A good-looking skewer by Tom Chawner...assayed not later than 1784...offered for thirty shillings...and you turned it down... It'd fetch ten guineas at Christie's. Besides, I wanted a skewer to open my letters with."

There was a dreadful silence.

Then –

"We'll go again tomorrow," said Daphne. "Tell me the dates again."

"Just go and buy it," said Berry. "Don't worry about any dates. I don't want you to turn it down because the Leopard is crowned." He sighed. "Don't bother about what I said. Forget the dates. Only remember this – that anything with ONLY four hallmarks is worth having, because that means that it was assayed before... Oh dear, there we go again. Well, never mind. Just absorb the fact that anything with ONLY four hallmarks is worth having."

"That's much simpler," said Daphne.

Shortly before luncheon on the following day she and Jill returned with Tom Chawner's skewer. They had also purchased the most hideous and revolting cream jug that I have ever seen. When this was produced to Berry, he stared upon it in horror and then averted his gaze.

"Remove that vessel," he said. "I don't doubt it's 'A Present from Margate', but it makes me feel physically sick."

"Well, we didn't like it," said Jill, "but it's only four marks."

This was quite true. *But it had been assayed in 1895.* And the duty mark of the Sovereign's Head was abolished in 1890, after a run of more than a hundred years.

My sympathies lay with Berry. One cannot think of everything. After all, he *had* said 'Georgian silver'.

*

Berry looked at me.

"When you and I," he said, "were members of Harrow School, we were more fortunate than we knew, for we came in for the very last years of the masters of the old school."

"What exactly d'you mean?" said Daphne.

"Well, when Boy and I were there, at least twelve of the masters had been born before the year 1850 and three of those had been born before 1840. So they may fairly be said to have belonged to the old school. All were men of letters, and their methods and their manners were incomparable. They showed no signs of age: their brains were clear: their eyes were not dim nor their natural force abated. All their lives they had applied themselves unto wisdom, so that, young and careless as we were, we could not help learning of them and picking up some of the crumbs that fell from their handsome tables. One or two of the younger men – notably N K Stephen – maintained the great tradition; but as a rule, when they died or retired, they were found to be irreplaceable. Now all those great leases expired while we were yet at Harrow or very soon after we left: so, as I said to begin with, we were very fortunate.

"What made me remember them was an absurd occasion when I was 'up to' Jack Stogdon, that is to say, I was due to receive instruction at his hands. 'Jack' was an institution. He was very quiet and gentle, seemed unaware of what was going on, yet never missed anything. When he was afoot, his eyes seemed always to be upon the ground; yet never in his life, when a passing boy touched his hat to him, did he fail to touch his mortar-board in return. It was always said that he used to salute such lamp-posts as he passed in this way. One of the new masters who arrived just before I left apparently considered it beneath his dignity to touch his cap in return and never did so. You may imagine the contempt with which such a breach of good manners was received.

"Well, when I was in 'Jack's' form – the First Fifth, I think – once a week he used to teach us English History. And the way he went about it was this. He would talk to us about some great matter, such as, for instance, the rise and fall of Cardinal Wolsey, in a friendly, informal way, inviting questions as he went. And we were supposed to take notes of what he said. During the following week we were required to write out, in the form of an essay, what he had told us. This, in our note-books. He never examined our efforts, but the next time he took us in History, he would pick two of us at random and desire us to read our essays aloud, before he began his new talk. As there were about twenty-five of us in his form, once you'd been picked, the probability was that you wouldn't be picked again that term, and any way we didn't bother very much, but trusted to luck. On this particular occasion, I'd forgotten all about the essay until the night before, and when I looked at my notes, they told me nothing at all. Boy was in the Second Fifth, so he couldn't help. Still, I did remember the subject, which was Mary, Queen of Scots, and, since the only history book I could find was Gilbert à Beckett's *Comic History of England*, in desperation I copied out some extracts from that and hoped for the best.

"The next morning, of course, 'Jack' picked me at once…"

"I can still hear the roars of laughter from the rest of the form, as I read out Gilbert à Beckett's ridiculous sentences. But 'Jack' declined to be amused and fairly put it across me, as, of course, I deserved.

"But worse was to come. When he'd finished with me, he called upon Guy Ridley, a most entertaining fellow and a younger son of the Judge. Now Ridley was not only entertaining, but he was enterprising and bold. Since 'Jack' had called upon him only the week before, he hadn't troubled to write an essay at all: but that didn't daunt him. To our unspeakable delight, he rose in his place and, holding his note-book before him, endeavoured to make a speech – upon what he remembered of Mary, Queen of Scots. As he progressed, frowning upon a manuscript which was not there, we were ready to die of

223

laughter which we dared not express. Ridley got through about three sentences. Then he began to hesitate.

" 'What's the matter?' said 'Jack'. 'Can't you read your own writing?'

" 'Not very well, sir,' said Ridley. 'I'm afraid I wrote it rather hastily.'

" 'Let me see if I can read it,' said 'Jack', beginning to understand.

"So Ridley took the book up...

" 'Jack' really was cross by now and fairly let Ridley have it. Happily the next fellow he picked put up a respectable show. But he was much put out, and Ridley and I, who had afforded our fellows entertainment of a high order, had our tails between our legs." Berry looked at me. "From the foolish grin on your face, I suppose you remember something worse."

"I remember a disaster," I said, "which occurred in the Upper Sixth. That was taken by Hallam, the grammarian. He was a corker and worked us terribly hard. I'm thankful to say I spent only two terms with him. Then I passed on into the still waters of 'The Twelve'."

"Where you did no work at all."

"Well, we went as we pleased – more or less. If we liked writing Greek Verses, we were encouraged to write them. It was a kind of sanctuary. And now let's get back to the Upper Sixth.

"Once a week, Wood, the Headmaster, used to take that form. And with him, we always read Homer. At the end of the hour he'd say what passage he wished us to prepare for the following week. And when the time came, each of us rose in order and translated aloud ten lines. Well, that was easy enough. Say I was tenth in the form, I was prepared to translate from line 90 to line 100 or thereabouts. But no more. You see, he always took us in order: so you couldn't go wrong. And then one terrible day, the second boy in the form had fallen suddenly sick. And the first thing we knew of his sickness was when he failed to appear...

"You may imagine the result. When Number Three broke down, Wood looked at him very hard, just said 'Sit down' and put on Number Four. When Number Four broke down, Wood never even said 'Sit down', but called upon Number Five. When Number Five broke down, Wood sat back in his chair.

" 'Has anyone here,' he said, 'learned more than his ten lines?'

"There was a dreadful silence.

" 'I see,' said Wood, coldly. 'In that case, you'd better listen to me while I translate the passage which you were asked to prepare.'

"With that, he rendered some two hundred and fifty lines of *The Iliad* in the most beautiful English.

"When he had finished, he closed his Homer and rose.

" 'We'll go on from there next time,' he said.

"His failure to punish or even upbraid us hit us much harder than could have any penalty: and every one of us had prepared the whole passage next time. But Wood was a great gentleman. When the time came, he put us on to translate in just the same order as before. First, Number One, then Number Two, and so on."

"Superb," said Berry.

"The old school," said I. "Can anyone wonder that we found him worshipful?"

There was a little silence.

Then Berry let out a squeal.

"My God," said Daphne. "Darling, must you do that?"

"Sorry, my sweet. But I have at last remembered what I have been trying to remember for more than a month. I've remembered it in Boy's absence again and again. But never in his presence, which, however undesirable, is in this case necessary. Of course my memory today is too awful. I rang up Coates at the Embassy the other day, and when he came through, I couldn't remember his name. I'd just asked for him, too."

"Whatever did you do?" said Jonah.

"Told him," said Berry. "I couldn't keep on saying 'you'. He was very nice about it."

"The things you get away with," I said. "Well, what is it you want to ask me? Or have you forgotten again?"

There was an agonized silence, while Berry clasped his head in his hands.

Then –

"It had gone," he said. "I only just got it back. I tell you, my memory today – "

" Look here," I said, "you'll forget it again in a minute. Why don't you say what it is?"

"I want to throw back," said Berry. "You remember that death-bed Will case Coles Willing took you to hear?"

"Vividly," I said.

"Well, we were all agreed that, if justice had been done the executors of the new Will would have gone to jail. Now if criminal proceedings had been instituted, what would they have been charged with?"

"With forgery of a Will."

"Forgery?"

"Yes. If the nurses were to be believed, the testatrix was as good as unconscious when, by the solicitor's orders, the pen was held into her hand and her signature was affixed. In such circumstances it could clearly have been maintained that that was 'the false making of a Will of a living person', and that is forgery."

"The Law is very jealous of Wills?"

"Of all to do with them. At least, it used to be. Some Judge once said, 'The testator must be allowed the utmost eccentricity.' By which, of course, he meant that however eccentric the directions, they must be observed. And anyone who is convicted of forging a Will or of destroying or even concealing a Will may be sent to penal servitude for life."

"I never knew that," said Berry. "Does the same apply to a Codicil?"

"Oh, yes. To any testamentary instrument. The Law very properly regards them as sacred things. After all, they are the spokesmen of the dead." I hesitated. "For all that, signed and attested as they may be, not all of them come to be proved."

"What ever do you mean?" said Daphne.

"This," said I. "Within a few hours of the testator's death, many an unwelcome Codicil has disappeared. Unless it has been properly drawn by a firm of solicitors, there is very little risk. And even then, who is to say that the testator didn't change his mind and destroy it himself?"

"*Adela Leith* did it, in *Period Stuff*."

"I know," I said, laughing. "She could have been sent to penal servitude for life. And there you are. Who was to know? The thing was too easy. A Will made in an hotel more than a year before, witnessed by the porter and a floor-waiter, and no solicitors employed. Nobody knew of its existence. You can't be surprised that the Law does its best to protect such very vulnerable things. And don't forget that the temptation is terrific. Take this imaginary case. A woman is the dutiful wife of a susceptible man. After a long illness, he dies. Going through his papers, she finds a recent, home-made Codicil, by which he has devised half his fortune to his designing young nurse. If you were the widow, what would you do?"

"Shove it in the fire," said Berry. "Without the slightest compunction. I should lock the door first, of course."

"Well, there you are. Penalties or no, the only safe place for a testamentary document is the strong-room of a solicitor."

Berry looked round.

"This book," he said, "will make some people think, won't it?"

"It may," I said.

"How many letters did you get after *As Berry and I Were Saying* about Trustees?"

"Quite a lot," I said. "But no one went empty away. I don't say that all were content. One or two of the younger generation, who wanted to blue their substance, seemed to think they were on a good thing. I was rather severe with them. But the responsible people who wrote to me, seemed to be satisfied with my replies. Once or twice I had to point out that we had not written a text-book, but that if they submitted their case to the Court of Chancery, what did they think that such a Court would say. To that, they had no answer. You were on very good ground."

"But, darling," said Daphne, "you don't suggest that Wills and Codicils are often destroyed?"

"Good lord, no. I should think it's extremely rare. But that such things have been done, I have no doubt."

"I feel," said Berry, "that *Her Grace the Duchess of Whelp* would have put it higher than that."

"She was very outspoken," I said.

"She knew her world," said Berry. "*Humanum est errare* – don't forget that. Inclination and Opportunity are a tempting pair; but when they are reinforced by Impunity – well, such a coalition is formidable indeed."

"That's very true."

"Darling," said Jill, "what is a home-made Will?"

"I gave it that name, my sweet. I meant a Will that has not been drawn by a solicitor. Any fool can draw a Will, if it's a simple one. It's only got to be signed by the Testator in the presence of two witnesses who must append their signatures. I think I'm right in saying that a Will consisting of the words 'All to my wife', duly signed and attested, has been admitted to probate. So long as its meaning is clear, the traditional phraseology may be omitted. Mark you, I don't recommend this. It's much better to write down what you want done and give it to a solicitor, who will then put your wishes into the shape and form in which they should be presented. You've no idea how easy it is for a layman to write down something which seems to him quite clear, which is in fact ambiguous. More than one very great lawyer has drawn his own Will and, when he has died, the construction of that Will has presented so much difficulty that the ruling of the Court has had to be sought before it could be proved. But over and over again in an emergency, the home-made Will has, so to speak, saved the game."

"How astonishing," said my sister, "that an eminent lawyer should have gone wrong."

"Yes, it is very strange. I believe I'm right in saying that the first Viscount Esher was one of the culprits. And he was the Master of the Rolls. I may be wrong, but it was either he or one of his predecessors. I think it was Esher – a most distinguished lawyer. He spent nearly sixty years at the Bar and on the Bench and only retired a few years before my acquaintance with the Law Courts began.

"Which reminds me that among the letters I got after the publication of *As Berry and I Were Saying* was a very civil one from a reader, venturing to deplore the words I had used of one of the Judges of my time. I had said, 'Such men are not bred today.' "

"Nor they are," said Berry.

"Well, that was all right. But he added that that was an unfair reflection upon the present Lord Chief Justice, Lord Goddard."

"How could it be?" said Jonah.

I shrugged my shoulders.

"Well, I've always had a great respect for Lord Goddard – or Rayner Goddard, as I remember him. And from all I hear and read – for I've never seen him on the Bench – he's a first-rate Lord Chief and fully maintains the traditions of his high office. So I wrote to the fellow at once, pointing out that, as Lord Goddard was seventy-four years old when I wrote those words, to construe them as a reflection upon his lordship was fantastic."

"So it was," said Jonah.

I sighed.

"Letters like that show that, careful as an author may be, he never knows when something he's written is going to be misread or misconstrued or misinterpreted."

"Have you been corrected lately?"

"Once or twice. One fellow wrote and said that if I presumed to write books, I ought to know better than to write 'receipt' when I meant 'recipe'."

"I trust," said Berry, "that you wiped the floor with him."

"No, I didn't do that. I simply said that I wrote 'receipt', because I happened to prefer that to 'recipe', but that in fact either word was as good as the other."

"I know some people say 'recipe'," said Jill, "but I shouldn't know how to spell it."

"It's Latin, my darling. And it means, 'Take'. In the old days doctors always used to write their prescriptions in Latin and their prescriptions always began with the direction, 'Recipe', that is to say, 'Take'. *Take two grains of calomel* etc. And so prescriptions came to be called 'recipes'."

"A slovenly derivation," said Berry. " 'Receipt' is the better form. And now that the word 'prescription' has displaced 'recipe', the latter should be retired. Have you got any more like that?"

"Not very many. 'Different to' is always cropping up – I mean, objections to that usage. Oh, one fellow wrote, saying that the 'shoot' in *Blind Corner* should have been spelt 'chute'."

"What did you say to him?"

I can't remember. I think I said I preferred using English to French. But they mean no wrong, you know, and it shows that they take an interest."

"Do they ever apologize? After you've written, I mean."

"Sometimes. And handsomely, too. But the worst offenders don't."

"Years ago," said Berry, "I read a book by a well-known novelist, which centred round an action for slander. I mean, that *was* the book – the slander, the preparation of the case, and finally the hearing in the Law Courts. And the plaintiff won her action. The slander was uttered at a sherry-party by one society girl of another. Very well and good. I've no doubt a lot of people enjoyed the book. And now for the slander. To the best of my recollection one girl said of the other that she was 'a little snob'. Is that a slander, Boy?"

I shook my head.

"The matter would never have got past the Master. He would have struck out the action. *De minimis non curat Lex* is a time-honoured saying. 'The Law does not concern itself with trifles.' It's not a slander to call somebody else a snob. Good God, if to say someone was a snob was to court an action for slander, everybody would be afraid to open his mouth. But I don't suppose that occurred to most people who read the book."

"All wrong," said Berry. "At least, I think it is. An author of standing has a responsibility to his public. I know that's your outlook."

"Yes," I said, "it is. So far as facts are concerned, one must be accurate: and where fiction is concerned, one must be reasonable. At least, that's my idea."

"Have you ever deliberately falsified the facts?"

"What a question!" said Daphne.

"I did once," I said, laughing. "I hoped it would be considered that I was availing myself of what I think is called 'an author's licence'. In *Berry and Co.* I brought on the action of *Pleydell against Bladder* very much more quickly than it could have come to be heard."

"That," said Berry, "was excusable. To have put off the case for six months would have thrown the whole book out of gear."

"I agree. I couldn't have done it. The chapter would have had to go."

"What is a slander?" said Berry. "And what is not? Can't you give us an answer that we can all understand?"

"Well, before I try to answer, let me say this. I'm speaking, as they say, off the record. It's more than forty years since I was at the Bar and to lay down the law of slander is beyond my power. But few of us have access to textbooks and I can give the general idea with more or less accuracy. Only, I don't want somebody to read this and then, when they get a writ, to write to me and say, 'This is all your fault.' "

"Proceed," said Berry.

"Well, I can say this – that for an action to lie, the statement complained of must be grave. In the book we were discussing, if the defendant had declared that the plaintiff was a drunkard, that would have been slanderous. I think the line must be drawn by common sense. Supposing a fellow says of a grocer in town, 'Don't you deal with —. He gives short measure,' that is a slander: but if he buys that grocer's car and says later, 'You know — swindled me over that car', that is not slander."

"Oh, I give up," said Daphne.

"I'm sorry, my sweet. The distinction is very difficult to define. But I'm sure you can see that if you could be run for slander if you said that so-and-so was a snob, or lived for food, or didn't know how to treat servants, or was mutton dressed lamb – well, life wouldn't be worth living, would it?"

"Not for my sex," said Daphne.

"Bear with me," said Berry. "Supposing you said of a bloke that he 'lifted his elbow'?"

"That would depend on whether he had a profession and, if so, what it was. If you said it of a butcher, it would not be slanderous: but if you said it of a surgeon, it would.

"Then again no action will lie if the words complained of are what is called 'vulgar abuse'. That you can understand. If A backs into B's new car and does fifty pounds' worth of damage, as like as not the shortcomings which B attributes to A in the presence of several bystanders will be unprintable. But that is not slander. Whether or no a statement is slanderous very often depends upon the circumstances of the case. If somebody said of a bachelor member of the Bar that he took out a different girl every night of his life, that might not be true, but it wouldn't be slanderous: but if the same statement was made of a clergyman who was married, it would. For obvious reasons, of course. Finally, to return to our starting point, when you consider the truly slanderous statements of which what is called 'gossip' is very largely composed, you will appreciate why an action brought by a girl because someone called her 'a snob' could never have got as far as a Queen's Bench Judge."

"Well, thank you very much," said Berry. "I can't say I'm very much wiser, but I do see the points you've made. I take it that such cases are rare."

"Very rare. For one thing the tale-bearer is usually most reluctant to come to Court. And a reluctant witness is no damned good. They'll always break down in cross-examination, even if they come up to their proof. Libel, of course, is a very different matter. If it's printed, as it usually is, it's far more serious and the printed word speaks for itself."

"When," said Jill, "you say 'come up to their proof', what do you mean?"

"Well, in the brief which is sent to counsel, there are copies of the statements which the witnesses he is to call have made to the solicitors. Such statements are called 'proofs'. Sometimes, when a witness is in the box, he declines to go as far as he did in the privacy of the solicitor's office. Well, that can be very awkward for the counsel concerned. And if the witness actually goes back on his proof, then counsel can hand the proof to the Judge and ask his permission to treat the witness as what is called 'a hostile witness'. And if the Judge gives his consent, he can cross-examine him, just as if he'd been called by the other side. I've known it done. But it's never any good. If a witness lets you down, you must let him go. At least, that's my opinion."

"Is that your last word?" said Berry.

I nodded.

"Then I'll take over." He sat back and closed his eyes. "Speaking," he declared, "as one whose portion has been unbridled slander for many years, who, of natural love and affection, has always refrained from seeking redress from the Courts, I trust – though without much confidence – that you four will now reconsider the propriety of subjecting your elder and better – "

The remainder of the period was not unnaturally lost, and, when order had been restored, we went to bed.

*

"I've remembered one thing," I said, "which happened to me, as an author, a long time ago, before the first war. I was writing *The Brother of Daphne*, and the short tales of which that consists were appearing one by one in *The Windsor Magazine*. As I think I've said before, I then had no idea that they'd ever be collected and published in volume form. They didn't appear every month, for I was then at the Bar and I hadn't much time to spare. Still, people seemed to like them and my name was getting known.

"One day I received a 'reply paid' telegram from, let us say, the Lake District. It had been directed to me c/o my publishers, who were then in Salisbury Square, and they sent it at once to my chambers by special messenger. It was the longest telegram I have ever received in my life – four or five pages in length – from a man I had never seen, of whom I had never heard. I still have that telegram somewhere. I wish that I had it here, for its burden was unbelievable. But I know you'll believe my report.

"Now this was what the telegram said. (I naturally can't remember it word for word; but it was the kind of message which you never forget, and I know that I'm not far out.)

"*I have for some time been deeply in love with a most attractive young lady who for some reason did not look favourably on my suit stop the set in which she and I move are ardent admirers of your work and it suddenly occurred to me that if I were to tell her in strict confidence that I was really the author of your stories and was concealing my identity under the pseudonym Dornford Yates this might persuade her to promise to be my wife stop accordingly a day or two later after swearing her to secrecy I told her that in fact I was Dornford Yates with the happy result that the lady was so delighted that there and then she consented to be my wife stop most unfortunately she did not keep her promise to tell no one what I had told her but told a great friend of hers who has never liked me and this evil-disposed woman actually went so far as to write to your publishers and ask if what I had said was true stop they naturally replied that it was not and in triumph she showed their letter to my betrothed who despite my entreaties and my assurances that the publishers were only obeying my instructions to conceal my identity immediately broke off our engagement stop Mr Yates I implore your help in this matter which means so much to me what I want you to do is to answer this telegram just saying that it is perfectly true that I am the author of the stories which appear under your name for if you will do this her friend will be discredited and she will again consent to be my wife it will mean nothing to you but all my happiness depends on your reply.*

"Then followed his name and address.

"I remember that, soon after the telegram reached me, the Editor of *The Windsor Magazine* rang me up and asked me very politely how I proposed to reply. (He admitted later that he was afraid lest the young and inexperienced author should yield out of kindness of heart to the sender's impudent appeal.) I'm not sure, but I think we discussed the matter – should I ignore the telegram or should I send a curt refusal to do as the fellow asked? At this distance of time, I can't be sure which I did: but I think we agreed that it was better to reply, sharply refusing his request. And that was the end of the matter, so far as I was concerned.

"Now, as I have said before, I know of more than one case in which men – and in one case a woman – have told their acquaintances that they were, in fact, Dornford Yates: but that is the only case in which the impostor has actually requested that I should support the lie. Indeed, for barefaced effrontery, I have always felt that that telegram was unbeatable."

"I remember it, darling," said Daphne. "You showed me the wire. I think it was rather longer than your version."

"I'm greatly relieved," I said, "for, to be perfectly honest, it is an incredible tale."

"Boy," said Jonah, "we've known you too long and too well to disbelieve what you say. But it's more than incredible: it's unimaginable. The man must have been besotted."

"And what of the girl?" said Berry. "She must have been raving mad." Before Jill could protest, "Seriously," he added, "are you sure that it wasn't a plant?"

"Made with some cock-eyed idea of presently cashing in on any money I made? I don't think so. You see the production of his telegram would have been the answer to any such attempt. Then, again, I could produce my manuscripts. Oh no. It was genuine enough. But it just shows the lengths to which some people will go to obtain their heart's desire. And, damn it, that's made me think of another case. Not nearly so gross, but it bears a certain similarity which you will immediately perceive." I put a hand over my eyes. "Bear with me a moment, while I go over the facts."

There was a little silence. Then I lifted my head.

"I've got it straight now…

"Now this happened much later on – in the nineteen-thirties, I think. A woman, of whose existence I had never dreamed, wrote to me from London and addressed her letter to White Ladies. Fortunately for me, I was out of England at the time: her letter was forwarded. It was very well and naturally written and one or two things she said were amusingly put.

"She said that her daughter was engaged to a most desirable young man. To contrive this engagement, she had left her humble lodgings and had taken an expensive, furnished house in a fashionable square. She had engaged good servants to run it and had lived there in style – on credit. At first the young man's parents had viewed the match with distaste; but when they had seen the handsome manner in which the girl's mother lived, they had withdrawn their objections and given their consent. And now Nemesis was knocking at the door – with the wedding-day still a fortnight away. The house-agents were demanding the rent. The servants were pressing for their wages and threatening to leave. Tradesmen were refusing to deliver until their bills had been paid. Almost worst of all, the telephone was about to be cut off. She believed that with two hundred pounds she could just keep things going until the marriage took place. After that, of course – the deluge. But that didn't worry her at all. *She desired me to remit this sum to her without delay.* I mean, it was essential, otherwise everything would crash. Could I possibly telegraph the money?

"I replied shortly, saying that I was not prepared to lend her money for any purpose, much less to subscribe to false pretences which could only come back on her child. When she got my letter, she cabled, virtually demanding the sum. When I took no notice, she cabled again, warning me that my failure to comply with her request would result in tragedy. And that was the last I heard of her.

"The two cases have this in common – that on each occasion I was desired to assist the petitioner to bring to a successful issue his or her deliberate deception of a third party. I mean they made no bones about it. In the first case, the girl was to be led to believe that she was about to marry the budding author for whose work she had a great regard: in the second, the man and his parents were to be sure that his fiancée had (or would have) plenty of money, when in fact she was penniless. I can only suppose that each of the suppliants perceived something in my work which suggested that I should sympathize with an attempt to obtain what they wanted by false pretences."

"How," said Berry, "did the lady propose to pay you back?"

"That question did not arise. I rather think that virtue was to be its own reward."

"Astounding," said Jonah. "Two hundred pounds down the drain...to a woman you'd never heard of...to maintain the shabby deception which she is practising upon the parents of her future son-in-law. And when you decline to play, she resents it."

"I think," said Daphne, "that her case was worse than the first. In the first case you were approached by a callow, lovesick youth: in the second, by a sophisticated woman of the world who did know how to behave."

"I agree," said Berry. "Both petitions were grossly impertinent and both were shameless. But while the first was lunatic, the second was designing. The second was a determined attempt to obtain your assistance to commit a misdemeanour."

"So was the first," said Jonah.

Berry looked at him. Then –

"By God, you're right," he said. "At least, I think you are. What does Boy say?"

"Neither of the petitioners," I said, "could have been prosecuted for false pretences – if the marriages had come off. In other words, both were within the law. But, judged by respectable people, both attempts were indecent."

"When the truth was discovered, could either marriage have been dissolved?"

"No, indeed," said I.

"Wicked," said Berry. "Have you got any more like that?"

I shook my head.

"All authors get begging letters – at least, I suppose they do. I've had very few of them. Four or five perhaps – in forty-five years. I fell for the first one, of course: but when the writer returned for a second helping, I saw that I'd made a mistake and hardened my heart. And now it's your turn."

"Sorry," said Berry, "but I can remember no more. It's not for want of trying. I've flogged my memory. So now it's up to you."

"I'm almost through," I said. "In fact, this next reminiscence will be my last. As no doubt you surmise, it belongs to the Law. But it had to do with the Bench, and not with the Bar.

"More than once I've mentioned The Clerk of Assize. Each Circuit – I think there are seven – has its own Clerk of Assize. For all I know, things have changed in the last forty years; but in my day the post of Clerk of Assize was greatly coveted. Whoever was to fill it had to be a Barrister-at-Law. The salary was worth having and the expense account was handsomely furnished. And the Clerk of Assize was a very important man. He ruled the Circuit: so far as the Circuit was concerned, his word was law. And the Judges deferred to him. After all, the Red Judge passed, but the Clerk of Assize went on.

"Now how was the Clerk of Assize appointed? I'll tell you. When a Clerk of Assize retired or died, his successor was appointed by the Judge who was going that Circuit at the time or was to go that Circuit the next time it was opened. In other words, the post was in his gift. Now a Judge can choose which Circuit he wishes to go: but if two Judges apply for the same Circuit, then the senior Judge has his way. Only no Judge can go the same Circuit twice running.

"In my day Channell J and 'Long Lawrance', two of the very best, were senior Judges; and it became an understood thing for several years that those two Judges took the Western Circuit in turn. No other Judge ever went it. It was reserved for them.

"Now why was this? Not because they liked it, although, to my mind, it is the pleasantest Circuit to go. The two of them went that Circuit because the Clerk of Assize was getting on. He was really elderly. And as Channell had two sons at the Bar and 'Long Lawrance' had one, each wanted to be in at the death."

"Really!" said Daphne.

"I know," I said, laughing. "I admit that it has it's grim side: but it was a jest in The Temple and bets were laid as to which of the two would win. Of such is patronage.

"At last, to Lawrance's annoyance, the old fellow died while Channell was doing his stuff; and Channell's elder son was appointed Clerk of Assize. (He was a very nice fellow, but rather delicate and, to everybody's regret, he didn't live very long.) It was really a barefaced business, for Channell and Lawrance had gone that Circuit for years. And the old Clerk must have known why."

"It makes me smile," said Daphne; "but it makes me feel rather ashamed."

"My darling, so it does me. Waiting for the dead man's shoes. What is more, I'll tell you this. I knew Channell very well, and I'll lay any money you like that he felt ashamed, too. But he wanted to help his son, and what on earth was the point of his standing aside when another and junior Judge was waiting to take his place? 'Long Lawrance' was tougher than Channell, and I don't suppose he gave the matter a thought."

"A valuable memory," said Berry. "And most entertaining. Her Majesty's Judges endeavour to improve the occasion. And I don't blame them at all. Only a fool, as you say, would have stood aside. And now one more."

"Sorry," I said. "I've pumped my memory dry."

"D'you mean that's all?" said Daphne.

"I'm afraid so, my sweet. I can't say yet if there'll be enough for a book."

"What did you say?" said Berry.

"I said that I didn't know if there'd be enough for a book. If there is – "

"D'you mean to say that you're actually contemplating the possibility of suppressing all we have composed in the sweat of our face? And what about *Old London Bridge*?"

I shrugged my shoulders.

"We cannot give the public short measure."

"Darling," said Daphne, "I'm sure this will make a book which is longer than many I've read."

"I know," I said. "Some books, especially novels, are today extremely short. But I've always given good measure. *Ne'er Do Well*, I know, was not a long book – and it worried me very much. But that was how the story came out, and after a lot of reflection I let it go."

"Darling," said Jill, "if you'd put in *The Tempered Wind* – "

"I can't do that," I said.

The others sat up.

"What's this?" said Jonah.

Jill shrugged her pretty shoulders.

"He's going through all he's written and tearing it up. It's simply grievous, Jonah."

"Much better *I* should do it," I said.

"I appreciate that," said Berry. "But what is *The Tempered Wind*?"

I smiled.

"*The Tempered Wind*," I said, "affords a perfect example of the failure of a book to take charge."

"What do you mean?" said Daphne.

"Well, over the years I've had a great many requests that I should turn again to *Etchechuria*: or, in other words, that I should write a sequel to *The Stolen March*. In the end, against my better judgment, I sought to comply – by writing *The Tempered Wind*. Well, as usual, the book took charge; and everything went like a train till *Etchechuria* was reached. It was hard to get there, of course. Wild country, no track to follow, the compass playing up. Still, two men and a girl did it – by the skin of their teeth. I think that up to that moment the adventure rang very true. But once the three had arrived, the subconscious brain stopped dead. Try as I would, I simply could not recapture the carefree inconsequence of life 'within The Pail'. The conscious brain struggled on, but what I wrote was laboured… In desperation, I made a short story of the book. But makeshifts are no damned good."

There was a little silence.

Then –

"How many pages had you written?" said Daphne.

"Fifty-one," wailed Jill.

I took her small hand in mine.

"I'm sorry, my darling. But it's just one of those things. You see, I shouldn't have tried. I was asking too much."

"There I'm with you," said Berry. "Somewhere in *The Stolen March* you speak of 'a spring, schooled into a fountain, playing beneath an oak'. Well, that exactly describes the artless *joie de vivre* of the book itself."

"Steady," I said. "I'm glad it appealed to you. But many of my fans can't read it. One of them wrote and said I'd gone round the bend. Say rather that, good or bad, the subconscious brain felt unable to do it again. And fifty pages is not a terrible lot. I wrote more than two hundred once – and tore them up."

"What ever happened?" said Jonah.

"I don't really know," I said. "I think I was worried at the time: but the book never settled down. Some of it wasn't too bad. Of course I was very foolish not to have stopped before."

"What was it called?" said Daphne.

"I don't think I'd thought of a title. It was a romance."

"Has this kind of thing often happened?"

"Only three times, I think: so I can't complain. Say, three hundred pages in all: about the length of a book. *Absit omen*. We don't want to have to scrap this."

Berry covered his face.

"Surely it's long enough," said Daphne.

"It may be – in the rough. But it's got to be pruned, you know."

"Not my monographs!" screamed Berry. "They're twice as finished as anything else in the book."

Jill, beside me, began to shake with laughter.

"I'm afraid you're a little too fond of The Wife of Bath."

"Damn the man," cried Berry. "I knew he was going to say that."

"I'm sorry," I said, laughing. "But we must not repeat ourselves. And some of the memoir, I think, should be considered again. Any way, I'll tell you next week."

Jonah laid a hand on my shoulder.

"One last look at The Temple, before you close down. I mean, after Lamb, strolling down Crown Office Row."

I leaned back, closing my eyes.

"Crown Office Row and The Cloisters... I can see Lord Cecil of Chelwood – then Lord Robert Cecil – striding along. A tall, notable figure, with a very definite stoop. Tall hat and short coat, always. He must be terribly old, for it's more than seventy years since he was called to the Bar... Darling J, very dapper as always – grey morning-coat suit and a grey top-hat, which he was continually raising, for every counsel that passed him uncovered his head. (Whether or no he knew you, you always raised your hat when passing a Judge.)...Sir Harry Poland, once, I think, of Treasury Counsel, old and wise and diligent, a small and bird-like man, on his way to the Inner Temple Library, where he spent most of his time: a pleasant, encouraging manner towards everyone that he met... Tiverton, son of Lord Halsbury, a little older than me. (I came to know him at Oxford, for though he went down the year before I came up, he used to return sometimes. He had been President of the OUDS. He was a most amusing fellow, later to become a QC. He used to go down in the country and defend motorists for the AA. If he couldn't do anything else, he took a point of law. His father, late Lord Chancellor, had given him his library, and he used to delve into long-forgotten Law Reports and discover some ancient case which suited his book. He'd take the volume with him and scare a country Bench with some monstrous argument, backed, so he said, by something some Judge had said in 1610. And he would produce the Report. I was in the Divisional Court on one occasion, when he was up on his feet. You see, the Crown had appealed against some Magistrates' decision in his favour: so 'Tivvy', as he was known, had to try and make good his contention before two Queen's Bench Judges – a very different thing to three Justices of the Peace. One of the two, I remember, was the Lord Chief – Alverstone. Of course he'd known 'Tivvy' all his life and I can see him now shaking with laughter at the ridiculous argument which 'Tivvy' was endeavouring to invest with some semblance of dignity. I'm sorry to say he died young, for he was most entertaining in all he said and did…) McCarthy, wan and abstracted, still at the Junior Bar… Jones, always ready with a jest, waddling rather than walking, simply because he was fat beyond all belief… Swinton – then Lloyd Greame – with a quizzical look in his eye, saying something which made his companions laugh… R D Muir, unsmiling and portly, very conscious of his importance as Senior Treasury Counsel, living for work… F E Smith, very well turned out and the picture of health, silk hat on the back of his head, with his supercilious air and, rarely, the ghost of a smile… And, nicest of all, Theo Mathew, short coat and silk hat on one side, wearing, I think, an eyeglass, radiating goodwill and good humour, so plainly finding the world an excellent place; though, able and charming as he was, he never met the success he most justly deserved. Finally, if you want it, myself, morning coat and striped trousers, silk hat just out of the straight, remarking the lively passage of famous men, finding the sunshine too brave to return to chambers and trying to make up my mind whether to lunch at *The Cock* or in Inner Temple Hall."

"Were you lucky, darling?"

"Yes, indeed," I said. "To vary Lamb's famous words, 'A man would be fortunate to have loitered in such a place.' "

EPILOGUE

(In the shape of a letter from Bridget Ightham to her brother, John Ightham, farmer, of Bilberry, in the County of Hampshire.)

Dear Jack,

Thank you for your nice long letter. I'm thankful young Arthur is shaping so well and ready to listen to you. It was very kind of Colonel Scarlett to send me such a nice message. Next time you see him, please thank him very much and say how happy we all are to think of him being in charge of White Ladies. It does make it better, you know. Fancy Bluecoat being an institution. I shouldn't be in a hurry to sell them the Dale. I mean, wait and see what sort of Institution it is. It might be for lunatics: and if it was – well, you wouldn't want to have them too close to the house.

All well here, thank God. Very quiet living, of course, but we're happier so. The Major and Madam seem exactly the same – so gentle and kind and natural, just as they always were. My lady as sweet as ever – always so gay and loving in all she says and does. Colonel Mansel is here a lot, I'm thankful to say, for it does us all good just to know he's about the place. But I'm worried about the Captain, for he is so very tired. You know, Jack, he works like he used to twenty years ago; and he's over seventy now, though he doesn't look his age.

Ed Fitch and I think we're lucky to be here and I know George Carson is always glad to be back. 'You want to be young,' he says, 'to live in England today.' It's quiet, of course, but we're all of us thankful for that. And the people are very nice. We've quite a good cook and three maids, as willing as ever you saw. And they take a pride in their work. Just like the old days, Jack. I've very little to do, except keep an eye on things, and I'm often with Madam and my lady. They're very sweet to me: if there's anything doing they never leave me out. They often take me to Lisbon: it's really a lovely city and heaps of lovely shops, and beautiful English films right up to date. And all in English, too. I don't know how the Portuguese get on, but the houses are always full. I had a perm the other day, and my lady says, 'We'll take you to our place, Bridget; but mind you're not shocked.' 'If it's good enough for you, my lady,' says I. 'Well,' says she, 'it's where all the ladies of the town go; but it's spotlessly clean and it's very much better and cheaper than anywhere else.' You know, if she hadn't told me, I'd never have dreamed. Their manners were that perfect. And I'll say they did me a treat, and most respectful. And I had a manicure. And some of the shops are a sight. Talk about dressing a window – London's got something to learn. And everything you can think of. Sometimes we three go in to see a film – Ed Fitch and George Carson and me. And when it's over we sit down outside a café and have a glass of beer. And all the foreigners so pleasant and so polite, you wouldn't believe. And then George drives us home.

The house – quinta, they call it – is very nice. It stands well back from the road, so it's very quiet. It's got a courtyard in front, with walls on three sides, and you drive in under an archway and up to the steps. It's quite an old house, you know, but it has been modernized: lovely big rooms, but rather cold in the winter so we have to keep up good fires: still, we get a lot of sun and in the summer it's lovely and ever so cool. Ed and George and I have a beautiful sitting-room and a splendid radio, so we get all the English programmes, and you know, Jack, I can't help feeling we're very fortunate. It's not as we was young. I'll soon be sixty-eight and Ed is older than me. And with all the changes at home – and what good have they done, Jack? That's what I want to know. I tell you straight, I'm glad to be out of it all. But here we're comfortable and happy, just as we used to be; and no one can ask more than that. It was a good day when I went to White Ladies, fifty-one years ago.

Dear me, what a long time that is. D'you remember Mary Anne – the strawberry roan that Father used to drive? Funny how one remembers little odd things like that. And old Chalk in his cottage garden, wearing his smock and tall hat and half asleep in the sun? He was very old when he died. Ninety-eight, I think. I know he was born in the reign of George the Third.

Well, goodbye, Jack, for the present. Give my love to Amy and write again when you can.

Your loving sister,

Bridget.

Dornford Yates

As Berry and I Were Saying

Reprinted four times in three months, this semi-autobiographical novel is a comic rendition of the author's hazardous experiences in France at the end of World War II. Darker and less frivolous than some of Yates' earlier books, he described it as 'really my own memoir put into the mouths of Berry and Boy', and at the time of publication it already had a nostalgic, period feel. A hit with the public and a 'scrapbook of the Edwardian age as it was seen by the upper-middle classes'.

Berry and Co.

A collection of short stories featuring 'Berry' Pleydell and his chaotic entourage established Dornford Yates' reputation as one of the best comic writers of his generation. The German caricatures in the book carried such a sting that when France was invaded in 1939 Yates, who was living near the Pyrenees, was put on the wanted list and had to flee.

DORNFORD YATES

BLIND CORNER

This is Yates' first thriller: a tautly plotted page-turner featuring the tense, crime-busting adventures of suave Richard Chandos. Chandos is thrown out of Oxford for 'beating up some Communists', and on return from vacation in Biarritz he witnesses a murder.

Teaming up at his London club with friend Jonathan Mansel, a stratagem is devised to catch the killer. The novel has equally compelling sequels: *Blood Royal, An Eye For a Tooth, Fire Below* and *Perishable Goods*.

BLOOD ROYAL

At his chivalrous, rakish best in a story of mistaken identity, kidnapping, and old-world romance, Richard Chandos takes us on a romp through Europe in the company of a host of unforgettable characters. This fine thriller can be read alone or as part of a series with *Blind Corner, An Eye For a Tooth, Fire Below* and *Perishable Goods*.

DORNFORD YATES

AN EYE FOR A TOOTH

On the way home from Germany after having captured Axel the Red's treasure, dapper Jonathan Mansel happens upon a corpse in the road, that of an Englishman. There ensues a gripping tale of adventure and vengeance of a rather gentlemanly kind. On publication this novel was such a hit that it was reprinted six times in its first year, and assured Yates' huge popularity. A classic Richard Chandos thriller, which can be read alone or as part of a series including *Blind Corner, Blood Royal, Fire Below* and *Perishable Goods*.

FIRE BELOW

Richard Chandos makes a welcome return in this classic adventure story. Suave and decadent, he leads his friends into forbidden territory to rescue a kidnapped (and very attractive) young widow. Yates gives us a highly dramatic, almost operatic, plot and unforgettably vivid characters.

A tale in the traditional mould, and a companion novel to *Blind Corner, Blood Royal, Perishable Goods* and *An Eye For a Tooth*.

OTHER TITLES BY DORNFORD YATES AVAILABLE DIRECT
FROM HOUSE OF STRATUS

Quantity		£	$(US)	$(CAN)	€
☐	Adèle and Co.	6.99	11.50	15.99	11.50
☐	And Berry Came Too	6.99	11.50	15.99	11.50
☐	As Berry and I Were Saying	6.99	11.50	15.99	11.50
☐	Berry and Co.	6.99	11.50	15.99	11.50
☐	The Berry Scene	6.99	11.50	15.99	11.50
☐	Blind Corner	6.99	11.50	15.99	11.50
☐	Blood Royal	6.99	11.50	15.99	11.50
☐	The Brother of Daphne	6.99	11.50	15.99	11.50
☐	Cost Price	6.99	11.50	15.99	11.50
☐	The Courts of Idleness	6.99	11.50	15.99	11.50
☐	An Eye For a Tooth	6.99	11.50	15.99	11.50
☐	Fire Below	6.99	11.50	15.99	11.50
☐	Gale Warning	6.99	11.50	15.99	11.50
☐	The House That Berry Built	6.99	11.50	15.99	11.50
☐	Jonah and Co.	6.99	11.50	15.99	11.50
☐	Ne'er Do Well	6.99	11.50	15.99	11.50
☐	Perishable Goods	6.99	11.50	15.99	11.50
☐	Red in the Morning	6.99	11.50	15.99	11.50
☐	She Fell Among Thieves	6.99	11.50	15.99	11.50
☐	She Painted Her Face	6.99	11.50	15.99	11.50

ALL HOUSE OF STRATUS BOOKS ARE AVAILABLE FROM GOOD BOOKSHOPS
OR DIRECT FROM THE PUBLISHER:

Internet: www.houseofstratus.com including author interviews, reviews, features.

Email: sales@houseofstratus.com please quote author, title and credit card details.

Hotline: UK ONLY: 0800 169 1780, please quote author, title and credit card details.
INTERNATIONAL: +44 (0) 20 7494 6400, please quote author, title and credit card details.

Send to: House of Stratus Sales Department
24c Old Burlington Street
London
W1X 1RL
UK

Please allow for postage costs charged per order plus an amount per book as set out in the tables below:

	£(Sterling)	$(US)	$(CAN)	€(Euros)
Cost per order				
UK	2.00	3.00	4.50	3.30
Europe	3.00	4.50	6.75	5.00
North America	3.00	4.50	6.75	5.00
Rest of World	3.00	4.50	6.75	5.00
Additional cost per book				
UK	0.50	0.75	1.15	0.85
Europe	1.00	1.50	2.30	1.70
North America	2.00	3.00	4.60	3.40
Rest of World	2.50	3.75	5.75	4.25

PLEASE SEND CHEQUE, POSTAL ORDER (STERLING ONLY), EUROCHEQUE, OR INTERNATIONAL MONEY
ORDER (PLEASE CIRCLE METHOD OF PAYMENT YOU WISH TO USE)
MAKE PAYABLE TO: STRATUS HOLDINGS plc

Cost of book(s):——————————— Example: 3 x books at £6.99 each: £20.97

Cost of order:——————————— Example: £2.00 (Delivery to UK address)

Additional cost per book:————— Example: 3 x £0.50: £1.50

Order total including postage:——— Example: £24.47

Please tick currency you wish to use and add total amount of order:

☐ £ (Sterling)   ☐ $ (US)   ☐ $ (CAN)   ☐ € (EUROS)

VISA, MASTERCARD, SWITCH, AMEX, SOLO, JCB:

☐☐☐☐☐☐☐☐☐☐☐☐☐☐☐☐☐☐☐☐

Issue number (Switch only):

☐☐☐

Start Date: **Expiry Date:**

☐☐/☐☐   ☐☐/☐☐

Signature: _____

NAME: _____

ADDRESS: _____

_____

POSTCODE: _____

Please allow 28 days for delivery.

Prices subject to change without notice.
Please tick box if you do not wish to receive any additional information. ☐

House of Stratus publishes many other titles in this genre; please check our
website (**www.houseofstratus.com**) for more details.